WE
CAN
SEE
YOU

Simon Kernick

WE CAN SEE YOU

CENTURY

1 3 5 7 9 10 8 6 4 2

Century
20 Vauxhall Bridge Road
London SW1V 2SA

Century is part of the Penguin Random House group of companies
whose addresses can be found at global.penguinrandomhouse.com.

First published by Century in 2018

www.penguin.co.uk

A CIP catalogue record for this book is available from the British Library.

ISBN 9781780894492
ISBN 9781780894508 (export)

Typeset in 11.75/17.25 pt Times New Roman
by Integra Software Services Pvt. Ltd, Pondicherry

Printed and bound in Great Britain by Clays Ltd, Elcograf S.p.A.

Penguin Random House is committed to a sustainable future for
our business, our readers and our planet. This book is made
from Forest Stewardship Council® certified paper.

For my girls, as always.

Part One

1

Wednesday night
Four days ago

Even the most perfect life can shatter in seconds, and Brook Connor's nightmare began approximately two minutes after she walked through her front door. For some reason she'd had an ominous feeling in her gut on the drive home, which was an unusual occurrence for her. As a child she'd been plagued by bad dreams – often recurring ones – and had grown up with a deep, irrational sense of doom that could manifest itself in periods of anxiety, especially when things were going well for her. Brook had learned, through long practice, to control those bleak, self-destructive thoughts, so she was surprised by the way this one had sneaked up on her.

It had been a long day. A round of newspaper and radio interviews in San Francisco to promote her second book, *Release*

Your Inner Warrior, had taken up the morning. These had been followed by two ninety-minute back-to-back private client visits at her office in Santa Cruz, both of which had been utterly exhausting. The first client was a twenty-seven-year-old dot-commer who had designed an app that had made him a multimillionaire overnight, but who'd developed a crippling addiction to internet porn, which made it impossible for him to develop normal relationships with women. Unfortunately there was no shortage of cases like his and, as far as Brook was concerned, he was part of a ticking time-bomb that was going to have huge ramifications over the next ten years.

The second client was an equally wealthy married housewife from San José who had completely the opposite problem. She couldn't stop developing relationships with the opposite sex and was having numerous encounters with men she met through various hook-up apps, even though she'd been happily married for more than twenty years to a man she claimed to love more than any other.

Brook considered herself a life-coach, not a sex therapist, and indeed both her books were guides to helping people create better lives for themselves by learning to deal with the stresses of the modern world. But it seemed that a lot of people's life goals revolved around sorting out issues with their love lives. Take sex out of the equation and she'd probably be broke.

It was just short of nine o'clock when she closed the front door behind her, already frowning at the heavy silence inside, and called out to no one in particular that she was home. Seven p.m. was Paige's bedtime. That was when her bedside light went off, after the two stories she was read every night (usually by Brook), so she'd be long asleep by now.

However, there was almost always some noise in the house at this time in the evening. Even if Logan wasn't home – and it didn't sound like he was – Rosa's Honda was in the driveway, so she should be around somewhere. She always kept the TV on in the kitchen, where she liked to sit in the evenings after she'd fixed dinner, trawling through Facebook so that she could find out what all her friends and relatives were up to, back home. And Rosa, who was what might best be described as a larger-than-life woman, was incapable of being quiet when she moved about. She banged; she crashed; she grunted with exertion; she cursed in Spanish. Logan, Brook knew, would have preferred someone prettier, because that was what he was like; but Paige loved Rosa, and so did Brook, who found her a warm, comforting and lively presence within the family – and that was why she picked up on her absence now.

'I'm home, guys,' she called out again, throwing down her purse and kicking off her heels. All the lights were on and it had only been dark for half an hour, so there had to be people here somewhere. Brook checked her cellphone. No missed calls, so there was no emergency she should know about. Maybe Rosa had broken her usual habit and fallen asleep, or taken an early night.

Brook hurried up the stairs, forcing a smile as she pushed away the ominous feeling and looking forward to the prospect of seeing her daughter. Paige always looked so angelic when she was asleep, surrounded by her teddy bears, her breathing so soft it was almost inaudible. Sometimes Brook would kneel down beside her bed and watch her for minutes at a time, relishing their closeness.

As quietly as possible, she pushed open Paige's bedroom door and peered inside, knowing she shouldn't wake her daughter, but secretly hoping that she'd stir.

The bed was unmade and had been slept in.

It was also empty.

Brook's heart lurched and she suddenly felt nauseous. What was going on?

She raced back down the stairs and headed straight into Rosa's bedroom, not even bothering to knock as she called out Rosa's name and switched on the light.

But Rosa wasn't there, either. Unlike Paige's bed, Rosa's was made and hadn't been slept in. Everything else in the room was scrupulously neat, as always. Rosa had worked for them for two years and never once had she not been here when she was meant to be. And she was definitely meant to be here tonight to look after Paige, because she'd known Brook's last appointment didn't finish until seven and that she was going to be late.

Brook checked her cell again, just in case somehow she'd missed a call. But she hadn't. No one had phoned.

She immediately phoned her husband, opening Rosa's wardrobe as Logan's cell rang and rang incessantly. Rosa's clothes were all there, so it was clear she hadn't decided to quit, out of the blue. But then of course she wouldn't do that. She was well paid and well-treated. She was part of the family. She was happy here. And, most importantly of all, her car was still in the drive-way. There was no way she or Paige had gone anywhere on foot. They were three miles from the centre of Carmel, on an unlit road with no sidewalk.

Logan's cell went to message. 'Call me as soon as you get this,' Brook said, striding back through the house. 'It's urgent. Paige and Rosa aren't here, and I don't know what's happened to them.'

Brook ended the call and focused on her breathing to calm herself down. There was almost certainly a logical reason why they weren't here. She just hadn't thought of it yet. She called Rosa's cell and almost immediately heard it ringing. For a second she couldn't pinpoint its location, then she realized it was coming from the living room.

Frowning, she strode inside and saw it vibrating on the coffee table. It was an old iPhone 5, and Rosa never went anywhere without it.

Except, it seemed, tonight.

Brook ended the call and paced the house, cell in hand, waiting for Logan to call her back, frustrated because right now she had no idea what was going on, and there was nothing she could do about it. She was a woman used to being in control. She'd worked for herself for most of the last fifteen years; had built up everything she had, through her own efforts; and when she saw an obstacle, she found a way around it. That was why she was successful and why people read her books. It was her unique selling point.

Her throat felt dry and she went into the kitchen to get a glass of water.

And that was when she saw it. A cellphone on the kitchen island with a charger attached, sitting on a folded sheet of A4 paper. The cell, a cheap Nokia handset that she didn't recognize, looked brand new. She put it to one side, unfolded the sheet of paper and, as she started reading, felt her whole body tighten.

The words, in a large, bold typeface, were cold and unrelenting:

We have your daughter. She is unharmed. If you want her back alive, you will do exactly as we say. If you call the police, you will never see her again. We can see you and we will know. We will call you with instructions on the phone next to this note. Keep it with you at all times. Now look in the cutlery drawer. We have left you a gift to show you we are serious.

Remember. We can see you.

Brook put down the note, her breathing much faster now. It felt like some kind of sick joke. And yet she knew straight away it was far more serious than that. She looked down at the cutlery drawer, put her hand on it, but held back from pulling it open. Somehow, while the drawer stayed shut, reality was kept at bay.

She hesitated a long time, wishing that Logan would just call her back and tell her everything was okay.

But he didn't. She was on her own. And finally ... finally curiosity got the better of her and she placed her fingers around the handle and slowly pulled.

Sitting in the knife tray was a tiny cardboard box decorated in a flower pattern, with a red ribbon wrapped around it.

Brook felt a deep sense of dread as she looked at the box, her curiosity fighting with a desire to run right out of the room. She knew she ought to put on a pair of gloves before she opened it, in case whoever had put it there had left fingerprints behind, but instead she steeled herself and, in one quick movement, picked up the box, pulled open the ribbon and lifted the lid.

It was then she realized that, without a doubt, this nightmare was real.

2

The police interview room
Now

Detective Tyrone Giant went to stroke his beard, remembered as he touched the bare skin that he'd shaved it off this morning for the first time in five years and then, feeling somewhat naked, stopped outside the interview-room door, his A4-sized notebook under one arm.

Twelve-thirty a.m. on a Monday morning was a hell of a bad time to be starting an interview, but there was a lot riding on this. The Chief, the local mayor, the media – they all wanted Brook Connor's head. And even more than that, they were desperate to hear the story of how she'd ended up as a fugitive on the run, wanted for mass murder. It had only been four hours since her arrest, but no one – least of all Giant – wanted to give her the breathing space to come up with a story to explain her actions over the past four days. He wanted to catch her out, get a confession and wrap up this whole thing.

It had been Giant and his partner, Detective Jenna King, who'd made the arrest, which was why they'd been given responsibility for conducting the interview. Giant was the more senior of the two, being five years older and with seven years more experience as a detective, but he knew that Jenna was the more respected amongst their colleagues. She'd been at the department for eight years, he'd only joined it nine months ago. And Jenna was very much one of the boys. Everyone liked her. She backchatted. She didn't take shit. And she was heavily decorated, having single-handedly shot dead two suspects in a firefight. There was no way Giant could compete with any of that. He was the first to admit that he was the more traditional kind of detective. The one who went out of his way to avoid violence and who, if he was honest, was dead scared of it.

But now he had a chance to change things. To become respected by everyone. It was something he badly wanted.

He turned to Jenna, still touching the bare skin of his chin. 'You ready?'

'I can't get used to you without a beard,' she said. 'You look younger.'

'And that's a good thing, right?'

She smiled, and Giant felt a frisson of excitement, as he always did whenever she smiled. 'Yeah, but the beard gave you a certain gravitas. Useful in an interview like this. Come on, let's get it over with. I'm pooped already.'

Giant opened the door and moved aside to let her in first, trying to work out whether Jenna preferred him with a beard or without, before going inside and taking his seat.

He cleared his throat and looked across the table at the two women sitting opposite him. Brook Connor looked tired but defiant – the kind of suspect who wasn't going to roll over and confess everything – which Giant knew didn't bode well. Her right cheek was swollen and an unpleasant yellowing bruise ran down to her jawline, making it look like she'd been punched hard in the face, which only added to her defiant appearance. Even now, though, rundown and devoid of make-up, with her hair short, badly cut and unkempt, she still looked pretty, and Giant could see why she'd done so well with her books and her cable-TV show. She had presence.

The woman next to her had presence, too, but in a very different way. Brook Connor's lawyer, Angie Southby, was small and whip-thin, possibly late forties, although it was hard to tell with all the work she'd had done, with very thick, jet-black hair pulled back into a tight bun, a tan so dark it had to be fake and a face that radiated a volatile mix of anger, disdain and haughtiness. Giant didn't know her – apparently she had a criminal-law practice in San Francisco – but she had a reputation as something of a ball-breaker, and she was expensive, too, which always spelled trouble. She'd do everything she could to get her client out of here, but unless she was a miracle-worker, that wasn't going to be happening any time soon.

Jenna spoke first – her voice calm, almost regretful in its tone. 'You're in a lot of trouble, Brook. I hope your lawyer's told you to cooperate with us.'

'My client intends to prove her innocence,' said Southby firmly.

Jenna raised an eyebrow. 'Really? Well, she's got a lot of proving do. But all we want to hear tonight is the truth.'

'And my client will give you that. But then I want her released and out of here tonight. She's been through a very traumatic experience.'

Giant took a deep breath and spoke for the first time. 'You must have some explanation, Brook,' he said, making a play of consulting his notes, before looking her right in the eye. 'Because, you see, what we've got here – on top of everything else from the past four days – are three dead bodies, a missing child and one suspect. And that suspect's you. So my first question is this: if you're as innocent as your lawyer here claims, then what the hell happened?'

Brook met his gaze, and when she spoke, it was with the languid British accent that had become her trademark. 'It's a long story.'

Giant leaned forward in his seat. 'You'd better start telling it, then.'

3

Wednesday night
Four days ago

Brook was pacing the hallway in her bare feet, unwilling to sit down or even stop moving, when her husband walked in the front door, dressed in a check shirt, jeans and boots, as if advertising the fact that he rarely, if ever, worked.

'Where the hell have you been?' she demanded.

Logan shut the door behind him and glared at her. 'Having a drink with a couple of the boys. You got a problem with that?'

He'd had more than a couple of drinks. She could tell. He was doing it more and more these days. She wasn't sure if it was a reaction to their failing relationship, or whether their relationship was failing as a consequence of it. Either way, she was pretty certain he didn't love her any more, and the love that she'd had for him had faded almost to nothing, too. It was something that had been weighing on her mind for the past few months, but right now, with Paige missing, their marital problems had been rendered utterly meaningless.

'Why didn't you call me back?' she asked him, trying to keep the anger out of her voice. 'I left a message for you almost an hour ago. I said it was urgent.'

He didn't even look at her as he pulled off one of his boots. 'I only picked it up a few minutes ago. Anyways, what's the problem?'

'Go into the kitchen. Read the note and look in the box.'

'What the hell are you talking about?'

'Just do it, Logan.'

He looked at her strangely, then pulled off the other boot and, with a shake of his head, stalked off to the kitchen. Brook followed a little way behind. She'd put the box on the island next to the phone and the note, and she watched as Logan read the note first, then carefully opened it, his back to her.

She heard his sharp intake of breath and watched his shoulders sag. Logan Harris was a big man, close to six four and built like a bear, but he seemed to shrink in front of her and, when he turned around, his face had turned a sickly grey.

'Jesus!' he whispered. 'Have you called the police?'

Brook shook her head. 'I didn't know what to do. I was waiting for you. What do you think they want?'

He looked confused. 'I don't know. Money? It has to be that. Why else would they take her and leave a note for us?'

'We're not that rich.'

'You're a celebrity, Brook. You've written bestselling books. You're on TV. Look at this place.' He gazed around him with an expression of disgust, as if his whole life was toxic. 'Look at what we've got.'

We, she thought bitterly. *Me*, more like. Logan was a semi-retired, bit-part actor and semi-pro tennis player turned coach. When they'd met, he'd been experiencing what he'd described as 'cashflow' problems, a situation that hadn't improved much since. 'Listen, Logan. There are probably a hundred people richer than us, just in Carmel – some much, much richer – but you never hear about their children getting taken like this.' It made Brook feel sick, saying the words aloud.

'Well, maybe it's because they pay a ransom.'

'No way,' she said emphatically. 'Something like that would get out. Look at what they did to Rosa, for Christ's sakes.' She pointed to the box on the island that the kidnappers had left. Inside was the freshly severed little finger of Rosa's right hand, still wearing the silver ring that Brook had given her the previous Christmas.

When Brook had first set eyes on it, it had been like receiving an electric shock. The finger looked like some sort of horror-film prop, but one that was a little bit too realistic. The flesh was torn and shredded where the finger had been sawn off, and blood smeared the soft paper inside. There was even a piece of protruding white bone, and Brook had felt sick at the sadism of whoever had done this to an innocent woman – someone she really cared about – and with fear of what they'd do to her child. 'This is personal, Logan,' she said. 'No one goes to this much trouble just for money.'

'How do you know? Are you an expert now?'

Brook let out a long breath. 'Because it's logical. People don't kidnap children for ransom any more. When was the last time you heard of it? So my question to you is: have you been pissing off the wrong people?'

'Of course I haven't,' he said, but she immediately spotted the hint of uncertainty in his expression. The thing was, she didn't trust Logan. She hadn't for a long time. He had dark, brooding good looks and an air of the celebrity about him, even though his acting career had been nothing to write home about, and the older he grew, the better-looking he seemed to get. Brook's girlfriends always said how lucky she was to have him. At least, to her face. But that was the problem. Women loved Logan, and he loved them right back. Far too much.

'Look, if you've done something wrong – something you're ashamed of – let's talk about it now, because frankly, I don't care. I just want to find our daughter.'

'I haven't done anything wrong,' he snapped, his voice loud in the room. 'What about you? Have you done anything you're ashamed of, Brook?'

It was, she thought, the typical response of the guilty. Deflecting blame.

'I've never done anything I'm ashamed of,' she said firmly, only vaguely aware that this wasn't true. 'And I don't have any enemies.'

'It could be one of your crackpot clients. Have you thought of that?'

'I life-coach people – people with money. I help them achieve their goals. I don't deal with the criminally insane.' She walked back out of the kitchen, putting some distance between her and the argument, and stood in the spacious hallway, looking around at the house they'd bought together only three years ago. The place that was going to be their family home. Now violated. 'They must have come when Paige was asleep, because her bed's been slept in,' she said almost to herself, suddenly thinking of something. 'And they must have come in and left by car, so they'll have been recorded by the camera on the front gate.'

Like most people living in a large, detached home, she and Logan were security-conscious. Their property was in a quiet development in the hills above Carmel, backing onto woodland and surrounded by a high brick wall. The only way in with a car was through security gates covered by a surveillance camera. They'd thought about installing more cameras at the rear of the house, in case anyone came over the back wall, but as most of the houses round there didn't even have front gates, it seemed like overkill. As Logan had pointed out, they weren't exactly living in a high-crime area.

However, the camera covering the front gate automatically began filming when the sensors underneath the tarmac detected movement, and automatically sent footage into the Cloud, which both Brook and Logan could access from apps on their cells. She pulled out her cell now and checked the app, as Logan came up beside her, putting a hand on her shoulder and giving it a gentle squeeze. He smelled of Creed Aventus aftershave. His favourite, and definitely not something you put on for a couple of drinks with the boys.

'Did the camera pick up anything?' he asked.

Brook's initial excitement faded as she opened the app and stared down at the screen. 'There's nothing,' she said quietly. 'It says the camera's offline. It didn't even record you or me coming in. They must have switched it off, or cut the cable. But how did they even know about it?'

'I don't know,' said Logan, his face crumpled in confusion.

Brook put the cell back in her pocket and, for the first time since she'd read the note, she felt like crying. She was terrified for Paige, who would be scared out of her wits, and who might even have witnessed the terrible thing that had happened to Rosa.

It was now becoming clear that these people were far cleverer than just simple criminals. But that's what they'd said in the ransom note, wasn't it? *We can see you*. What if they'd planted cameras in here and were watching them right now?

As if on cue, the sound of an old-fashioned sing-song ringtone came from the kitchen.

She and Logan looked at each other, and it was Logan who hurried into the kitchen and picked up the cell. He didn't speak and it was clear he was listening to instructions from the other end, but he had his back to her and she couldn't hear what was being said.

After what seemed like a long time, he said the word 'Understood' and placed the cell back on the kitchen top.

'What is it?' she asked him. 'What did they say?'

Logan took a deep breath. 'It was a man. He says they want two hundred and fifty thousand dollars for Paige's safe return.' He paused, steadying himself on the worktop. 'We've got until tomorrow night at ten p.m. to get it. We'll hear from them again then. And they only want to talk to me. Not you.'

Brook frowned. 'Why not?'

'I don't know, he didn't say. And there's something else.'

'What?'

'They knew it was me, even before I picked up the phone. They've got cameras everywhere. They're watching us.' He looked around the room, his expression that of a hunted animal, before fixing his gaze on Brook. 'I haven't got that kind of money. Can you get a quarter of a million dollars by tomorrow?'

But alarm bells were already sounding for Brook. She couldn't believe the kidnappers had only asked for such a relatively small sum of money. They'd mutilated Rosa and probably couldn't afford to let her go now, meaning she was likely to be dead. Surely they wouldn't murder a woman, kidnap a child and risk ending up on death row, all for a quarter of a million dollars? Potentially split more than one way.

It didn't make sense. None of this made sense.

But for the benefit of any camera that might be in the room, she nodded. 'Yes,' she said. 'I can get the money by tomorrow.'

4

How can you sleep when you've just found out that your five-year-old daughter's been abducted by strangers who've already shown their ruthlessness by sawing off her nanny's finger?

After the phone call from the kidnappers, Brook got Logan to put the box containing the finger in the freezer, so it was out of sight, but still available in case it was needed as evidence at a later date. She then paced the house like a caged animal, unable to settle, while Logan sat hunched silently in his den, with only a bottle of Jack Daniel's and his thoughts for company, the kidnappers' phone on the table in front of him. Brook had been tempted to tell him that now was not the time to be drinking, but in the end she'd decided it wasn't worth it. As long as one of them remained sober, it didn't matter. She was desperate for a drink herself, if only to take the edge off everything, but it would have been a show of weakness and she couldn't allow herself that now.

Eventually, at 2 a.m., Logan staggered up to bed and, when exhaustion set in half an hour later, Brook headed up, too.

Logan was already asleep when she slipped under the sheets, still fully clothed in case the kidnappers had a camera here and were watching.

We can see you. It was a phrase that made her skin crawl.

She looked down at Logan, wondering how he could manage to sleep with his daughter in danger, but then she also knew from her work how easily some men can detach themselves emotionally from situations. She'd once had a number of one-to-one coaching sessions with a high-ranking San Francisco executive who was trying to improve his interactions with his staff. He'd come across as a nice guy, but it had turned out that he hadn't seen the two children of his first marriage for close on ten years, having left their mother when they were still at kindergarten age. He hadn't financially supported them, either. It was as if they no longer existed for him. Brook had tried numerous exercises to cultivate empathy within him, but eventually gave up when it was clear he was never going to feel any and dumped him as a client. Having lost her own family, she simply couldn't understand how someone could be so blasé about voluntarily leaving theirs behind. Unlike a lot of people, she was fussy about who she worked with.

Worryingly, she was also certain that Logan was capable of that kind of behaviour, and not for the first time that night, a nagging thought crossed her mind. Could her husband be involved somehow? Their marriage had been going badly for months now, maybe even longer, and he always needed money. They'd always had their own bank accounts and, although she covered all the household expenses, she no longer gave him any handouts, and she knew he resented the fact that she was the breadwinner and that she kept a tight lid on the finances. Maybe this whole kidnapping was some warped money making scheme of his. She'd also noted that when he'd been on the phone to the kidnappers earlier, he hadn't begged for his daughter to be returned home safely or demanded proof that she was alive, like they did in the movies. He'd simply listened and then put down the phone. Was that the behaviour of an innocent man? It wasn't something she would have done.

Yet it was what had happened to Rosa that made her dismiss his involvement. Logan was many things, and he could shout and scream with the best of them, but he wasn't a violent man and would never have countenanced hurting Rosa, and he did genuinely love Paige. Brook had seen the way he was with her, and you couldn't put that on.

Yet still he managed to sleep, and he looked peaceful, too, as if he didn't have a care in the world.

Brook shut her eyes and concentrated on her breathing. She had a whole chapter in her first book containing different exercises to relieve stress, but the kind of stress she was feeling now – the abject fear for the safety of her daughter – wasn't something that any exercise was going to alleviate, and she tossed and turned in the bed, her sweat cold on the sheets, until finally she fell into a shallow, fitful and terrified sleep, where the nightmares that she'd suppressed for so long rose up out of the darkness of her unconscious to plague her once again.

A thin shaft of daylight was coming through the gap in the curtains when Brook woke with a start.

She'd seen the old lady in her nightmare – the one she used to dream about as a child. There was nothing pleasant about this old lady. She looked like the witch in *Snow White*, with a long, hooked nose and bulbous, staring eyes, and in the dreams she would always appear at the edge of a forest, wearing a black dress and beckoning Brook inside with an eerie smile. Although Brook always tried to stop herself, something would always drag her towards the forest, as if she was under some kind of spell, even though deep down she knew that the old lady meant her harm. The dream would then go one of several ways. Either the spell would be broken and Brook would turn and run towards freedom – sometimes chased by the old lady, sometimes not. Or she would take the old lady's hand, powerless to resist as she was led further and further into the forest, until all around her was darkness, and she knew this was the place where she would die.

In the dream this time, Brook had been unable to resist the old lady's coaxing. But the old lady hadn't taken her into the forest. Instead she'd guided her down a quiet residential street of pretty, well-kept houses with neat front lawns and picket fences, until they came to a parked car. The day was gloriously sunny, and Brook had even begun to relax a little as the old lady opened the car door and helped her inside.

And then, as she sat down, all the doors suddenly locked and at the same time night fell and the world was transformed into a cold, dark, terrifying place. The old lady climbed in beside her, and Brook saw the cruel, sadistic look in her deep-red eyes as she repeated the same phrase over and over again: '*You're mine now.*'

For several seconds Brook felt an overwhelming relief that she was no longer trapped inside the nightmare. And then the reality of her situation hit her with a sickening inevitability and she felt like crying. She looked at the bedside clock: 6.55 a.m. Logan, incredibly, was still asleep beside her, although she'd felt him move about restlessly in the night, as if he too had been haunted by his dreams.

She got out of bed and went into the bathroom, spending the next five minutes searching around for hidden cameras. According to Logan, the kidnappers had warned them both not to look for, or disable, any of the cameras that they claimed had been planted all over the house, but there was no way Brook was going to be watched while she was in the bathroom. She couldn't find anything out of place and concluded that they hadn't planted one in here. In fact, the more she thought about it, she more she was convinced they could only have planted one or two cameras at most. They wouldn't have had a lot of time in the house the previous night, and much of it would have been spent neutralizing Rosa, cutting off her finger and then getting her and Paige into the car and out of the property, while also at some point disabling the security camera covering the front gate.

Unless, of course, they had inside help.

She threw off her clothes and stepped in the shower, letting the hot water flow over her, her mind already trying to make sense of why they'd been targeted, because it couldn't be purely about money. Maybe if the kidnappers had asked for two and a half million, she'd understand (not that she had that kind of cash). But two hundred and fifty simply wasn't worth the hassle. No, this was personal. Brook wondered briefly if it might be someone jealous of her success, but in the end she wasn't that famous. Yes, she'd done well for herself, having written a self-help book that had sold half a million copies, and she had her own segment on a TV show. But a lot of writers sold more than half a million copies, and the TV show was a local one on cable, with a regular viewing audience of fewer than a hundred thousand. She wasn't exactly Oprah.

And it wasn't anything in her personal life, either. Brook was proud of the fact that she'd never knowingly made enemies and always tried to do the right thing.

But Logan … he was another matter. He was the key to this, Brook was sure of it. And she hadn't liked the fact that, when she'd asked him if he'd pissed off the wrong people, he'd hesitated for half a second before answering her, as if it had just occurred to him at that moment that maybe he had.

But if Logan had been doing anything bad, she was going to know about it. She'd already taken steps in that department. Perhaps it was time to get some feedback.

She got out of the shower, dried herself and, with the towel still covering her, went back into the bedroom.

Logan was awake now and sitting up in the bed. He stared at her, his face crumpled and defeated, his eyes bloodshot. 'I thought it was a nightmare,' he said.

'Don't worry, honey, we're going to get through it,' she replied, kneeling on the bed and pulling him close to her. 'Meet me at the summerhouse in ten minutes,' she whispered, conscious that he still smelled of alcohol and expensive aftershave, before pulling away from his grip and throwing on some clothes.

As she walked out onto the wraparound interior balcony and glanced across at Paige's empty room, Brook took a deep breath, telling herself she had to remain strong. *We can get through this. There's always a way.* Wasn't that the theme of her latest book? If you can release your inner warrior and work towards your true potential, then anything's possible.

Even getting your kidnapped daughter back.

They'd had the summerhouse built a couple of months after they'd moved in. It was tucked away in the shade of a mature oak tree, beyond the main lawn in the corner of their property, and Brook liked to sit on the rocking chair outside when it was warm enough, watching Paige play and contemplating all that was good in her world. Saturday had been an unseasonably hot day for the beginning of May, and she'd been outside then, reading a book and drinking an iced tea, relishing the time alone for once. Logan had been out coaching tennis to one of his clients, and Paige had been at a friend's for a sleepover. It was hard to believe that had only been a few days ago. The world had been a completely different place and she hadn't had the faintest idea of the cataclysmic event coming their way.

Brook checked the framework of the summerhouse, and even the oak tree facing it, to make sure there were no cameras, but there was nothing. Next to the summerhouse, set amongst the shrubs that obscured the brick wall, was the back gate. It led onto a tree-covered hill that ran down to the road on the other side of their property, and was the same height as the wall, at approximately seven feet. The gate was locked and bolted, as it always was. However, that wouldn't have stopped someone determined climbing over and getting into the house that way. Because of the trees and the space between the houses, they wouldn't have been seen. The only problem was there was no way they'd have been able to lift Rosa back over it (or Paige, for that matter), so they would have had to leave through the front. The whole thing would have been a very tricky operation, because they were running the risk of being discovered by either Brook or Logan. So either the kidnappers were real risk-takers or they'd known that she and Logan were out and wouldn't be back.

She frowned to herself and turned to watch as Logan came out the back door, dressed in the clothes he'd had on the previous night, and walked towards her, his shoulders hunched and his head bowed, looking more like a condemned man than ever.

Surely he wasn't that good an actor, she thought. Seeing him now, it was hard for her to believe that he could ever have been involved.

'Is it safe to talk?' he asked, stopping in front of her and looking round.

She nodded and stepped forward so that she was close enough to whisper. 'I've checked for cameras. There aren't any. And I think we need to go to the police.'

Logan shook his head emphatically. 'No. We can't risk it. If they find out, we'll never see Paige again.'

'We can't do this on our own. We've got a much better chance of finding her with the police helping. They've got the resources.'

'We've got to do this on our own. If we get them the money, they'll release her unharmed.'

'You see, that's what I don't get, Logan. It's only a quarter of a million they want.'

'Only? It's a lot of money, Brook.'

'But it's not. This house cost ten times that. And they'd have needed two people to have overpowered Rosa and taken her and Paige like that. That means they're looking at a hundred and twenty-five thousand each. It's not enough money for the kind of risk they're taking and the amount of jail time they're looking at.'

'Not all criminals are Einstein, Brook.'

'Maybe not, but these ones are definitely no fools. So it's personal. And if it's personal, they're going to want to make us suffer. And that means they're not going to want to give Paige back.'

Logan's face dropped, as if this had only just occurred to him.

'Is there anyone you can think of who might hate us so much as to snatch our daughter and injure – maybe even kill – her nanny as well? I know I asked you last night, but I'm asking you again. In fact I'm begging you, for Paige's sake. Tell me, if there is. We can work through this.'

He met her gaze with an expression that she'd seen him use before, and which was more often than not the prelude for a whopping lie. But still there was the tiniest hint of doubt in his eyes as he said once again that no, he couldn't think of anyone. 'No one hates me that much,' he added hopefully.

'We need proof that Paige is alive,' said Brook. 'Next time they phone, you're going to have to insist on it. I'm not paying them any money until we know. We have to take back some control in this situation.'

He nodded. 'Okay, I'll make sure I ask them.'

'Don't ask them,' she said firmly. 'Tell them. We need a photograph. One that proves she's unharmed.' As she spoke, she wondered what it was that had made a strong, confident woman like her go for a man like Logan: strong on the outside, but weak, needy and narcissistic underneath. It was a question she'd avoided asking herself for years, and she still didn't know the answer now. Like most people, she was a lot better at psychoanalysing others than she was at analysing herself.

'They're not going to like us making demands,' said Logan. 'We've got to be careful.'

She gave him a withering look. 'I don't care. If you want, I'll take the phone and I'll be the one to tell them we want proof.'

He shook his head. 'No. I told you last night. They want to do all the negotiations through me. That means I have to keep the cell.'

Brook frowned. There had to be some reason why they would only talk to Logan, and whatever it was, it made her suspicious. She took a deep breath, knowing she needed to think about this, and started back towards the house.

'Where are you going?' he called after her.

'Where do you think?' she said over her shoulder. 'To get the money.'

5

Brook knew it was a total cliché, but she'd never meant to fall in love with a married man.

She and Logan had met, predictably enough, when she'd hired him to give her tennis lessons. She'd spent her formative years in England, after her parents had moved there when she was five, and she'd never learned to play tennis. So when she'd returned to California eight years previously, aged twenty-eight, she'd vowed to take it up. However, since then her game had been flat-lining, and Logan had been recommended to her by a girlfriend as a man who could improve it.

From the moment she'd set eyes on him, Brook had felt a strong physical attraction. He might have been close to ten years older than her, but he was a good-looking guy – tall, tanned and well built, with dark, curly hair flecked with only the merest hint of grey and a wide, friendly smile. But Brook knew he was married, so she kept her distance. And to be fair to Logan, so did he. He was friendly and charming, but he was also respectful and avoided physical contact. In fact, he did everything right. She knew that some of his other clients flirted with him, but she didn't hear any gossip suggesting he was unfaithful.

He was a good coach, too. After three months of twice-weekly sessions her game had improved markedly.

And then one day everything changed. It was a sunny, warm morning in midsummer, and when Logan walked onto the court at the beginning of the lesson, his head was bowed and he looked troubled in a way he never had before. Their interaction had always been very businesslike. Because Brook was so attracted to him, she went out of her way to keep their conversation centred on the lesson itself rather than on personal matters, and she never gave too much away about her own life, or asked too many questions about his. But seeing him like that, she'd asked if he was okay.

'I've had some bad news,' he answered, 'and I guess I'm having trouble processing it.'

She'd asked him if it was anything he'd like to share, half-expecting him to say no.

But he'd told her without hesitation. 'We've just found out my wife's got skin cancer. It's melanoma, and her chances aren't good.'

Brook had been shocked and sympathetic. She'd told him there was no need to continue the lesson if he'd prefer to be with his wife, but Logan had insisted they carry on. 'I'd prefer to keep busy,' he told her. 'It's easier that way.'

In hindsight, maybe Brook should have guessed that, by choosing not to be with his wife, it said something less than flattering about Logan's character. But she hadn't. Instead she'd read it as stoicism and, ironically, it gave her a new respect for him.

And so over the next few weeks they'd begun to talk about more personal matters. She noticed that Logan's jaw tightened when he was fighting to contain his emotions, and especially when he gave her updates on his wife's progress (it wasn't good, she was going downhill quickly). Looking back, Brook should have noticed that it was odd he never talked about her by name, always preferring to refer to her as 'my wife', until Brook finally brought him up on it, and Logan told her that she was called Anna.

But at the time it had never occurred to her that his de-personalizing of Anna suggested that he had deeper, more worrying, personality issues. Instead Brook tried to keep his spirits up by being as optimistic as possible. 'You can't let yourself lose hope until the very last breath' was one of the lines she'd often used in their conversations, and which was lifted straight out of her first book, *You Can Be the Hero*. She'd really believed it then, too. Now she saw it as the clichéd statement of the obvious it so clearly was, and it made her cringe.

And then one day Logan – big, strong Logan who'd always held it together – had broken down in tears during a lesson. It was late on a cloudy, unseasonably chilly afternoon, and they were alone on the court, with no one to see them. She remembered walking up and putting her arms around him, immediately conscious of his warmth and masculine scent, and she felt an intense, almost animalistic yearning for him that was sudden, unexpected and, most of all, hard to resist.

But resist she did, even as he put his own arms around her and held her close, the strength in his muscles intoxicating to her. The urge she felt to kiss him was close to overpowering. She'd never felt like this about a man, and only when he told her that the doctors had informed them the previous day that Anna's cancer was terminal – and that she could expect only months, not years, of life – only then did Brook's lust (because that was in essence what it was) begin to fade, although in her heart she already knew that her resistance was only temporary.

And it was. One evening, a few days later, Logan called her at home. He told her he needed to talk and asked if he could come round. He sounded as if he'd been crying and Brook felt sorry for him. Once again, in hindsight, she should have been suspicious of the fact that he didn't have other people – close friends – he could talk to, but that was her weakness. Because, in the end, she wanted him to come round, and she justified it in her head by saying that she could give him some good support and advice, knowing that she had nothing to be afraid of with Logan, as he'd always been totally respectful in her presence.

An hour later, he was on her doorstep. He looked tired and down, but he'd dressed well and was wearing aftershave. His eyes were no longer red, if they ever had been.

Brook had known what was going to happen as soon as she let him in, but it hadn't stopped her. The close hug had come first, accompanied by the talk about how hard Logan was finding everything, how he'd been looking after Anna all day, how he'd just needed to get out; then the staring into each other's eyes as she told him that he had to be strong, for Anna's sake; then came the kiss, followed with grim inevitability by the clothes being ripped off.

They hadn't even made it as far as the bedroom.

Afterwards, both of them had expressed their guilt over what they'd done, but it hadn't stopped them doing it a second time half an hour later, this time upstairs on Brook's bed.

Logan had left soon after that, but not before he'd told Brook that, in spite of himself, he had very strong feelings for her. Brook hadn't replied, but in the end she hadn't really needed to. Her actions had told him everything he needed to know.

And, of course, when you've sinned once, it becomes so much easier to do it again, and very soon, despite Brook's rather weak protestations, she and Logan had begun a full-blown affair.

The guilt she felt wasn't easy to handle. It kept her awake at night sometimes. Logan had told her that the guilt was weighing on him, too – and he'd certainly acted like it had been. But that was the whole point with Logan. He was an actor. It had taken her a long time – years rather than months – to realize that he was always playing a part, depending on who he was with. He seemed to have difficulty expressing genuine emotions, and she wondered if, like the businessman client she'd dumped, her husband was incapable of feeling empathy, and if, beneath the surface of his smile, there was nothing there.

Brook had had plenty of chances in those early days to spot the warning signs and terminate their affair. But she couldn't remember whether she'd not seen them or whether, more likely, she'd chosen to ignore all the negatives. Either way, her failure was why she was in her current situation, driving to the bank in the nearby Carmel Rancho shopping centre to withdraw a quarter of a million dollars in cash, having just phoned Paige's kindergarten to tell them that her daughter wasn't feeling very well and wouldn't be in that day. It had been an almost impossible task to sound cheerful as she'd spoken to Paige's teacher, Mrs Day, but somehow she'd pulled it off.

'I love you, baby,' she whispered aloud in the car as she parked in the lot across from the bank and cut the engine. 'I'm going to make you safe.'

At that moment, her cellphone rang.

It was Logan and he started talking rapidly. He sounded breathless. 'They've sent me a photo of Paige. I asked for proof of life, like you said . . .'

Brook felt her heart lurch. 'Is she okay? They haven't hurt her, have they?'

'No, she's fine. She looks fine, anyways. She's in a room somewhere. I don't recognize the place.'

'Can you send me the photo on WhatsApp?'

'They told me to delete it straight away and definitely not share it on other phones.'

'Are you in the house now?'

'No. I'm in the car.'

'Then send it to me. They'll never know. I'll delete it later.'

'I don't think it's a good idea.'

'Please, Logan,' she said. 'I'm the one about to get that money. I need to see proof.'

'Okay,' he said reluctantly.

'I'm guessing the kidnappers called you. What did they want?'

'They wanted to make sure we were getting the money and we hadn't done anything stupid. They said they were still watching us the whole time.'

Something still didn't feel right about how the kidnappers were handling this, but in the end Brook was just happy to have it confirmed that Paige was still alive. 'Was it the same man on the phone as last night?'

'Yes.'

'And does he disguise his voice?'

'He speaks quietly, but he sounds local. Not foreign.'

'And you don't recognize it?'

'No, of course not. Why are you asking me all these questions? I'm trying to give you some good news about Paige.'

Brook took a deep breath and saw her reflection in the rear-view mirror. She'd put on make-up and was wearing a smart suit, wanting to look as businesslike as possible for her visit to the bank, but it was impossible to hide completely her exhaustion and agitation. 'I know you are,' she said. 'Thank you.'

'I'll send the photo now,' he said, with a tenderness in his voice that had had been missing too long. 'She's going to be okay.'

'I know she is.'

'Are you at the bank?'

'I'm just parking.'

'Good luck in there.'

Brook said goodbye and ended the call, eager to receive the photo of Paige.

She didn't have to wait long. Less than a minute later her cell bleeped to say she'd received a WhatsApp message. Her whole body tensed as she opened the app and enlarged the photo. For several seconds she was too overcome with emotion to take in what she was seeing. She blinked back tears, slowed her breathing, then examined the picture properly.

Paige was a beautiful child. She had rich, dark hair and golden skin; a round, cherubic face with big brown eyes full of life and innocence; and a cute gap between her front teeth. You couldn't really see any of that in the photo, though, which was a full-body shot taken from a few feet away. Paige was in an unfamiliar room, with only dark wooden floorboards and a blank wall visible, and she was wearing an equally unfamiliar red-and-white hooded sleepsuit, with the hood bunched up behind her head. She was only half-looking at the camera and her face registered confusion, but not, thank God, fear. At her feet was a small Sylvanian doll's house with a handful of pieces scattered about it. Other than that, the room appeared empty. There were no clues as to its location or to the identity of the person taking the photo.

But the point was, she was definitely alive. She'd been taken somewhere, put in new clothes and given access to toys. She didn't look scared. These were all positive signs and, for the first time, Brook experienced an almost elated sense of relief. Maybe they'd even be getting her back as soon as tonight.

But mixed with the relief were nagging questions about the kidnapping. And yet, as Brook got out of the car and retrieved a holdall from the back seat, she pushed such thoughts from her mind.

Paige was alive and, right now, that was all that mattered.

6

Brook had called ahead to the manager of the bank where she'd kept her money for the best part of the last ten years, and he was waiting in the lobby when she walked in.

Ralph Byfield was a short, overweight man in his fifties with an inflated air of his own importance and a moist handshake. There was nothing likeable about him, and Brook imagined him to be the kind of man who'd achieved his promotions by subtly undermining his colleagues. He'd been the bank's manager for three years now and she tended to avoid him when possible, especially as she knew he had a bit of a thing for her.

Today he was dressed in a charcoal-grey three-piece suit a size too small for him and polished Derby brogues that looked like they were pinching his feet.

'Ms Connor, always a pleasure to see you,' he said, putting out a pudgy hand and trying not to look too interested in the empty holdall she was carrying.

'Thanks for making the time to meet me, Mr Byfield,' she said, as he led into her through a side door and down to his office.

'Of course – you're one of our best customers, and we at the bank always like to be on hand to help whenever we can. Please,' he said, motioning her to take a seat.

Brook put down the holdall and sat opposite him across his outsize desk.

'First of all, can I offer you some coffee, or green tea perhaps?' he asked, his smile unctuous.

She'd mentioned on one of her appearances on the TV show that she drank green tea to relax her, and it unnerved her that Byfield had obviously seen it. 'No thanks,' she said. 'I'm fine.'

'So what can we do for you? You mentioned that it was urgent.'

Brook had already worked out her story. 'My husband and I have been given an excellent investment opportunity in Mexico – one that we've checked out and are happy with – but we need to make a deposit in cash to secure the best deal. I need two hundred and fifty thousand dollars in cash today.'

Byfield's smile evaporated and was immediately replaced by a surprised expression that was only just the right side of suspicious. 'Ms Connor, I think any investment that requires a cash deposit of that size – especially one taking place outside US jurisdiction – is one that you and your husband should think very carefully about. We hear lots of stories about fraud ...'

'We know what we're doing, Mr Byfield. We just need the money. And we need it today.'

Byfield looked on the verge of panic. He clearly wasn't used to requests like this. 'That's not going to be possible, Ms Connor.'

'I believe that I have four hundred and thirty-eight thousand dollars in the standard savings account I have with you' – Byfield started to speak, but Brook put up a hand to stop him – 'as well as a further one hundred and forty-five thousand in my business account, and forty-three thousand in my personal checking account. That, if I calculate correctly, is six hundred and twenty-six thousand dollars. So clearly I have the money to cover this transaction and, according to the bank's terms, I'm entitled to immediate access to it. '

'We don't keep that kind of cash on the premises,' he said, his forehead glistening now.

'Then please could you get it for me? I need it by close of business this afternoon.'

'I don't think you understand, Ms Connor. I would need to inform the relevant authorities of a transaction of this size, under the terms of the Bank Secrecy Act. There are forms that need to be submitted. It's certainly possible to get you the money at some point in the next five business days, but it won't happen much before then, if at all. I'm sorry, Ms Connor, but my hands are tied.'

Brook's earlier elation was fading fast. The kidnappers weren't going to wait that long. And the fact that it was her own money, and she was entitled to it, frustrated her even more. She forced herself to remain calm, but coming on top of the stress of the last twelve hours, it was hard.

'You say that you don't hold that amount of cash here, but you have other branches. In an emergency, you could get the money together by close of play today, yes?'

Byfield looked interested now. 'Is this an emergency? Are you in some kind of trouble?'

'It's a hypothetical question,' she said. 'Humour me. Like you said: I'm one of your most valuable customers.'

He didn't like that. 'I suppose, in an emergency, yes. But an investment in Mexico isn't an emergency. Unless it's something else. Something we may be able to help with.'

There was no way Brook was going to let him know anything about her predicament. But she was playing for high stakes now, and she had to choose the way forward carefully. 'I respect your position, Mr Byfield, and I'm happy to sign whatever paperwork needs signing, but I want my money today and I know you can get it.'

'I think we're going round in circles here—'

'No, we're not. Because if you don't get it for me, not only will you lose me as a customer – and I'd like to remind you that as well as the six hundred and twenty-six thousand dollars in *cash* that I have in this bank, I have a further one-point-eight million dollars in investments with you. You'll not only lose all that, but I will also walk straight out of here and tell every customer and would-be customer who comes through your doors today, tomorrow and the next day that you haven't got the cash reserves to fund withdrawals. I'll tell them that you won't even give me my own money. And then we'll see exactly how long it takes to start a run on your bank.' Brook delivered this whole spiel with a calmness in her voice that belied the seething emotions she was experiencing inside. She'd considered trying to sweet-talk Byfield, but she didn't think this approach would get her the quarter of a million by the time the bank closed, whereas the threat just might.

It was clear she'd put him on the spot. His face was red, and he looked flustered as he fiddled with the papers on his desk. 'You're a very valued client, so I really wouldn't advise you to do that, Ms Connor,' he said, but there was uncertainty in his voice.

Brook thought of Paige, all alone in a strange place, and pressed her advantage. 'I don't care what you advise. That's what's going to happen. If it doesn't, I'll also bring up the issues I'm having with your bank, and you personally, on the TV show.' She wouldn't, of course – they'd never let her – but now wasn't the time for subtlety.

'I don't know why you're doing this,' he said, looking so genuinely confused that she actually felt sorry for him. 'Are you in some kind of trouble?'

'All I want is a portion of *my* money, Mr Byfield,' Brook said, almost soothingly, knowing that it's always good to follow the big stick with a carrot. 'That's all I'm asking for. Nothing more. And I just want you to get it for me by the end of today.'

Byfield took a deep breath and met her gaze.

The moment of truth. Brook could hear her heart beating a rapid tattoo in her chest.

'Come back at four o'clock and we'll expedite your request,' he said, getting to his feet .

7

Brook had barely been inside the bank for ten minutes, but she already had a missed call from Logan. She put on her sunglasses and looked around before walking back to the car, checking for any suspicious-looking characters who were hanging around, but the parking lot was empty.

As soon as she was back inside the car, she returned Logan's call.

'Did you get the money?' he asked immediately.

'I've got to go back and collect it later this afternoon,' she told him. 'It wasn't easy. There are rules about withdrawing large sums of cash.'

'But they're going to give it to you, right?'

'Yes. They're going to give it to me.'

'That's great.' He sounded relieved. 'Are you coming home?'

Brook sighed. She needed time to think. 'No, not yet. I'm going to take a drive, clear my head.'

'Don't be too long, babe. I need you here with me.'

She was suddenly very tired of Logan. 'I'll be back when I can,' she said, trying to inject some enthusiasm into her voice.

'Did you get the photo of Paige?' he asked her.

'I did. It was a real relief.'

'She looks okay, doesn't she?' he said brightly. 'We're going to get her back, Brook. We deliver them that quarter mill and hopefully Paige will be sleeping in her bed tonight.'

'There's no "hopefully" about it, Logan. They don't get the money until we see Paige. No way. The money gives us leverage. Without it, they've got no incentive to cooperate.'

'I'll make sure they know that.'

'Please do, because we can't afford to screw this up.'

'Don't you think I know that, Brook? She's my daughter.'

'Yes,' she said, too mentally exhausted to get into an argument. 'I know she is. I'll see you later.' She cut the call, no longer wanting to talk to her husband, and reversed the car out into the traffic.

What Brook couldn't understand was Logan's apparent lack of concern for Paige's safety. He'd always been a pretty assertive guy – at least on the surface – and yet he wasn't being at all pushy with the kidnappers, letting them dictate things totally when, as Brook knew from past experience, you had to wrest back control, get your opponents to show you respect. The money seemed to interest him more than Paige did, which would stand to reason if he knew for a fact that she was safe and well.

The only way he'd know that for sure, however, was if he was a part of the kidnap.

But in the end she couldn't think of a good reason why he'd do this. If he needed her money that much, he could simply divorce her. They hadn't bothered signing a prenup – mainly because, even now, Brook wasn't exactly super-wealthy, and when they'd wed two and a half years ago she'd been worth a lot less – so there'd been no obvious need for one. With hardly any assets of his own, Logan would be able to claim a sizeable slice of her money anyway – far more than a quarter of a million dollars – and do the whole thing completely legally.

Even so, Brook was certain that Logan was the key to all this. And if she could find out how, then she might be able to get a clue as to the identity of the kidnappers, because she wasn't at all confident they were going to deliver Paige home safe and sound, even after getting the money. If they had a personal grudge, they'd keep the torment going as long as possible.

Only one person could help Brook find out what was really going on. Someone she'd been trying to get hold of for the past three days, until Paige had gone missing. But the thing was, Chris Cervantes hadn't been returning her calls, even though she was paying him good money for his services.

Chris Cervantes was a private investigator. Brook had found him on the Net. She had no idea how good he was but, according to his résumé, he'd been a police officer for twenty-eight years – twenty of them as a detective – before opening up his own PI practice four years earlier, so he certainly had the experience. She'd hired him three weeks earlier to find out what Logan was doing when he wasn't with her. She knew – or at least guessed – that he played around, but she needed to know whether it was the occasional drunken fumble or something more serious. A lot of women would have said it was better not to know. As long as everything remained fine at home – and largely it did – Brook had Paige; she and Logan got along fine most of the time; they still made love at least once a week then, why rock the boat by finding out things you know aren't going to make you happy?

But Brook knew the reason why. It was because she didn't want to risk losing Paige, and she was a great believer in the maxim that forewarned is forearmed. So if Logan was planning on leaving her, she wanted to know about it now, so she could be prepared.

She'd arranged with Chris Cervantes that he'd send her weekly reports every Sunday before midnight to a Hotmail address to which only the two of them had access. The first report hadn't contained anything out of the ordinary (Logan was doing his usual mix of tennis coaching, hanging out in bars and going to the gym). The second report had been a little more interesting. Twice, Logan had made journeys of an hour and a half in the day (the first up to San José, the second down to King City). They were both places that, as far as Brook was aware, Logan had no business in, and on neither occasion had he mentioned being there. In San José, his car had been parked for three hours in the downtown area, while it had been parked for just over four in King City, but on neither occasion had Cervantes been able to find out what Logan had been doing. There might have been an innocent explanation for both trips, but the fact that they'd been made in secret had aroused Brook's suspicions.

She hadn't confronted Logan about it, preferring to wait and see what came out of the next weekly report.

Except that the report had never arrived. It had been due the previous Sunday, and when it hadn't turned up by Monday morning, Brook had emailed Cervantes, asking where it was. When he hadn't replied by Tuesday, she'd called him on his cell and left a message, before sending another email.

Now, two days later, she still hadn't heard a thing back from him, which was interesting in itself. The timing seemed coincidental and Brook knew from all the detective shows she watched, and books she read, not to trust coincidences.

She thought about calling Cervantes now, but decided it might be easier just to turn up at his place in Monterey. But then it occurred to her that the kidnappers could easily have planted a miniature tracking device somewhere on or in her car.

They might even be tracking her movements on a computer right now, just as she was sure Chris Cervantes had done with Logan. How else had he managed to track him down to San José and King City? She felt sick, knowing that they might be able to see exactly where she was going. There was no way she could turn up at the office of a private detective now. It was too damned risky. Instead she drove into Carmel and parked her car in one of the two-hour slots a little way up from the beach.

She and Logan had picked Carmel to live in because it felt like the best place to bring up Paige. A picture-postcard little seaside town on the central Californian coast, two hours south of

San Francisco, and made famous by the fact that Clint Eastwood had once been mayor, it was a place of art galleries, independent shops and restaurants, with plenty of green spaces, wildlife, state parks on the doorstep, and a magnificent beach that never seemed to get too crowded. The deep-red sunsets across the Pacific were breathtaking; the people were friendly; vehicles stopped for pedestrians crossing the road. It was safe. It was perfect.

And now, in just one day, it had lost all its charm, the thin veneer of safety suddenly wrenched away.

Brook wandered aimlessly around the shops, trying to pass the time before she collected the money from the bank, and feeling like a complete outsider amongst all the people going about their daily lives without a care in the world. Every so often she looked over her shoulder, but no one was following her and, even if they were, she was simply walking. And yet all the time she couldn't get it out of her head that she ought to try to get hold of Cervantes. That he might have a clue for her.

Finally, she stopped for a coffee and bagel at a café opposite the beach. In her current state of mind, the bagel tasted like sawdust, but she forced it down, knowing she needed to eat, before going to the washrooms and locking herself in the cubicle, cellphone in hand, ready to call him. There was no way the kidnappers could have got to her cell. Like everyone else these days, she kept it with her at all times. And yet she was also aware that there were so many ways now of tracking your every move. Was it possible that the photo of Paige they'd sent to Logan, and which he'd sent on to her, contained some kind of viral attachment that could monitor what she was looking at on the phone, or who she was calling? If she called Cervantes and they found out about it, it could cost Paige her life. The stakes were that high.

And Brook knew that losing Paige now would mean the end of her own life. With her family gone, and her husband not the man she thought he was, Paige had become the one person who truly mattered to her. Take her out of the equation and Brook would be left staring into the abyss.

She had no choice but to follow the kidnappers' instructions, deliver them the money and hope they came through. With a sigh, she put the phone away, got to her feet and exited the cubicle.

8

Life had never lived up to expectations for Logan Harris. At school, he'd had so much promise. A handsome, popular boy with a talent for drama and sports, he was the one voted most likely to go places in his class. The girls loved him. So did the boys. Everyone wanted to be his friend. Everyone agreed that Logan was an all-round good guy. Even his home life was great. His parents were liberal, caring, well enough off that nothing was ever too hard and, best of all (or so it seemed at the time), they never pushed him too hard.

When, aged twenty-two, he'd left California State University with a degree, very little debt – thanks to his tennis scholarship – and plenty of optimism, the world had been Logan Harris's oyster, and he was ready to launch himself upon it and make the kind of mark that befitted the faith his former school friends had placed in him.

Except it had never quite worked out like that. Logan had become the perpetual nearly-man. Nearly a successful actor. Nearly a pro tennis player. Nearly a good businessman. Nearly even a good husband – at least with his first wife, Anna. But that was the problem. In the end, nearly didn't count for anything.

And now, as he stood staring at his reflection in the mirror, he realized that his life had finally fallen to pieces.

Anna – the love of his life – was dead. His second marriage, made on the rebound, had been falling apart almost from the moment it had started, and now Paige was gone. Logan hadn't realized until now how quite much he loved his daughter. Perhaps because he'd always taken her presence for granted. She was cute and pretty, and he loved how small and precious she felt in his arms when he picked her up, but then a few seconds later he'd always put her down again and find something else to do. He just hadn't been that interested in her as a person. Until now, when it was too late.

Now she was gone, it hurt him like a physical pain. What hurt him even more was that he had a very good idea who was behind her abduction, and if he was right – and by God, he prayed he wasn't – then he was never going to see his daughter again.

He'd ruined everything. How the hell could life have been so cruel to him? 'Why did you do it?' he snarled at his reflection in the bathroom mirror, sickened by the man who stared back at him, and especially by the handsome, chiselled face that had seemed like such a gift growing up, but had now become a curse, leading him into a succession of bad decisions, culminating in the one he'd made only a few weeks ago – the one that now looked set to destroy all of them.

He lifted a fist, feeling all the anger and frustration welling up in him, and launched it at the mirror, wanting to shatter it – and the man it represented – into a thousand pieces.

But the mirror didn't break. Because his fist never reached it, stopping two inches in front of the glass. He couldn't even manage to do that right – the prospect of a painful cut hand overriding his rage, like the coward he was.

Shaking his head in disgust, he stalked out of the bathroom into the cavernous entrance hall, with its grand spiral staircase and expensive, abstract paintings of nothing lining the walls. He'd never felt at home in this house. It had been Brook's choice. Brook's project. Everything had always been about her, which was why he'd made the decision to end the marriage and leave to start a new life.

His thoughts were broken by the sound of a cellphone ringing. It was the one the kidnappers had left and he ran into the kitchen, picking it up from the worktop where it was charging.

'Hello,' he said breathlessly, relieved that the kidnappers were still in contact.

'Have you got the money?' demanded the man at the other end – the same one who'd called on the previous two occasions. His voice was low and deep and Logan was convinced he was a young man in his twenties or thirties and that he was American and probably local.

'My wife's going to collect it later. It takes the bank time to get the cash together.'

'If you get the money today, and do everything you're told, you'll have your daughter back tonight. Otherwise, the deal's off.'

In spite of himself, Logan felt a surge of hope. 'We'll do anything you say. Just don't hurt her.'

'We haven't hurt her,' said the kidnapper. 'She's fine. You saw that from the photo we sent. Have you deleted it now?'

'Yes, I have,' Logan lied without hesitation. He'd always been a good liar. 'I didn't share it, either.'

'Not even with your wife?'

Logan tensed, wondering if they'd found out somehow. 'No, I told her about it, but that was it. We're obeying all your instructions, I promise.'

'Keep it that way. And do not, under any circumstances, involve the police.'

'We haven't. We just want Paige back unharmed.' He deliberately used her name, hoping it would elicit some human emotions in the kidnapper.

It didn't. The kidnapper's tone was deliberately cruel as he asked his next question. 'Would you do *anything* for Paige, Logan? *Anything* at all.'

'She's my daughter, of course I would,' he answered, but he was conscious of the uncertainty in his voice.

'When you deliver the money tonight, there's something else that you have to do. Something that you must not discuss with your wife under any circumstances.'

Logan tensed. 'What's that?'

'It's not going to be very pleasant, Logan. Not very pleasant at all. But if you do it, your daughter will be sleeping in her own bed tonight.'

'Tell me,' he hissed through gritted teeth.

'You're going to have to betray your wife,' said the kidnapper. 'But then you're used to that, aren't you?'

9

It's true what they say about time. When you want it to go slowly, it speeds along relentlessly, seemingly accelerating all the time. And when you want it to go quickly, it crawls inch by interminable inch.

Brook sat in their family living room opposite Logan, the holdall containing two hundred and fifty thousand dollars open in front of them, wishing she could smoke again. She'd quit six years ago, the day after her thirtieth birthday, and had never even come close to going back to it, even though before that she'd had a regular ten-a-day habit. But now, sitting there constantly looking at her watch, willing the hours away until the kidnappers called with instructions, she knew that if there'd have been a pack in front of her on the table, she'd have gone through half of the cigarettes by now.

Instead she drank strong coffee, wanting to keep awake and alert. She was now on her third cup of the evening, and was so wired she doubted if she'd be able to sleep at all tonight. A day ago she wouldn't have countenanced drinking coffee at this time. She only allowed herself one cup a day usually, always in the morning. A day ago her body had been her temple. Today, none of it mattered.

In the end, it hadn't been that hard to get the money, although she'd been nervous when she'd got back to the bank that afternoon, in case Ralph Byfield had lost his nerve and called the police, or the bank regulator, or whoever the relevant authorities were. But no, he'd been true to his word. The money had been there on his desk, neatly stacked in twenty-five separate ten-thousand-dollar piles, each containing a mixture of fifty- and hundred-dollar bills. He'd offered to let her count it, but she'd declined. 'I trust you,' she'd said.

'And I hope you know what you're doing,' had been his reply.

She didn't, but there wasn't much that could be done about that now. So she'd loaded the money into her holdall, put it over her shoulder, thinking it didn't weigh as much as she'd thought it would, and walked out of there, imagining the stares of the bank's tellers and customers boring into her back, as if everyone in there knew how much money she was carrying and what it was going to be used for.

She looked at her watch yet again: 10.15 p.m. 'What time did they say they'd call back?'

Logan sighed and rubbed his eyes. He looked exhausted. The kidnappers' cellphone was on the coffee table next to him. 'I told you. They didn't give a time. They just said they'd phone later with instructions about where to deliver the money.'

'We're doing an exchange, right? We're not parting with that money until we see our daughter alive and well in front of us.'

'I told them that,' he said.

'And what did they say?'

'They said that's okay. They'll bring her with them to the rendezvous. When they've checked the money's all there, they'll release her.'

'That all sounds pretty simple.'

He shrugged. 'It's a business transaction. We pay them money. We get Paige back. There's no need for it to go wrong.'

'Hasn't it occurred to you that they might double-cross us?'

'Of course it has. But we've got to play by their rules, Brook. They're the ones holding Paige.'

'They're not touching that money until I see that she's safe and well,' she said fiercely.

'Hey, this isn't all about you, you know!' he yelled. 'This is *my* daughter we're talking about.'

'She's my daughter, too,' Brook said quietly. 'And all I want is for her to be back here safely where she belongs.'

Logan let out a low groan and put his head in his hands, before looking back up at her. The pain etched on his face looked real enough and she could see that his eyes were wet. She felt sorry for him then and guilty for her lack of trust.

'I'm sorry, Brook,' he said. 'I didn't mean it like that. I'm just stressed. And I know I haven't been the best husband, either. When all this is over, I'm going to change. I promise you. We're going to be a proper, happy family again. We're going to make everything work.' A tear formed at the corner of one eye as he spoke, and there was an almost childlike desperation in his voice, as if he was willing her to believe him.

It was a plea straight from the heart, but she remembered Logan sitting here and making a very similar plea soon after their wedding, when she'd found explicit texts on his cellphone from another woman – a woman that it turned out he'd already been seeing when he first met Brook.

She'd forgiven him then, because he'd sworn blind that he'd only seen her once since they'd been together, that he'd been drunk at the time and that he was now racked with guilt and would never cheat on her again.

But she knew he had, and she also knew that he'd never change. Because men like him never did. Logan was a fraud. The question was: how much of one?

It angered her that she'd stayed with him, because it went against her whole philosophy of becoming strong through self-respect and independence. 'You write about it, now live it,' she told herself.

'You believe me, don't you?' said Logan now, giving her the kind of look that would have charmed anyone who didn't know him. 'I mean it.'

'I know you do,' she said, getting to her feet and walking out of the room.

'Where are you going?' Logan called after her, sounding nervous.

'I can't just sit there, stewing all night. I need to move around.'

But she was lying. She might not have been quite so suspicious of Logan as she had been, but she didn't trust the kidnappers an inch, and she wanted some kind of security in case things went wrong. She was going to get the gun.

It was a cheap Kahr nine-millimetre pistol that Brook had bought herself for security some years before. Logan hated it. He'd never fired a pistol in his life, but for Brook it was a necessary evil. There were plenty of bad guys out there with access to firearms. If one turned up at her house in the middle of the night, then she wanted a level playing field, which was why, when she was single, she'd always kept the gun in the drawer of her bedside table. However, since they'd bought this place, it had been kept in the bedroom safe because neither of them wanted Paige to find it by mistake. Logan had asked Brook to get rid of it on several occasions, but she'd always resisted. Every now and again she liked to fire it over at the range between Monterey and Salinas, just to keep in practice, knowing that there might come a day when such practice came in handy. She truly hoped that today wasn't that day.

And then, when she was only halfway up the staircase, she heard it. The tinny, sing-song ringtone of the kidnappers' cellphone. She continued up the stairs, not daring to increase her pace, in case she was being watched. She heard Logan say a few muffled words, then his footfalls as he came striding out into the hall.

Brook was two steps from the top of the staircase when Logan called up to her. 'We've got to go. Now!' He was already pulling on his coat and the kidnappers' cell was in his hand.

'We've got fifteen minutes to get to the turn-off to the parking lot up at Garland.'

She froze, not sure whether to tell him to wait a minute or not. He looked agitated. Suddenly she was struck by indecision. The gun was a huge risk. Just pulling it out of the safe might mean she was caught on-camera. The kidnappers probably still had eyes in the house. And if they saw her get the gun, they might call the whole thing off and then she would never see Paige again.

'Come on, Brook. We need to go. Now!'

Making her decision, she ran down the stairs.

Logan handed her the car keys. 'We'll take the 4Runner. You drive.'

She frowned. 'Why?'

'Because I need to talk to them on the phone and get further instructions. I can't do that and drive at the same time.' He took her by the arm and gave her a push. 'Come on. We've got less than fifteen minutes to get there.'

Unarmed, unsure and definitely unready – the exact opposite of what someone going into a difficult encounter should be, in one of her books – Brook grabbed her coat and walked out the front door and into the night.

10

The night might have been cold, as was typical of the central Californian coast at this time of year, but Logan Harris was sweating. He sat in the passenger seat with the cellphone on his lap and Brook beside him, driving.

They were heading down the Carmel Valley road away from the sea and towards Garland Regional Park, a popular hiking destination. The Santa Lucia Mountains rose up on either side of them. This was rural, wine-producing country – lush and beautiful – and a place that Logan far preferred to the upmarket boutiques and art galleries of the town of Carmel itself. It had been Brook's idea to move down here, away from the San Francisco suburb of Pacifica where they'd first met, and where Logan had spent most of his adult life. They'd both wanted to escape the negative attention their relationship had attracted from the people around them, who were never going to accept the fact that they'd got together when Anna was barely in the ground. Logan had wanted to move to the relative anonymity of Oakland or San José, where it was lively and there was plenty to do, but as always Brook had got her way, and he couldn't help thinking that if he hadn't met her, and had instead settled down with someone with the same kind of easy-going personality that Anna had, he wouldn't be in this situation now.

It was Brook's fault. He just needed to remember that.

Traffic was sparse at this time of night. Even so, Logan had asked Brook to keep within the speed limits. There were often cops on this stretch of road after dark, and it would be hard to explain the quarter of a million dollars in cash in the holdall on the back seat if they were stopped. According to the Waze app on his cell, they'd get to the main entrance to the park at 10.28 p.m.

He looked at his wife as she stared straight ahead, watching the empty road. She was a beautiful woman. Tan, lithe and fit – the epitome of a successful life-coach. Her face was girl-next-door pretty, rather than right-out-there gorgeous, but she had one of those warm, lively smiles that lit up her whole face and was pretty much irresistible.

Logan had fallen in love with her at first sight. By the end of their first lesson, he knew he was going to have to be with her. Unfortunately he had two problems. First, he was already married. Second, he was also seeing another woman. Logan knew how bad that kind of behaviour would look to outsiders, but as far as he was concerned, he had his reasons. He and Anna had already known she had cancer and that the prognosis wasn't good. It had been her second bout of it, and had spread to her bones. They'd both fought it hard the first time, and they'd fought it hard the second time, too, but the pressure of watching his wife slowly deteriorate had got to Logan and he'd sought solace with someone else.

He wasn't a good man, he knew that. But he wasn't such a bad one, either, and when he'd fallen for Brook, he'd known she was the one – just as Anna had been when he'd first met her. Anna had never known about Brook (at least Logan hoped she hadn't), but she'd definitely given her blessing to him moving on.

Unfortunately, things hadn't turned out as he'd hoped. Brook might have had a good heart, but there was also a ruthlessness about her that unnerved him, and a determination that bordered on the pathological. She kept her focus and she never gave up, whatever the cost. She had plenty of acquaintances but very few, if any, real long-standing friends, and her past . . . well, whichever way you looked at it, her past was dramatic. She adored Paige – there was no question of that – but Logan had known a long time ago that Brook didn't feel the same way about him and that their love had faded to a shell of what it had once been.

Even so, the thought of what he had to do to her to get his daughter back filled him with dread. The kidnapper had given him specific instructions earlier but, looking at Brook now, he wondered if he could physically carry them out. He was a big man and naturally muscular, the kind people didn't pick a fight with. But it was all an act. When it came down to it, Logan knew he was a pussycat. He hated physical violence, and always had. The last time he'd hit someone had been back in college, when he and the other guy had been so drunk their punches had hardly even connected. It had been more of a scuffle than a fight, and he'd been hugely embarrassed about it afterwards. In the end, he was a lover, not a fighter, and that, of course, was the root cause of so many of his problems. Take attractive women out of the equation and he probably could have won the Nobel Prize.

Instead, here he was, frightened and confused, wondering why his daughter's kidnappers were so keen to hurt his wife. They'd demanded a quarter of a million for Paige's safe return and they were going to get it. So what did Brook have to do with anything?

The problem was that Logan also had a possible answer to that question, and it was one that truly made him nauseous. Because if he was right, Brook would only be the first to die. Paige would be next. And then, finally, it would be him.

Logan had a sudden urge to throw up, and he could feel himself shaking in his seat. He told himself to calm down, that he might well be wrong. But it didn't work. He was a physical wreck, and he knew it.

Brook, though, looked different. Tense, yes. But also strong, focused, her jaw set firm. Always the alpha female.

He saw her check the rear-view mirror. 'There's a car behind us,' she said. 'It's been that distance for the last five minutes.'

Logan turned round in his seat and saw headlights in the distance, maybe two hundred yards back. He swallowed. The moment of reckoning was coming. He looked at his watch: 10.27. They were almost there. He wondered whether Brook had any inkling of his betrayal. He had to act as naturally as possible, but however hard he tried, he couldn't get out of his mind the picture of Brook dead on the ground covered in blood, with Paige lying beside her.

She looked at him. 'Are you all right?'

'Feeling the pressure,' he said, taking a deep breath. A thought occurred to him then. 'Did you bring the gun?'

'No. I thought about it, but thought it was too risky.'

Logan wasn't sure if he was relieved or not. Obviously it made his task easier, but somehow Brook having the gun wouldn't leave them quite so vulnerable and exposed, especially if the car behind them contained the kidnappers.

The turn-off to Garland appeared ahead, and Brook headed down the track that led to the parking lot. The lot itself was next to a thick line of trees which marked the park entrance, and was hidden from the main road by a high, grassy bank on the other side. The park shut at sunset so the place was completely empty.

Logan looked around again to see if the car had followed them in, knowing that if it did, they'd be blocked in, since there was no other way out.

But it kept going. They were alone.

Brook left the engine idling as she looked out the window into the wall of trees. Behind them, the narrow and very shallow Carmel River flowed through the valley towards the sea, ten miles distant. There were plenty of paddling and swimming spots along the river's banks, making it a popular picnic spot in summer. They'd brought Paige here more than once, to play in the water and enjoy the peaceful surroundings, and Logan had fond memories of being here that were about to be erased for ever. As long as he lived, he would never come back to this place. In fact if he somehow wriggled his way out of this situation and got Paige back, then the two of them – no one else – would definitely leave California and start again, somewhere a long way away, just as he'd always been planning.

He looked at his watch again: 10.31. He picked up the phone, holding it tightly in his hand, unsure whether he wanted it to ring so they could get this over with, or whether he'd prefer to continue to keep the unknown at arm's length for a little while longer. He'd never been so scared in his whole goddamned life as he was now. He wished he could talk to Brook about it. Jesus, he wished Anna was there to comfort him and tell him it was all going to be all right. Anna had always known what to say to calm a situation – even when it was her own imminent death. Or even his mom, who'd always had a backbone of steel beneath the smiles and would have told him immediately what he had to do to save his daughter. He missed his mom. They'd been close. But she'd divorced his dad ten years ago and now lived with her female partner in San Diego, and he hadn't seen her since he couldn't remember when.

There was no one to help him. The nearly-man was going to have to do this on his own.

'I wonder if they're watching us right now?' said Brook, breaking the tension. 'Where are you, you bastards? Show yourselves.'

But there was only silence.

10.32. 10.33. A bead of sweat ran down Logan's forehead and he wiped it away angrily. 10.40. How long are they going to torture us? he thought.

And then the cellphone rang, the ringtone loud and taunting in the car.

'There's been a change of plan,' said the kidnapper.

11

Brook waved at Logan to get his attention, knowing she had to take control.

'Proof of life,' she hissed at him.

He nodded, then leaned away from her, talking into the phone. 'Paige is going to be there, isn't she?' he said, the uncertainty in his voice angering her. He had to be more assertive, otherwise there was no way they'd take him seriously. Showing confidence when you go into a negotiation – even if you don't feel it – is 70 per cent of the battle. It feeds doubt into the other side otherwise. Right now, Logan was sounding like a pushover, and neither she nor Paige could afford that.

She moved closer, trying to hear what was being said by the man on the other end of the phone but Logan moved away, leaning his head against the passenger window, making it all but impossible, although she could just make out that it was a man's voice. 'What are you doing?' she mouthed at him. 'I need to hear.'

He shook his head at her, then said, 'I understand' into the phone, before finishing the call.

'Why are you trying to hide what's being said from me?' Brook demanded, suddenly suspicious of her husband again. He looked like a condemned man, pale and drawn, a glistening sheen of sweat on his forehead, in no state to bring his daughter back safely, if that was even what he wanted to do.

'I was trying to hear what he was saying,' he answered breathlessly. 'I needed to concentrate.'

'And what did he say?'

'We need to get to the intersection with Tassajara Road. We'll get further instructions then.'

'Why are they messing us around like this?'

'I guess they want to make sure we're coming on our own, and that the police aren't involved.'

Brook stared out into the night. If there was someone watching them now it would mean there'd only been one person waiting for them at the rendezvous, unless there were more than two conspirators, and she didn't believe that. More than two of them would be too risky. Plus the cut of money per person wouldn't be enough to outweigh the risk, even if this whole thing was personal rather than financial. And there was no point directing them to different places just to make sure the police weren't nearby. All the police would have needed to do was place a tracker on the 4runner and they could have followed them anywhere from a distance, and she couldn't believe the kidnappers didn't realize this. So why keep up this whole charade? It didn't make sense. None of it did.

'Let's go,' said Logan, interrupting her thoughts. 'They're calling again with further instructions in ten minutes.'

Brook reversed, did a rapid turn and drove back out of the picnic area and onto the empty road. 'Put the phone on speaker,' she said as they drove. 'I want to hear their instructions when they next call.'

Logan looked petrified at this. 'That's not a good idea. They might find out you're listening in.'

'So what? I'm Brook's mother. I'm a big part of all this. And it's my money we're paying them with.'

'*Our* money,' he snapped back. 'We're married, remember?'

She took a long, slow breath as she drove through the quiet town of Carmel Valley and into the silent, sparsely populated countryside beyond, knowing that arguing would do neither of them any good. 'We can't fight like this, Logan. We've got to work together. That's the only way we're going to get Paige back.'

'Then let me handle this, Brook. I'm not going to do anything that puts her at risk. Let's just do what they say. They want to talk to me – and me only – okay?'

'But why? It's not like I'm not involved.' She could feel her anger building again and forced it back down. And yet it was true. There was no good reason for Logan not to put the cell-phone on speaker.

Not unless he was hiding something.

For the next twenty minutes she drove in silence through the narrow, winding valley, the night around them black and silent, the traffic almost non-existent. This road, she knew, meandered along for many miles, getting slowly worse, before it finally hit Highway 101, somewhere a long way south. It scared her to be moving this far from people. Out here, anything could happen.

As they approached the intersection with Tassajara Road they'd been told to drive to, the kidnappers' cell rang again. Now Brook was certain they'd put a tracker on her car.

Logan picked up, without putting it on speaker. 'Yes, yes,' he kept saying into the phone, then to Brook: 'Turn right.'

She did as she was told, continuing down an unlit road, with a vineyard to their left and a steep hill rising to their right. Logan remained on the phone, telling her to turn left as they came to another junction. They were now in woodland, and the road had become narrow and rutted.

'There's an old plant nursery up here on the left,' Logan told her. 'We need to park up outside and go in on foot.'

Brook knew the place he was talking about. She'd bought some mature grape vines from there when they'd first moved into the house, and she remembered thinking at the time that it was a strange place to locate a business, in the middle of nowhere and a long way from any customers. She'd read somewhere that there'd been a fire at the nursery a few months ago and that it had since closed. She didn't like this. She didn't like it at all.

A few seconds later, the track that led down to the entrance appeared in the headlights and Brook turned onto it and drove to the padlocked gates at the entrance.

'We're here,' said Logan into the phone and ended the call.

A narrow track ran into the trees to one side of the gates and Brook pulled the car in there, stopping underneath a tree with a pile of old hoardings stacked against it. There were no other cars visible, but then of course, that was to be expected. The kidnappers were relying on an element of surprise..

'The gates are locked,' said Brook, cutting the engine. 'So where are we meant to go now?'

'There's a hole in the fence just down this track. We get into the plant nursery that way.' He started to get out of the car.

She grabbed his arm, stopping him. 'Then what?'

'We walk down to the other end of the nursery and we'll get another call then. Let go of my arm. We've got to go.'

Brook made a decision. 'I want the phone.'

He frowned. 'What? No way. I told you—'

'I know what you've told me. But I need to be the one who negotiates with these people, whoever they are. We've given them too much of an easy ride so far.'

'Look, for Christ's sakes. Don't screw this up.'

'I'm not. I just want to make sure we see Paige before we part with the money. And I'm sorry, Logan, but I don't trust you to do that.'

'I don't care what you think,' he said, pulling away from her grip and opening the car door. 'This is how it's going to happen.'

'Give me their phone or I drive away with the money.'

'No, you won't,' he said. 'I'm taking the money.'

'Fine. Take the money. But I'll leave here and call the police.'

He stared at her in disbelief. 'You wouldn't? Jesus, Brook. What the hell are you doing?'

'I'm going with my gut, Logan. I'm the best person to negotiate with them.'

'That's you all over. You're a fucking control freak.'

'It's your choice,' she said. 'Make it now.'

He continued looking at her for a couple of seconds longer, clearly trying to work out whether or not she was serious, before deciding she was. With an expression of sheer disgust, he slammed the phone into her hand, then got out the car and pulled the holdall from the back seat, before slamming the door and walking away up the track, switching on the flashlight app on his phone so that he could see where he was going.

Feeling slightly better now, Brook got out of the driver's seat and shoved the car keys in her jeans pocket and then, with the cell clutched tightly in her right hand, followed a few yards behind Logan. She didn't turn on her own flashlight app, preferring not to be seen too easily.

'Here it is,' whispered Logan, stopping at a large hole the size of a small person in the chain-link fencing. The hole looked as if it had been made with strong bolt-cutters. Logan stepped through it, scraping the holdall on the ends of the frayed wires, and waited for her on the other side.

Brook stepped through it, too, and saw they were on a paved walkway about five yards across, with the burned-out skeleton of a main building on one side and a row of large greenhouses, some of them with their windows caved in, on the other. Already the edges of the walkways had become overgrown with weeds and tangled bushes, and there were piles of junk that had been salvaged from the abandoned buildings dotted amongst them.

She stopped and looked round. The night was clear and there was an almost-full moon sitting low in the sky, bathing the nursery in its pale-blue light. There weren't, she thought, many places for the kidnappers to hide and, aside from the occasional hoot of an owl off in the distance, she couldn't hear anything, either. It was hard to imagine that Paige was somewhere nearby, but Brook had to hang on to the hope that she was.

'Come on!' hissed Logan. 'We've got to head to the other end. He said to go in a straight line.'

Brook wondered how the kidnappers could possibly know when they got to the other end unless they were watching them, but maybe they'd set up cameras here, too, just as they had in their home. If that was true, it meant she'd been constantly under-estimating them. It also confirmed that this was about way more than a quarter of a million dollars.

The walkway crossed another and then narrowed, as the greenhouses gave way to a path running through overgrown brush about chest-height on either side, where Brook vaguely remembered they'd kept all the outdoor plants. She kept looking round, making for the line of trees up ahead that signalled the nursery's boundary.

A cold breeze shook the leaves on the trees and a bird cawed up ahead. Brook shivered, realizing almost with surprise that she was now leading the way, even though she hadn't switched on her flashlight app. She turned and saw that Logan was five yards behind her. He was gazing from side to side, presumably searching for any sign of the kidnappers.

But it felt as if they were alone out here, and now she wished she'd brought the gun. She was a good shot, and fast, too. When someone had once asked her if she could ever shoot another human being, her answer had been a resounding yes. That if her life, or the life of someone she cared about, was in danger, she'd do whatever it took to save them, even if it meant killing. And she'd meant it. Now, she felt naked without the gun.

She stopped. She'd reached the treeline. The fence had been ripped away entirely here and, just ahead of her, the ground suddenly gave way to a steep twenty-foot drop down to a dirt track that ran parallel to the treeline below, and beyond that, more forest.

Brook took a step back and turned round.

Logan had stopped too, a couple of yards away. He put the holdall on the ground and gave her a strange, very intense look. 'Give me the phone, Brook,' he said quietly. 'Please.'

He took a step towards her.

Brook took a step back. She didn't like the expression in his eyes. 'Let me talk to them,' she said. 'Then I'll hand it back to you.'

'You don't understand,' he said. 'I have to have it.' His eyes were pleading, but there was a wildness in them that she'd never seen before, and which scared her.

He kept coming, and she knew she couldn't retreat any further without going over the edge of the bank.

'Why are you doing this?' he demanded, shaking his head angrily. And then, quick as a flash, his hand shot out and grabbed her right wrist, squeezing it much harder than she was expecting, to get her to release the phone. 'Give it to me,' he hissed, twisting her wrist painfully.

Brook had done a lot of self-defence training over the years. She didn't believe you could be a truly confident person without the ability to defend yourself from physical attack, and although she was shocked by this sudden assault, because it was not at all like her husband, she reacted fast, instinctively launching a palm-strike to Logan's nose with her free hand.

He howled in pain – the sound causing a bird to fly out of the tree overhead – and let go of her wrist, then bent over, holding both hands to his face. 'You bitch!' he cursed in muffled tones. 'I can't believe you just did that.'

Brook exhaled and bounced on the balls of her feet, the adrenalin pulsing through her. She couldn't believe she'd done it, either: she'd never struck anyone before in anger. She half-expected the phone in her hand to ring at any moment, with an angry kidnapper demanding to know what was going on. She even looked down at it, and so she wasn't ready when Logan silently rose up to his full height and slammed his fist straight into the side of her face.

The force of the blow sent Brook stumbling backwards, the phone flying out of her hand.

And then she was falling through the air, smashing hard into the dirt and rolling down the steep incline, hitting bushes and tree roots, until finally she stopped at the bottom.

Her head swam. She tried to open her eyes, but couldn't. Her whole body burned with pain. She thought she heard Logan give a frustrated animal-cry that echoed through the trees, but she really couldn't be sure.

Then the world seemed to drift away from her and she slipped into semi-consciousness.

12

Brook lay there, dazed and unmoving, for what felt like a long time. She half-expected Logan to scramble down the bank and tell her he was sorry and see if she was all right. But he didn't. No one had come down here. It was as if she'd simply been discarded.

Slowly, she lifted her head. It hurt like hell and, when she opened her eyes, her vision was blurred for a few seconds before slowly coming back to normal. Groaning, she rolled onto her back, staring up at the night sky. Logan was no longer at the top of the bank, and she wondered where he'd got to. She felt her jaw where he'd punched her. The skin was hot and tender and her face was already badly swollen, but it didn't feel like anything was broken. Even so, the blow had been a good one, connecting perfectly and delivered with real anger. She still couldn't understand why he'd done it. Just because she wouldn't give him the phone? Logan might have been under a lot of pressure, but Brook would never have expected him to do anything like that. And then to have left her there, injured, maybe even dead. It shocked her.

Breathing slowly, trying to ignore the pain, she listened to the sounds of the night.

And that was when she heard it. The sound of a car pulling away somewhere off in the distance. It was coming from the direction of the nursery entrance, where she'd parked.

At first she thought Logan had abandoned her. But then she remembered that he couldn't have done, because she still had the car keys. She reached into her jeans pocket, just to confirm they were there, and immediately felt the oval key fob with Paige's face on it, which had been a present from her daughter for her thirty-sixth birthday.

This confused her even more. Because if it wasn't her car that she'd heard, it had to be the kidnappers'. In which case, where was Logan? And, far more importantly, where was Paige?

The thought that her daughter might be nearby spurred Brook into action. She sat up far too fast and immediately her vision blurred again and she thought she was going to throw up. She took a series of deep breaths and the fuzz in front of her eyes faded. Moving slowly this time, she got to her feet and pulled out her phone: 11.19. According to the dashboard on the car clock, it had been 11.04 when she'd parked the car, and it had only been a five-minute walk to get to the top of the bank, so she must have been lying there for around ten minutes.

She wondered what she'd missed during that time, and how Logan had managed to communicate with the kidnappers after he'd struck her, because she was certain that their cellphone had fallen down the bank with her and was around here somewhere. She stood still for a second, looking around and listening. Again, the only sound was the breeze in the trees.

She switched on the flashlight app on her own phone and shone the light across the ground in front of her, searching for the kidnappers' cell. If she had that, there was at least a slim chance she could talk to them. She thought about the money then. Had Logan simply handed it over to them? It wouldn't have surprised her. After the way he'd attacked her just now, nothing he could have done would have surprised her.

The flashlight picked up something up on the bank a few feet above her, resting against a tree root. She climbed up closer and felt an irrational surge of excitement as she realized that it was indeed the kidnappers' phone. She picked it up and pressed the home button, lighting up the screen. The phone looked undamaged, and she checked the call log. There were four incoming calls recorded, all marked as coming from the same cellphone. The photo of Paige that the kidnappers had sent them earlier was no longer on it.

Four calls. She was sure Logan had only told her about three. So what had the other one been about?

She leaned against a tree for support, knowing that she had to think logically about what had happened. Paige was almost certainly still alive. She might be up in the nursery somewhere, either alone or with Logan. They might even be looking for her ...

Except they weren't. She was still within ten feet of where she'd landed, so she wouldn't have been hard to find.

Knowing she wasn't going to solve anything by staying down here, Brook put the phones in separate pockets and then, slowly and carefully, climbed up the bank, using the tree and plant roots to help her. She almost fell back down twice and had another dizzy spell halfway up, but eventually she managed to half-scramble, half-roll over the top and lay there for a moment, breathing heavily, before getting to her feet.

The nursery was exactly the same as it had been earlier. Dark and empty. There was no sign of Logan or the kidnappers. The only explanation was that he'd gone somewhere with them. Maybe to collect Paige. But when she thought about it, she realized that didn't make sense at all. The kidnappers were going to do as much as possible to protect their identities, so they weren't going to want Logan in their car, or travelling with them to wherever it was they were keeping her.

Slowly she made her way back through the nursery the way she'd come. She called Logan's name. Quietly at first, then louder. Then she called Paige's, this time at the top of her voice.

There was no reply, and she felt a sudden aching loneliness, as if she was the last person left in the world.

Taking out the phone, she called the kidnappers' number, but wasn't surprised when an automated message came back saying that it was no longer in service. They weren't going to be that stupid.

But they weren't going to be geniuses, either. At some point – and it might have happened already – they were going to make a mistake, and it was that which would lead her to Paige. Now, though, was the time to involve the police. She couldn't do this alone.

She climbed through the hole in the fence and immediately saw her car in the shadows where she'd parked it.

Wary of an ambush, Brook approached it as silently as possible, all her senses alert, keeping a few yards away as she checked it out back and front to make sure no one was hiding there. Then she looked inside the windows. She'd seen a movie once where a woman driving a car had been attacked by a man concealed in the back, and she wasn't going to have that happen to her. But the car was empty.

She opened the door and got inside, half-expecting someone to come running out of the trees and attack her, and now she felt a real urgency to get out of there. Starting the engine, she turned the car round in a cloud of dust and accelerated back up the track onto the road, before turning right towards home.

She drove fast, making the journey in less than half an hour, ignoring the pain in her jaw and her throbbing headache, hoping against all the odds that somehow Logan would be back there with Paige, and that Paige would be unhurt and mentally unscathed, not even realizing she'd been abducted, and they could all be a family once again. Brook knew she wasn't that easy to live with, and now that she was at risk of actually losing everything she held dear, she regretted her own behaviour. If the three of them could be together again, she'd make far more effort to make her marriage work.

Please be there . . .

The lights were still on as Brook turned into the driveway and drove up to the front of the house, but no one came out to greet her, and she couldn't see anyone inside. Rosa's Honda was still there, a terrible reminder of what had happened to her and of how, even if Logan and Paige were okay, nothing in any of their lives would ever be the same again.

Brook swallowed, fighting back tears. Rosa meant a lot to her. She was kind, maternal and good fun, too. She'd taught Brook how to make the perfect enchiladas, her chief tip being to fry the tortillas briefly in hot canola oil before filling and rolling them, to prevent them soaking up too much of the sauce and disintegrating. Sometimes they'd drunk beer together out in the yard, and Rosa had told her about her childhood growing up in a dirt-poor village near Guadalajara. They'd grown close. They would have grown closer over the years. But now, even if she was still alive (and Brook didn't think it likely), Rosa would be horrifically traumatized.

Brook backed the car into the garage, already playing over in her head what she was going to say to the police.

It was only when she'd got out of the car that she saw it – a glimpse of something through the tinted rear window of the trunk, an area she hadn't bothered checking when she'd got back in the car earlier.

Brook's heart started thumping, her imagination already going into overdrive. She looked closer. There was something in there that hadn't been there earlier. Something big.

She walked round the back of the car, feeling a sense of dread, and stood there for a long moment, before finally forcing herself to pop the trunk.

It opened steadily with a faint hiss and, as she saw what was inside, Brook reeled in shock.

This was not how it was meant to end.

13

The police interview room
Now

'So what was in the trunk, Brook?' asked Detective Tyrone Giant, knowing full well what the answer was.

Brook took a drink of water and wiped her mouth. 'It was Logan,' she said at last. 'He was lying in the foetal position. His eyes were closed and there was a ...' She paused. 'There was a knife sticking out of his side, with a lot of blood around it. He was obviously dead.'

'And are you sure about that?' asked Giant gently.

She nodded emphatically. 'I'm sure. I felt for a pulse. First in his neck, then on his wrist, but there was absolutely nothing. He was gone.'

Giant had been watching Brook like a hawk as she'd been recounting her version of events, listening out for any contradictions in her story. It had been his and Jenna's plan to hand Brook the rope and let her hang herself with it. Liars, however good, always made mistakes, especially when the stories they told were as elaborate as this one. However, so far Brook Connor had sounded like a woman telling the truth about a terrifying ordeal. The emotions in her voice, and on her face, had been almost visceral in their intensity.

It was, he thought, time to up the pressure.

He sat forward in the plastic chair and shook his head, as if in disappointment. 'I still don't understand why you didn't come to us in the first place, when this whole ordeal began. It would have been the logical thing for any concerned parent to do. We could have helped. And not only would you have saved yourself from this, but you would have saved a lot of lives.'

Brook sighed and ran a hand roughly through her newly short hair. 'I know that now, but as I told you, we were both too scared. These people were professionals. They were watching us.'

'Really?' said Jenna. 'We searched your whole house from top to bottom, and we didn't find any signs of cameras anywhere.'

'Well then, maybe they removed them.'

Jenna looked sceptical. 'They seem to have been able to move very freely around your house.'

'They kidnapped my daughter. They knew what they were doing.'

'And that's the other thing that's bothering us,' said Giant, not liking what he was about to say next.

Brook looked at him. 'What?'

'Paige is not your actual daughter, is she?'

14

The shock of seeing Logan there had been enough to make Brook cry out. For a moment she thought Paige might be dead in the trunk, too, which would have been too much for her to bear, but Logan was alone, and Brook felt a guilty sense of relief. They hadn't killed Paige. Amidst all this carnage, that at least was something.

But even as she felt for a pulse, knowing instinctively that she was too late and her husband was already dead, it was also dawning on her that this looked very bad for her indeed, and that her plans to call in the police were going to have to be put on hold. At least temporarily.

In the meantime, she knew who she had to call.

*

Two hours later she was sitting at the centre island of the family kitchen, nursing a large gin and tonic to calm her nerves and holding an ice-pack to her left cheek to combat the swelling where Logan had struck her, while a few feet away stood her lawyer, Angie Southby, hands on hips, dressed in a smart two-piece business suit and immaculately made-up, considering the hour, and doubtless wondering why she'd been dragged out here in the middle of the night.

'Okay, Brook,' she said, 'before you start talking, you have to appoint me as your lawyer. That way, anything you tell me is covered by attorney–client privilege.'

'Consider yourself appointed,' said Brook, her voice sounding woozy to her own ears. She was on her second drink and she'd already taken a couple of painkillers. Knowing that she had to keep a clear head, she pushed the drink away.

Angie looked round. 'Where's Logan?'

Brook didn't speak for a moment, steadying herself, and then came out with it. 'Logan's dead.'

Angie couldn't keep the shock off her face. It hit her hard and she wobbled a little on her feet. She and Logan had been friends years back in San Francisco, which was how Brook had initially met her.

'I'm sorry,' said Brook. She stood up. 'Can I get you a drink?'

The shock seemed to pass. Angie was a tough woman, which was why Brook had wanted her as her lawyer now.

'What happened?' Angie's voice was tight and she looked uncomfortable as she glanced around the room, as if she half-expected Logan to leap out of one of the cupboards and shout, 'Surprise!'

'It's a long story,' said Brook. 'And before you get any ideas, it wasn't me who killed him.'

'Did he to do that to you?' Angie motioned towards her swollen cheek.

Brook nodded, realizing how that must make her look. Her husband punches her. Now he's dead in the trunk of the car. 'Like I said. It's a long story.'

'You'd better tell it, then,' said Angie, opting to remain standing, the glint of suspicion already showing in her eyes. 'And if you don't mind, I'm going to record everything. It's all covered by client confidentiality, so no one – apart from you and me – will ever hear it, but I find it a lot easier than making notes.' She removed a portable tape-recorder from her purse, set it on the table and pressed Play.

Brook cleared her throat and, starting from the beginning and putting in as much detail as she could, told Angie everything, finishing up with the part where she opened the trunk to reveal her husband lying there.

Angie didn't interrupt the whole way through, nor did her expression change, remaining cool and inscrutable right up until the final revelation. Only then did her eyes widen. 'Jesus Christ!' she whispered, finally sitting down, although on the other side of the island from Brook. 'So how do you think he got in the trunk in the first place?'

'Well, I guess the kidnappers put him there,' said Brook.

'But that doesn't make sense. Even if they killed him and took the money, it would be a needless complication to carry him over to the trunk of your car, with the murder weapon sticking out of him, and manhandle him in there.'

'That's what happened,' said Brook, sensing the suspicion in Angie's tone. 'I promise you.'

'I'm your attorney now, Brook, so everything you tell me is in confidence. I need to know, because it'll help me construct the best possible defence. Did you kill your husband?'

'No, of course I didn't. Why would I do that?'

'Why do people do anything? Who knows? But the point is that they do. Husbands and wives fight. Things get out of hand.'

'That's not what happened. It's exactly as I told you.'

'But Logan did punch you in the face. You need to get that looked at, by the way.'

Brook put the ice-pack down. It was making her face too cold. 'I don't know why he did that,' she said. 'He's never hit me before. I think the pressure must have been getting to him.'

'And what happened to the money?'

'It's gone. The kidnappers must have taken it.'

Angie nodded slowly, looking worryingly unconvinced. 'And Paige is still missing. I've got to be honest with you, Brook. This doesn't look good. Especially when you consider that you're not her birth mother.'

The words were like a hammer blow to Brook. 'You're not her birth mother.' How many times over the years had people given her looks that told her that was that was exactly they were thinking? 'You're not her real mom.' Paige had been less than

94

a year old when Brook had met Logan. The fact that she'd had an affair with a man whose wife was dying of cancer was bad enough, but the fact that there was a child involved made it even worse. And yet Brook had always sought to do the right thing and bring up Paige in a way that would have made her mother proud. She even encouraged Paige to look regularly at the photo album that she and Logan had put together for her, full of pictures of her with her mom when she was a baby. Brook had never wanted to replace Anna. She'd just wanted to do the best she could.

'I know how it looks,' she said wearily. 'But I'd give my life for Paige without a second thought.'

Angie looked as if the idea of that kind of sacrifice was completely alien to her, which it doubtless was. 'I know you love her, Brook. I've always been able to see that, but the fact remains that if you and Logan had ever split up, you'd almost certainly have lost Paige. And that gives you a motive.'

Brook was only too aware of that. It was, in truth, the main reason she'd hired Chris Cervantes. It was also why it was so hard to say what she had to say next. 'There's something else as well. The knife used to kill Logan … it's one of ours.' She pointed at the knife block in the corner of the kitchen, where the handles of eight different knives jutted out from the foam. 'There's one missing. I recognized it immediately.'

'Had you noticed it missing before?'

Brook shook her head. 'It could have been taken at any time. With everything that was going on, I was never going to spot a missing knife..'

'You said the kidnappers cut off Rosa's finger and left it for you in a gift box. Is it still here?'

Brook nodded. 'I got Logan to put it in the freezer, in case we needed to show it to the police. I couldn't face having it in the fridge. Do you need to see it now?'

Angie frowned through her Botox. 'I can't think of anything I'd rather see less, but I think I'm going to have to, so I know exactly what it is we're dealing with here.'

'I'll get it.' Brook got up and went over to the freezer. As she bent down, a magnet on the door with a photo of Logan, her and Paige, all grinning at the camera, stared back at her. It had been taken at the Children's Fairyland theme park in Oakland two years ago, when things were still pretty good between her and Logan, and she was suddenly hit with a devastating feeling of gloom. Logan was dead, and she was never going to speak to him again. Everything he'd ever felt and experienced was gone. Rosa was almost certainly dead, too.

For a second, Brook thought she might collapse under the strain of it all, but then she steadied herself. There'd be time to grieve later. Now she had to concentrate on saving herself and Paige.

Logan had told her he'd put the gift box in the bottom drawer of the freezer, away from all the food, but when she checked it now, it wasn't there. Her heart thudding, she checked the other drawers, and then the fridge, but there was no sign of it.

The evidence was gone.

'It's not there,' said Brook, walking back to her chair and picking up her drink, sinking the contents in one go and noticing that her hand was shaking. 'But I know that was where he put it.'

Angie didn't say anything. Her expression was grim.

'I'm telling the truth, Angie, I promise you. I saw that finger with my own eyes, and it belonged to Rosa, and there's no sign of her – or it – anywhere.'

'Okay,' said Angie, not giving anything away. 'Have you still got the phone the kidnapper, or kidnappers, left you?'

'Yes.'

'Can I see it?'

Brook took it out the back of her jeans and pushed it across the worktop. 'It hasn't got the photo of Paige on there any more, though. Logan removed it, like the kidnappers told him to.'

'I'll have one of my people run a trace on the number they called you from,' said Angie as she inspected the contents of the cell, 'but unless they're fools, it's going to be a burner.'

'I also think Logan might have been involved in some way. There are four calls on that cell from the kidnappers' number, but he only told me about three of them. It's hard to imagine he'd be a party to the kidnapping of his own child, but ...' She let the sentence hang in the air, unfinished.

'I know Logan pretty well, Brook, and that doesn't sound like him. He wasn't the most perfect guy in the world, but he did love his daughter.'

'Maybe so, but he was hiding something. And he punched me in the face and left me unconscious at the bottom of a ravine.'

'It's possible they were blackmailing him somehow. Does – did – Logan have any enemies that you know of?'

Brook shook her head. 'I don't think so. He was just a tennis instructor.'

'He was also a tennis instructor who had an affair with you. I know it's not something you want to think about, but could he have been having an affair with someone else?'

Brook had thought about it plenty of times. It was why she'd hired Chris Cervantes. 'It's possible, I guess, but if it was like an angry husband or something, then surely he'd have taken out Logan. He wouldn't go to all this trouble and make a five-year-old child suffer, would he?'

'It depends on who that person is,' said Angie. 'Some people do crazy things, Brook. But the point is this: only two explanations for what happened to Logan make sense. One, you killed him and you're making up this whole story to deflect suspicion away from you. Or two, someone's setting you to take the rap for the murder of your husband, and potentially your daughter and the nanny, too.'

The thought that someone could do this to her made Brook feel nauseous. And confused, too. She was certain she didn't have any real enemies – not ones who'd go to such lengths to destroy her. She'd worked hard in life to stay on the right side of people. She ran her business ethically. She wrote books, for Christ's sake! How could she inflame in someone the kind of passions necessary to kidnap a five-year-old girl? It had to be something to do with Logan. Or there was a third explanation that they hadn't thought of yet.

'Right now, the only people who can help you find Paige are the police. As your attorney, I strongly advise you to hand yourself in and tell them your story. I will do everything I can to stop them pressing charges, but I can't guarantee anything.'

'You think they'll charge me?'

'It's possible. But I should be able to get you bail.'

Brook didn't like the sound of 'should be'. If she went to the police station voluntarily, it was possible – maybe even probable – that she wouldn't be emerging again. 'No,' she said. 'I can't hand myself in. Not with Paige out there alone. I need to find out what's happened to her.'

'The police can do that a lot better than you can, Brook. And if you don't report what happens, it will make you look even more guilty of Logan's murder.'

'Don't turn me in, Angie. Please.' She knew her voice was shaking and hated herself for it.

'I can't. Everything you say to me is confidential. But remember that every hour you remain free now increases your chances of being charged with murder. Sleep on it if you have to, but your husband's body is in the trunk of your car, so now's not the time for long contemplation. We'll speak first thing in the morning and discuss what we're going to do.'

Brook nodded. 'I understand.' She pointed to the tape-recorder on the island. 'Can I borrow that? If the kidnappers call back, I want to be able to record the call. It might help prove my story.'

'Good idea. Here, I've got a spare I always carry.' Angie took it out of her purse and handed it to Brook.

They looked at each other. Angie gave her a reassuring smile, but there was something a little bit forced about it. Although Brook had known her ever since she'd got together officially with Logan, they'd never been great friends. They'd had Angie and her boyfriend, Bruce, over to dinner a couple of times, and had been to dinner at their place in Half Moon Bay, but a year back Angie and Bruce had split up and the dinner dates had ground to a halt. The point was that Angie had been Logan's friend, not Brook's, and it struck Brook as she walked her to the front door and watched her leave that she might have made a mistake by calling her.

Maybe Angie didn't have her best interests at heart after all.

15

Brook slept surprisingly well. It must have been exhaustion, but she didn't wake up until gone 8 a.m., having slept right through the night.

For those blissful first few seconds of consciousness she had no memory of her current predicament and, as she opened her eyes and saw the sunlight streaming around the edges of the blackout blinds, it felt like another ordinary May day in California.

And then – bang, it hit like a sledgehammer. Her husband was dead in the garage; her daughter had been abducted; and very, very soon she was going to be a murder suspect.

She sat up fast in bed. Both her cellphone and the kidnappers' were on the bedside table. The kidnappers hadn't rung, and she doubted if they ever would now, although, as it was her only link with them, she was determined to keep the cellphone with her at all times. She'd put her own cell on silent and saw that she had a missed call from Angie at 7.35. Brook knew that Angie was going to keep putting the pressure on her to go to the police. She also knew it was by far the most logical step forward.

Except for one overriding issue. And that was that the evidence really was stacked against her. Logan was dead in the trunk of her car. He'd been stabbed with one of their kitchen knives. Brook's DNA was bound to be on it somewhere. It wouldn't be hard to create a story in which she and Logan had had an argument, he'd punched her and she'd stabbed him. For all anyone knew, she could have killed Paige and Rosa, too. Unless one or both of them suddenly appeared to back up her story of the kidnapping – and the more time that passed, the less likely that was proving to be – Brook would be the prime suspect in their disappearances. She'd be under suspicion for three murders. There was no way she'd avoid charges, let alone post bail.

No, for the moment she was on her own, which meant it was time to go to work.

And she knew exactly where to start.

Ninety minutes later she parked her car on a quiet residential street in east Monterey and got out. Earlier that morning she'd googled how to find trackers on a car and had searched hers inside and out for one, but had found nothing.

Chris Cervantes, the private detective she'd hired three weeks earlier, was a divorcee who lived alone and used his house as his office. 'No point spending your money, when I don't need to,' he'd told her when she'd first visited him there to talk through her concerns about her husband, and it had seemed a valid enough point.

The house itself was a small two-bed place in need of a lick of paint, older than the ones around it, and set back in the shade behind a couple of orange trees on a private, corner plot. As she walked up to the door, Brook was relieved to see Cervantes's car – an oldish white Dodge Avenger – parked in the driveway, which meant he was almost certainly home.

She thought about ringing the doorbell, but decided against it. He was clearly avoiding her and he had a camera above the front door, so it was going to need to be a surprise visit.

The room he used to meet clients in was at the front of the house, facing out onto the orange trees, and Brook couldn't see from the angle she was at whether or not he was in there, so she crouched down and crept beneath the window, then continued through an unlocked gate at the side of the house and into a scruffy back yard. It occurred to her that, rather worryingly for a PI, Cervantes didn't seem to have much in the way of security. This feeling wasn't alleviated when she discovered that his back door was unlocked.

She hesitated before opening it, as it occurred to her that the reason she hadn't heard from him for the past few days might be because something bad had happened to him, in which case, if she went inside and found his body, it would probably make things even worse for her.

In the end, she stepped inside anyway. She was about to call his name when he appeared out of a side door, leaning on his walking stick and dressed only in a T-shirt and underpants, both of which had seen better days. His hair was a mess and it was clear he hadn't been out of bed long.

The moment he saw her, Cervantes jumped back in shock, banging his head against the wall and only just managing to stay upright. 'Jesus!'

Brook eyed him coolly. 'We need to talk.'

He put up his free hand as if he was scared she was going to hit him. 'Look, I'm sorry. I should have called. I was going to refund your money. I'll write you a cheque now.'

'It's too late for that.'

He looked puzzled. 'What do you mean?'

'I mean I need some answers from you. Why don't you throw some pants on and we can talk in your office?'

'This isn't a good time right now,' said Cervantes.

'It's not a good time for me, either. Which is why we need to talk.'

Cervantes gave a resigned sigh. 'Give me five minutes.'

She waited in the hallway while he went back into the room he'd just come from, and when he reappeared a few minutes later he'd shaved and was dressed in a suit and tie, with his hair combed.

At one time Cervantes would have been a good-looking guy, and he still had the vestiges of those looks, with a full head of black hair, touched with only the faintest hint of grey, and brooding dark eyes. But his face was that of a heavy drinker, with clusters of broken capillaries across his deeply-lined olive skin, and this – coupled with the limp that he carried from an old police injury – gave him the appearance of an old man.

He didn't offer her anything to drink but instead walked straight into his office, leaving Brook to follow. It was clear he didn't want her there, and that simply piqued her curiosity even more.

She took a seat opposite him, across an ancient wooden desk piled high with files that didn't look like they were in any order. Cervantes definitely needed to improve the way he marketed his business, but then maybe he was going for the shabby, Colombo-style maverick-gumshoe look, in which case he'd got it down to a tee. But Brook remembered that when she'd first met him he'd had an air that suggested that, where detective work was concerned, he knew exactly what he was doing.

So it was something of a surprise when he told her he hadn't been able to find out anything useful about Logan's movements during the time he'd been tracking him. 'I'm sorry,' he continued. 'That's just the way it goes sometimes.'

It seemed a curious turn of phrase for him to be sorry he'd found out nothing untoward about a client's husband, when that client suspected the husband was up to no good. Cervantes didn't look very happy about it, either. He looked like he wished Brook would get up and walk straight out his front door, never to return.

'I don't believe you,' she said. 'In the last forty-eight hours my life has turned upside down. I'm in a lot of trouble. So is my husband. And I need to know the reason why'

Cervantes fidgeted in his seat for a couple of seconds. 'Is your husband all right?' he asked.

'No, he's not,' Brook said, aware that the more detail she gave him, the more vulnerable she made herself.

'What's happened to him?'

'That doesn't matter right now. I just need to know what you found out.'

Cervantes took a deep breath and stared at the ceiling. 'Look, I don't want to be involved in any of this. I'm sorry your life's in trouble, but it's nothing I can help with.'

'I'm not leaving until you tell me what you've found out.'

Cervantes opened a desk drawer and took out a packet of cigarettes and a lighter. He lit one, not bothering to ask if she minded him smoking, and made little effort to avoid blowing the smoke at her.

Fair enough, she thought. It was one way of trying to get rid of her but, like the others, it wouldn't work. Brook could be stubborn when she needed to be.

They stared at each other for a while and Cervantes broke first. 'Okay,' he said at last, looking at her through the smoke. 'You want to know. I'll tell you. I think your husband's having an affair. And if I'm right, he's picked probably the most dangerous woman in the whole state to have it with. I'm going to give you a piece of advice now, Ms Connor. If I were you, I'd put some distance between you and Mr Harris. Kick him out. Do anything. But get rid of him. He's toxic.'

Brook leaned forward in her chair. 'Tell me about this woman.'

Cervantes shook his head. 'The less you know about it, the better it is for you. And, more importantly, the better it is for me.' He pulled on the cigarette. 'Do not get involved in this, Ms Connor. It really won't end well.'

'It's too late for that,' said Brook, knowing she had to lay her cards on the table. 'My husband's dead, and our daughter's been abducted.'

Cervantes frowned. 'Then it means he's found out.'

'Who's *he*?'

'Someone I don't even want to mention by name. Have you been to the police?'

Brook shook her head. 'No. Whoever killed Logan framed me for his murder. That's why I'm in so much trouble. I have to find Paige, Mr Cervantes. She's only five years old.' She took a smiling photo of her daughter from her purse and, unable to look at it herself, pushed it across the desk so that it was directly under his nose.

Cervantes didn't want to look at it, but couldn't seem to help himself. It was clear his self-interested side was having a wrestling match with his conscience, and it was turning into a close fight. He didn't say or do anything for a good thirty seconds or so. Finally he picked up the photo and examined it, before pushing it back across the desk to Brook. 'Tell me what happened,' he said. 'Right from the start.'

She told him and, by the time she'd finished, he'd lit another cigarette.

'Now it's your turn,' she said. 'Tell me what you know.'

'On one condition. Whatever happens, you keep me out of this.'

Brook nodded. 'Done.'

'The woman your husband was having an affair with is called Maria Reyes. Now Ms Reyes's husband is a very high-powered

Mexican-American businessman who's suspected of having strong connections with a major Mexican drugs cartel. And when I say "suspected", I mean that he is actually a senior member of the cartel himself, although no one's managed to prove it yet. However, one thing is beyond doubt. You do not cross Tony Reyes under any circumstances. Certain people have done so, of course. There was an assistant DA down in LA who was trying to set up a case against him, and who ended up dead in a hotel room with a prostitute. There was a financial advisor who fleeced Reyes out of some money that he was supposedly laundering, and who disappeared without a trace, along with his wife. And that's the thing. Bad things happen to people who cross Tony Reyes. And sometimes to their whole families, too. He's the devil incarnate, Ms Connor. He has a ruthlessness that most ordinary people can't even comprehend.'

Brook felt a cold sweat on her forehead as she listened to Cervantes speaking. The thought that Logan could have got himself entangled with the wife of a man who killed off whole families made her feel sick. 'Are you absolutely sure they were having an affair?'

He nodded. 'As you know, I had a tracker on your husband's car and last Thursday I followed him down the coast to Andrew Molera State Park. I watched the two of them walk together on the beach down there. They were definitely intimate. I didn't realize who she was at the time, but I got an old colleague of mine to run the plates, and that's when I found out. That same colleague told me to keep well away from her, which was the reason I didn't return your calls. I was trying to work out whether

I should tell you I'd found nothing, and risk you getting caught up in the whole thing, or tell you the truth and advise you to leave your husband before Tony Reyes found out about him.'

'And in the end, you did nothing.' It wasn't a question.

He sighed. 'No. I did nothing. I'm good at that.'

'And now my daughter's missing. How do you feel about that?' Brook sat back in the chair and wiped the sweat from her brow, experiencing a potent mixture of anger and panic.

'I feel sorry about it. I really do.'

'Do you think Tony Reyes is the one behind her abduction?'

'I don't know,' he said. 'It doesn't sound like his MO to organize a whole complicated kidnap and ransom drop. If he'd found out your husband was sleeping with his wife, it's very unlikely he'd kill him quickly. He'd either have Logan abducted and taken some place where he could spend time taking him apart piece by piece. Or, if he was feeling particularly vengeful, he'd have all three of you abducted, and then make Logan watch you and Paige die before finishing him off.'

Brook felt sick, as the full enormity of what she was up against took hold. 'Would he really do something like that?'

Cervantes gave her a look that said, *You really don't understand*. 'These people take murder to a whole new level, Ms Connor. It's one of the reasons they're so successful. But Tony Reyes is first and foremost a businessman, so it could be that he had Logan killed and then sets you up for the fall. That way, no suspicion settles on him. I'll be honest, if he's got Paige, then I . . .' He paused. 'Then I don't think she's still alive.'

The words knocked Brook sideways, but she held herself together. She couldn't lose hope. Not yet.

'But it's still possible Reyes has nothing to do with this,' continued Cervantes hurriedly. 'Last Friday, the day after I saw your husband and Mrs Reyes at Molera State Park, and before I'd had it confirmed who she was, I was parked at the tennis courts where your husband coaches. As he was getting back in his car after the session, a guy in a suit appeared out of nowhere and got in the car with him. They talked inside for seven minutes, according to my watch, and it looked as if, during the course of the conversation, the guy handed Logan something, which they were both looking at. Then the guy got out and walked into the park next door, so I didn't get a chance to see what car he was driving. I did get a photo of him, though.' He dug out a cardboard file from the pile on the desk and leafed through it until he found what he was looking for. 'Do you recognize him?' he asked.

The photo was the side view of a fairly ordinary-looking black man in his mid-thirties, with short hair and a roundish face that was partially obscured by a beard, and a cheap suit that looked like it had been bought when he'd been a few pounds lighter.

She shook her head. 'I've never seen him before. He doesn't look much like a Mexican gangster.'

'No, he doesn't. So maybe he might have something to do with Paige's abduction.'

'Can you find out if your police contact recognizes him?' Brook asked, clinging to the faint hope that this man might be the one who had Paige, and comforting herself that he didn't look like the type who could hurt a child.

'I'm sorry, Ms Connor, but I don't want anything more to do with this case. I've already told you more than I feel comfortable with.'

'If you'd told me it before, my five-year-old daughter would have been safely with me, instead of God knows where.'

It was a low blow, and an effective one, too. Cervantes looked genuinely hurt. 'I'll see what I can do,' he said reluctantly.

'Can I have the file as well?' she said, putting out a hand. 'After all, it does belong to me.'

'You need to go to the police, Ms Connor.'

'I need to find my daughter, Mr Cervantes. If I go to the police, I'll probably be arrested. And right now I'm the only person Paige has got left. So I'm going to find out where she is and, if she's alive, I'm going to take her home – and then I'll go to the police and face whatever consequences need facing. And if Paige is dead, then I'm going to find who did it, and I'm going to kill them.'

In the years since her parents had died, Brook had always preached a gospel of independence, determination and positive thinking. The first line in her debut book, *You Can Be the Hero*, said it all:

Do you want your life story to be something you read with pride or shame?

Brook had always fought to live by that ethos. At times, especially in the past thirty-six hours, it had been incredibly hard, but sitting there now, in Cervantes's smoky little office,, she knew she had to fight back, whatever the cost to her. She owed it to Paige.

Cervantes saw the change in her expression. It looked like he was about to say something, then he clearly thought better of it and handed her the file.

'Be careful,' he said as Brook got to her feet.

'It's a bit late for that,' she answered, and walked out the door.

16

The police interview room
Now

Detective Giant cleared his throat and interrupted Brook Connor's story.

'The problem we have, Ms Connor, is that your husband's body was discovered in the trunk of *your* car in *your* garage, having gone unreported by *you*, and the murder weapon is one of *your* kitchen knives. You've admitted that you and he had a fight, and that he struck you in the face, causing a severe swelling, which is still visible now, three days later. And, most importantly, at this moment we have no one who can back up any aspect of your story.'

'And you've even given us your motive,' said Jenna, making a play of consulting her notes. 'I quote: "I knew that losing Paige now would mean the end of my own life." That's what you said, isn't it, Brook? I'm sure we can go back and play it on the inter-view tape, if you want us to.'

'I know that's what I said,' said Brook testily. 'But I didn't mean it like that.'

Angie Southby put a hand on Brook's arm, motioning for her to stop talking, before speaking herself. 'What my client said shows how much she cares for her daughter, and proves there's no way she would ever harm her.'

Jenna shrugged. 'If your client thought her husband was going to take Paige away from her, it's not inconceivable that she ended up killing them both. There's a long, long list of cases where a parent kills a child to prevent them from being taken away. And let's be perfectly frank. It's not even as if Ms Connor is a blood relation of Paige.'

'Fuck you!' snapped Brook, and for a split second Giant thought she was going to jump out of her chair and strike Jenna, but she managed to compose herself. 'I love that child with all my heart,' she said tightly. 'Jesus, she *is* all I've got.'

'It's ridiculous to suggest that my client murdered her daugh-ter,' said Southby, in that aggressive tone of hers. 'You've been through her family home from top to bottom, as well as both the family cars. Have you found any evidence that any harm might have come to Paige?'

'Not yet,' said Jenna, meeting her eye. 'But we're still looking.'

'And are you simply looking for evidence of my client's supposed guilt or are you actually looking for her five-year-old daughter? Because you're going to look very, very bad if she's out there alive somewhere and you're in here, accusing her mother of her murder.'

'We've had the full resources of the US Marshals Service searching for Paige for the past thirty-six hours,' said Giant, who always got annoyed when his, and his colleagues', competence was called into question. 'And as you both well know, Paige Harris's photo has been all over the media, which means that pretty much everyone in the whole country knows about her. And yet so far we haven't had a single reported sighting. Not one. Which suggests to me that she may be dead.' He looked at both client and attorney in turn. 'Now don't get me wrong. There's nothing I want more than for us to find Paige alive and well, but given the time that's passed since she was last seen and the lack of recent news, we wouldn't be doing our jobs if we weren't preparing for the worst.' He thought about adding that right now they had cadaver dogs searching for any sign of a child's body in the grounds of the house where Brook had been arrested earlier that night, but he was still finding it hard to believe that the bruised, dishevelled woman in front of him would have killed the little girl – stepdaughter or not.

As he laid out the facts for her, Giant could see Brook getting paler. She swallowed several times in quick succession, and he was about to ask if she was all right when she spoke.

'Listen,' she said. 'I know how at least some of this looks. I didn't love Logan, not any more. I told you that. And I did hire a private detective to follow him, because I thought he was almost certainly seeing other women and I wanted to be prepared, in case he left me for someone else because, yes, I didn't want to lose Paige.'

In spite of himself, Giant found himself feeling sorry for her, but that had always been his problem. He couldn't help getting emotionally involved in cases. It had almost destroyed him in the past, and he had no desire to repeat the process. 'But that's the thing, isn't it, Ms Connor?' he said gently. 'There was nothing you could have done if your husband had decided to leave and take Paige with him. He was her biological parent. So what was the point of hiring a private detective?'

'I guess, first of all, I wanted to find out if Logan was actually seeing someone seriously. I think if he'd chosen to leave me, I'd have tried to get him to agree to joint custody or, failing that, I'd have made him a financial offer. Logan didn't have much money of his own.'

'But he wouldn't need your financial offer, would he, Ms Connor?' put in Jenna. 'He could just have divorced you. Taken 50 per cent of your wealth, as well as Paige. And there would have been nothing you could have done about it. In fact the only way of avoiding a scenario like that – given that your marriage, by your own admission, was on the rocks – was if your husband was dead.'

'I would never have killed my husband,' said Brook firmly. 'There would have been another way. There's always another way.'

But this was Giant's one big problem with her story. Whichever way you looked at it – and Giant had been looking at it plenty of different ways – the only satisfactory outcome for Brook was her husband's death.

He exchanged looks with Jenna, then leaned forward across the desk. 'This isn't the first time you've been caught up in murder, is it?'

Brook's eyes narrowed. 'Are you referring to my parents?'

'What the hell has that got to do with anything?' demanded Angie Southby.

'The circumstances surrounding your parents' deaths have always been controversial,' continued Giant.

'The case was closed,' said Southby.

'And there have been several attempts to reopen it.'

'All of which have failed. It's been proven as a case of murder/ suicide.'

Giant ignored Southby, knowing he couldn't let this go. 'You were the sole beneficiary of their will, Ms Connor, and in many ways the money you inherited has been the foundation of your success.'

Brook gave him a withering look. 'Not only are you suggest-ing that I killed my parents, but that even my success is nothing to do with me? What the hell else are you going to accuse me of? Getting someone else to write my books?'

Giant's expression didn't change. 'In my experience, light-ning doesn't usually strike twice. A coincidence of this size makes us naturally more suspicious, that's all.' He had no idea whether Brook had been involved in her parents' death or not. In truth, it didn't look that way, from what he knew of the case – but it was his duty to take this line of questioning, even though he didn't enjoy doing it. Brook had been proclaimed innocent of all charges, and all he was doing was sticking a particularly sharp knife into an old wound.

And she did look genuinely hurt by what he was saying.

But then, as her lawyer intervened yet again to complain about the line of questioning, Giant saw Brook's expression change. It was as if a light bulb had suddenly gone off in her head, and she stared at him, her mouth forming a weird little smile.

'I don't believe in coincidences, either,' she said, her words quietening the room.

Giant frowned. 'What do you mean?'

'You know I told you that Cervantes saw my husband talking to a black man in his car at the tennis courts a week ago Friday. I didn't recognize the man in the photo at the time, because he had a full-face beard. But I recognize him now.'

She fixed Giant with a stare that made him want to look away. 'And who is he?' he asked.

'I think you know the answer,' said Brook. 'It was you.'

Part Two

17

A week ago
Friday

Right back from when he'd been a young kid, Tyrone Giant had wanted to be a cop. Even the death of his father, a Los Angeles patrolman shot dead by an armed robber when he was only twelve years old, didn't deter him. Nor did his mother's desperate requests for him to do another, safer job instead. His older brother became a truck driver, and his sister a marketing executive, so at least two of the three siblings did as they were told. But for Tyrone there was no alternative. As far as he was concerned, his father had believed in what he was doing. It may have got him killed, but Tyrone knew he'd be proud that his son had become a cop. 'Someone's got to bring the bad guys to justice,' his father had told him once when he was a young kid.

'And if you wait for other people to do it, you could be waiting a hell of a long time.'

The reality of being a cop didn't quite fit Tyrone's fantasy, though. He might have had a big name, but he wasn't a big guy, and he didn't have a tough demeanour. He carried too much puppy fat, especially on his face, which was round and cherubic, and however much exercise he did, his jawline remained weak and ill-defined. But he still got through the training, ignoring the ribbing of his fellow trainees, and became a patrolman working out of one of the more upmarket ends of Oakland.

His very first arrest was of a drunk outside a bar in Berkeley and it went badly. The drunk – a middle-aged man who could hardly stand up – turned on Giant and they'd ended up on the floor, rolling around and fighting in a heap while passers-by stood and stared, until finally backup had arrived and, when they'd finished laughing, had pulled them apart. A few days later, some wag had stuck a flyer on Giant's locker with his face superimposed on the body of a heavyweight boxer rippling with muscles. Even his sergeant, who was a decent, paternal sort nearing retirement, had taken Giant aside and asked him if he was really in the right job.

But Giant was nothing if not determined. He started hitting the gym every day and took up boxing. The puppy fat remained, largely because of his addiction to fried food, and although he'd never win any awards for his pugilistic skills, he learned enough that there were no more embarrassing struggles during his arrests, and his colleagues came to accept him, even if he never did truly feel like one of the boys.

But Giant's ambition had never been to remain in uniform. He considered himself a lateral thinker who liked to solve puzzles and so, as soon as he was able, he applied to be a detective, and passed all the exams with flying colours. He was good at it, too – mainly because he was very observant, and was good at putting all his observations together to make a whole. His patch was downtown Oakland, so there was plenty to keep him busy, and he gained something of a name for himself when his diligent detective work led to the arrest of a serial rapist who'd been targeting women living alone. After weeks of trawling for links between the five rapes, often working alone and late at night, Giant had worked out that all the victims had had takeout pizzas delivered to their homes at some point in the three months before they'd been attacked. Although those pizzas had been ordered from three different outlets several miles apart, Giant was convinced he was on to something, and through a combination of checking the employee records of the outlets, plus on- and off-the-record interviews with the managers and delivery drivers, he'd found the culprit. Miguel Sanchez, a twenty-seven-year-old illegal immigrant, had worked for all three outlets off the books, and had delivered the pizzas to each of the victims before coming back, sometimes weeks later, to rape them. He'd ended up being sentenced to twenty-five years, and for a long time afterwards Giant had been known (affectionately, he liked to think) as Mozzarella Man.

But as a general rule, Giant's career was largely uneventful, and the guys he put away were often sad and unlucky rather than bad.

And then, one bright sunny morning four years ago, he finally came face-to-face with true evil.

The first person to respond to the call that day had been a young uniformed patrolman called Pico Vasquez. Apparently, the Hernandez family hadn't been seen for several days and their children had not turned up at school. When Vasquez arrived at their house in a rundown district of east Oakland, there was no answer at the door and all the curtains were drawn. He'd gone round the back, tried the door and, finding it unlocked, had gone inside.

The smell had hit him immediately and, although he was relatively inexperienced, he'd known exactly what was causing it. A few seconds later, as he walked into the living area, he'd realized that what had happened in the Hernandez household was way above his pay grade and, when he'd finished throwing up, he'd put in an emergency call to the station.

By now, Giant was a homicide detective and it was his job to go the Hernandez house and secure the scene. And it was a scene that would stay for him for the rest of his life. The body parts of Pablo Hernandez, aged thirty-four; his wife Gina also thirty-four; and their two children, Pepe, nine, and Adalina, seven, were scattered all over the living room like broken, shredded dolls. The blood was everywhere. Up the walls, across the furniture, staining the windows. It was as if someone had come in and given the place a particularly sloppy coat of red paint.

It wasn't the gore or the smell that affected Giant. As a homicide detective he'd seen plenty of corpses before, some of them pretty badly damaged and, after the first one, had always been able to tolerate it. It was the sheer wanton cruelty of these killings that had stayed with him. The perpetrators – and Giant worked on the premise that there had to have been more than one of them, in order to subdue the whole family – had to have been complete sadists. They'd tortured the children for some time in front of the helpless parents – almost certainly until they'd bled to death – and had then spent some considerable time afterwards torturing the parents who, according to the coroner, had both died several hours at least after the children.

Giant had secured the scene, called in forensics and set the murder inquiry in motion, but he'd done the whole thing almost in a state of total shock, as if it was someone else doing it and not him. He and a dozen other detectives had worked round the clock to bring the killers to justice, but it had rapidly become clear that it wasn't going to be an easy one to solve. Pablo Hernandez, it turned out, was a mid-level drug dealer working for a major Mexican cartel, and it was almost certainly cartel members who'd killed him and his family. The problem was that the family lived in a poor, predominantly Hispanic area where gang influence was strong, and apparently no one had seen or heard a thing. The case initially made headlines thanks to the brutality of the murders, but it quickly faded from view. Maybe, Giant thought, if the victims had been a wealthy white family, there would have been a lot more coverage, and maybe they'd have got a break. As it was, everything ground slowly to a halt, with detectives being moved off the case one by one, until finally there were none of them left.

Giant had pleaded with his boss to let him stay with it. It was anathema to him that the killers might somehow get away with slaughtering a whole family. And it wasn't as if they didn't know who was behind it. According to the FBI, the cartel's top representative in northern California was a successful Mexican-American businessman called Tony Reyes, and the killings would have had to be sanctioned by him. But Reyes ran legitimate businesses, had a stable of top-notch lawyers, and kept himself a long, long way from the action. He probably didn't even know the identities of the killers. So in the end they couldn't touch him, and Reyes clearly ran a tight ship, because there were no weak links amongst the layers of cartel employees, and therefore no leads.

But Giant didn't want to give up. It wasn't in his nature. Look long enough and he knew they'd find the lead they were looking for and, if nothing else, at least ID the actual killers. But he was overruled. 'You've got to learn to let things go, Ty,' his boss, a thirty-year veteran, told him. 'If you carry too much, it'll break you eventually.'

The case hadn't broken Tyrone Giant, but it had steadily eaten away at him. He'd seen the torn-apart bodies of the Hernandez family in his dreams; he'd lost his Christian faith. He had intense mood swings, and periods of black depression. He had to fight just to get up in the morning. His fiancée left him.

Although he never gave himself credit for it, a lesser man would have collapsed under the strain, but Giant fought his way out of his depression and nine months earlier had taken a transfer out of Oakland to Monterey, where he was now. He still had to deal with some serious crimes, including homicides, but nothing like what he'd seen in the Hernandez household.

But neither did he forget about Tony Reyes, who'd moved out of San Francisco himself and now lived in a huge house with a ranch attached, down in the Carmel Valley, right within Giant's jurisdiction. Except that Reyes was still untouchable. Now a construction magnate with a reputed net worth of close to a hundred and fifty million dollars, he paid his taxes and, if he was on the FBI's radar, they didn't seem to be doing much about him, because he seemed to be living very happily and still having people killed at will. There was the case of the financial advisor with unproven links to the cartel, who'd gone missing from his home in Salinas along with his wife six months earlier, never to be seen again. Then there was the old lady, two years back, who'd refused to sell her home over near Modesto to a development company owned – in all but name – by Reyes, thus holding up a multimillion-dollar housing project, and who'd subsequently been found dead on her yard patio with serious head injuries (the coroner ruled it an accident, and the development went ahead). The way Tony Reyes flouted the law pissed Giant off mightily, but he'd also learned not to carry the burden and to bide his time. He watched and he waited, and when his opportunity came, it was completely by accident.

He'd been driving not far from the beach in Santa Cruz when he'd seen Reyes's wife, Maria, get out of her car. He recognized her instantly, having made it his business to know everything there was to know about Tony Reyes. Maria was a thin, elegant Hispanic woman, somewhere at the upper end of her forties, and the way she was looking round furtively set Giant's alarm bells ringing straight away, because it was clear she didn't want to be seen. The traffic was heavy, so he had time to watch in his rear-view mirror as Maria walked down the street in his direction, pretending to look in shop windows, before heading into the entrance of the kind of hotel that looked beneath her.

And that was when he'd known she was having an affair. Maria and Reyes had been married for twenty-six years. They had two adult sons, both attending good universities, and Reyes had a reputation as something of a ladies' man. Maria was probably lonely and looking for some excitement. That had been Giant's theory anyway, and he'd spent the last month looking to prove it, knowing that here was a potential chink in Reyes's hitherto impenetrable armour.

Which was why he was here today, sitting on a bench in the shade of some trees, waiting as Logan Harris said goodbye to the latest bored housewife he'd been coaching at tennis and headed back towards his car. Giant waited until Harris was putting his kit onto the back seat, before emerging from the trees and, as Logan climbed in the driver's seat, Giant got in beside him.

'Hey, what the hell's going on?' demanded Harris, looking shocked and angry.

He was a lot bigger and stronger than Giant, who'd long ago stopped going to the gym every day, now that he had less to prove, but Giant already had his badge out. 'Police, Mr Harris. I'd like to speak to you.'

'What the hell about?' demanded Harris, staring at the badge and then at Giant.

'Maria Reyes,' said Giant, watching as Harris turned a whiter shade of pale and seemed to deflate in his seat.

'I don't know who you're talking about,' he said.

Giant couldn't help it, he was enjoying the power he wielded over Harris, who was exactly the kind of jock who'd have ignored him in school. 'I think you do,' he said. 'You're having an affair with her, and I've got proof.' He pulled the A4 envelope out of the inside pocket of his suit jacket, unfolded it and threw it on Harris's lap. 'Have a look.'

At first Harris didn't move, but then slowly, reluctantly, he opened up the envelope and stared at the black-and-white photos Giant had taken of him and Maria kissing each other in Harris's Toyota 4Runner. They'd been taken in a quiet parking lot at Pfeiffer State Park a week earlier, where Giant had followed them on one of his days off. They were good shots, too, but then Giant had had plenty of time to take them, from his position in the trees barely twenty yards away.

'I've got film as well, from the Elliot Hotel in Santa Cruz,' Giant lied, using the location where he'd first spotted Maria the previous month. 'That footage is a little more explicit than those, as I'm sure you can imagine.'

Harris looked like he was about to be sick and his hands were trembling. He might have been a big man, but at that moment Giant could have flicked him on the nose and he'd have gone over. 'What do you want?' he said eventually, his voice hoarse.

'I want you to tell Maria Reyes what you've just seen, and I want you to persuade her that it's in her best interests to help us bring her husband to justice. You know who her husband is, don't you?'

Harris nodded weakly. 'Yeah, I know.'

'Then you also know that if he found out about the two of you, he'd have you fed to his dogs. Alive. You've got a family, haven't you?'

'You know I have, otherwise you wouldn't be asking.'

'Well, at the moment you're putting them at risk just as much as yourself. These Mexican cartel guys enjoy punishing the wives and children of their targets. Yours aren't safe while you're carrying on like this. If we can find out what you and Maria are up to, then so can Tony Reyes. It's not like you've even been that subtle. I mean, he might even know already and be planning something.' Giant paused to let the words take effect – which they duly did – before producing his carrot. 'But you've got a way out, Mr Harris. Persuade Maria to meet us. We can guarantee her security. You tell her to say she turned up voluntarily and to make no mention of this meeting, or these photos. We'll take things from there and let her know what we need her to do.'

Harris looked at him suspiciously. 'Are you sure you're a cop?'

'Look at the badge, asshole.' Giant held it up again, for longer this time. 'I'm a cop.'

'Maria won't agree to it. She's terrified of her husband.'

'Not terrified enough, if she's prepared to sleep with you. Show her these photos. I think that'll help persuade her. Then shred them. Because we don't want them falling into the wrong hands, do we?'

'Are you blackmailing me?' Harris looked again at the badge. 'Is that what you're doing, Detective?'

In reality, that was exactly what Giant was doing. And he didn't like it, either. He had no fight with Logan Harris and, if Harris hadn't been a married man having an affair with a married woman, Giant would almost certainly have left him out of it. But Harris was in the wrong place at the wrong time, and now he was going to have to be the fall guy. Although if he played his cards right, he'd escape from this situation unscathed, which was exactly what Giant told him now. 'I'm giving you an out, Mr Harris. You deliver Maria to us and then you go back to your wife and daughter, with no one any the wiser. Or you can ignore what you've heard today and take your chances. But in my experience, every risk-taker's luck runs out in the end, and the end for you isn't going to be pretty.'

Harris stared down at the incriminating photos on his lap, then gave Giant an imploring look. 'Can I have some time to think about it?'

Giant wasn't in the mood to be charitable, but he also knew better than to force things. 'I'll be back in touch in a week. By then you need to have talked to Maria Reyes and got her to agree to the meeting. Otherwise all bets are off.'

He put away his badge and got out of the car without taking the photos, knowing that he'd crossed a major line here. He was working alone, breaking the very law he'd always sworn to uphold, and if he was caught, then his career – indeed his whole life – would be over.

18

The police interview room

Now

As he sat in the claustrophobic atmosphere of the interview room, the ramifications of the line that Giant had crossed the previous week were suddenly as clear as day to him. The revelation, right in the middle of the interview, that Brook Connor had not only recognized him from the photo at the tennis courts, but was prepared to identify him, hit him with the same kind of physical shock that a decent head-punch in the boxing ring used to do. It had never occurred to him that Brook Connor was having her husband followed as well. Jesus, who hadn't been following that clown? The most important thing now, though, was for him to take possession of the photo that the PI, Cervantes, had taken of him with Logan Harris, and make sure that no one else saw it, because that photo was going to be very hard to explain away.

He kept his cool now, just as he'd been taught to do in the boxing ring, and immediately went on the attack, conscious that Jenna was also looking at him, evidently seeking answers herself. 'I think you must be mistaken, Ms Connor,' he said evenly. 'I've never met your husband.'

Brook Connor met his eye with the kind of gaze that was hard to hold without exhibiting signs of guilt. 'I'm not mistaken,' she said. 'It was you in the photo in the parking lot.'

'And have you got the photograph in your possession?' he asked, calculating (and desperately hoping) she hadn't.

'No,' she answered, still looking at him. 'But I know what I saw.'

Giant gave an exaggerated shrug, although his insides were churning as the fear and shame of potential discovery ate away at him. 'Well, that may be so,' he said, somehow still managing to keep his voice even and authoritative, 'but I can tell you quite categorically that I have never met you or your husband before.'

'It was you,' repeated Brook firmly. 'Why were you with him?'

Giant knew he had to move things along. Leaning forward in his chair, he glared at Brook and her lawyer in turn. 'We're going around in circles here, and I'm not going to keep repeating myself. You, Ms Connor, are meant to be the one answering the questions. So would you mind continuing with your story?'

She held his gaze for another couple of seconds, then turned to her lawyer, who gave her a little nod.

And with that, she continued, leaving him safe for the moment.

19

Friday
Two Days Ago

After she left Chris Cervantes's house, Brook had no idea what her next move was going to be. Logan's body was still lying in the trunk of the car in the garage at home. She now had three missed calls from Angie Southby as well as well as a message, delivered in exasperated tones, telling her to get in touch immediately, and warning once again that the longer she left it to report Logan's murder, the worse it would look for both of them. Angie had concluded the message by saying urgently: 'We need to get this over with, right now.'

Brook knew she was placing Angie in a difficult position but, as a mother – and that was what she was – she had no choice but to put Paige first. If she was arrested for Logan's murder and denied bail, then who would be looking out for her? And if Paige was in the hands of this thug, Tony Reyes, and if he was as untouchable as Cervantes claimed, then the police weren't going to be able to put pressure on him to reveal her whereabouts. Somehow, Brook herself was going to have to get Reyes to talk, although God knows how that was going to happen.

She needed to come up with a plan, and the best way to do that was to walk somewhere quiet with her phone off and think. In both of her books, Brook had written at length of the power of walking as a stress-reliever, and she knew from her own experience how effective it was, even when things were looking as bleak as they were now. It helped even more to walk in a place where nature was at its most majestic, so Brook drove north on Highway One, away from Logan's corpse and the chaos surrounding it, past Santa Cruz and along the beautiful, rugged central Californian coastline, until she came to the Big Basin Redwoods State Park – a huge, deep forest that stretched from the sea up into the hills south of San José.

Brook parked her car down by Waddell Beach, which was the entrance point to the park. The beach was empty at this time on a weekday morning, but would be filled with kite-surfers later, taking advantage of the huge Pacific winds that constantly battered this coastline. She remembered coming here the first summer after she'd returned to the States, with her boyfriend at the time. His name had been Josh and he'd run a plumbing business. They would come down from San Francisco, then park and hike inland before returning, tired and hot, to the beach. They'd strip down to their underwear and run laughing into the waves, staying as long in the frigid water as they could manage (which didn't tend to be that long), and then dry themselves out on the sand in the warm sunshine. She remembered how happy she'd been and, standing there now, with the wind in her hair, she regretted that they'd broken up. He'd been a good guy.

She'd brought Paige here, too, late last summer when Logan was away in San Francisco, supposedly meeting old college buddies for a reunion. Brook had taught Paige to swim when she was three years old, and the two of them shared a love for the sea. The day they'd come up here had been cool, with an even stronger wind than usual, but Brook remembered the two of them messing about together in the freezing-cold water, and Paige's infectious fits of giggles as she'd splashed Brook with the cold salt water.

Tears stung Brook's eyes as she walked up and down the beach, letting the memories flood over her like the tide. In many ways she'd led a blessed life, with far more ups than downs. But the downs, when they'd come, had been shocking and brutal.

Like the sudden death of her parents seven years previously. She'd always had a close relationship with her mom and dad. They'd moved to the UK when Brook was five years old, after her father had taken a teaching post at the University of Sussex, and she still had fond childhood memories of the English countryside and family vacations driving their campervan through Europe. She'd been eighteen when her parents had decided to return to the States, and it was a time when Brook had been trying to assert her independence, so she'd opted to stay behind and go to university in London. She'd stayed in London for another four years afterwards as well, working in marketing for a City bank, then as a freelance consultant, but the pull of family and sunshine had eventually brought her back to California. She'd lived with her mom and dad for a while, then got a job in San Francisco and moved out, but saw them once every couple of weeks at least. It had been a happy time.

And then it happened. Brook was at work one morning when two grim-faced male detectives had turned up at her desk. They'd told her there'd been an incident involving her parents. They wouldn't give her any further details, but instead drove her to the police station in Modesto, close to where her parents lived, and said they were going to ask her some questions. They'd offered her a lawyer but, because she'd done nothing wrong, she'd turned it down. By this time she was frantic to know what had happened, but still no one told her. Instead they'd sat her down in an interview room and asked her to tell them where she'd been the previous two nights. They'd also wanted to know if anyone could vouch for her whereabouts. Brook had been pretty naïve in those days, but even she could guess that something bad had happened to her mom and dad, so she'd come right out and asked the detectives if they were dead.

The more senior of the two detectives had nodded slowly and told her that yes, he was sorry to say they were, and that the circumstances were suspicious. So that was how Brook had found out. In a hot, stifling police interview room, where her interrogators refused to give her any details about how they'd died, but instead had questioned her for the next hour as a suspect, until it became clear to them that she wasn't going to slip up and incriminate herself as the killer.

Brook was released without charge, but she had been told not to leave the state without first getting permission from the investigating officers. And then finally, a month later, she was called back to the station by the lead detective on the case, who informed her that, after much deliberation, they'd concluded that her parents' deaths had been a murder/suicide. Their theory was that Brook's mom and dad had had an argument, and that her dad had struck her mom several times with a rolling pin in the kitchen, killing her, and then, in a fit of remorse, had killed himself. Her mom's body had been found on the kitchen floor where she'd fallen, with the rolling pin a few feet from her. Her dad's body, meanwhile, had been slumped in the chair in his study. He'd suffered a single gunshot wound to the temple, and the gun he'd used – an unregistered pistol missing its serial number – was lying on the floor at his feet. There were no signs of forced entry into the house.

Brook had told the lead detective she didn't buy their theory. Her mom and dad weren't the perfect couple. She'd heard them argue enough times before, especially when she'd been growing up. Mom could be pretty fiery at times, and in a moment of confidence she'd once told Brook that, in their younger days, Dad had had more than one affair and she'd actually come close to leaving him. But in later years they'd seemed much happier. And that was another thing that had bugged Brook. Her father was the least aggressive man she'd ever met. Even when he raised his voice, there was no threat to it. There was no way he was capable of the savagery they'd attributed to him.

'You'd be surprised the kind of mild-mannered people who one day just flip,' the detective told her, 'and no one sees it coming, least of all the people close to them.'

'Then why didn't you conclude that straight away?' she asked. 'You would have saved me a month of misery.'

'We needed to look at every angle. As you say, there was no history of domestic violence between them and,' he lowered his voice here, 'there were elements of the crime scene that looked too perfect. Almost as if they were staged.'

'Then why aren't you still looking for the killer?'

'If I had my way, we still would be,' he'd answered, 'but we've got finite resources and the doubts aren't strong enough to warrant keeping them on this. I'm sorry.'

Brook thanked him for his efforts, but as she got up to leave he said something that surprised her.

'You're going to be quite a wealthy woman now, aren't you?' he said, eyeing her closely. 'Spend it wisely.'

She knew, the moment he said those words, that he still wasn't entirely convinced of her innocence.

Brook sighed. 'It's no compensation for losing the only two people in the world you love – and who love you – unconditionally,' she told him. Then she walked out of there.

But she'd been carrying that burden on her shoulders ever since. The loss of her parents so violently and suddenly was hard enough to bear, but to know that some people, including the lead detective, believed she might have had something to do with it was even worse. Because it had never allowed her to get full closure.

Brook was indeed the sole beneficiary in the will. Her mom came from money, so as a family they'd always been very comfortably off, and the estate her parents left behind was worth a little over five million dollars, after taxes. Not enough to make a person super-rich, or to retire on, but more than enough to change a life or, she supposed, to give someone a motive to kill. She'd invested the money wisely and spent some of it financing life-coaching courses and taking time out to write her first book.

At the same time, she would have traded it all in, just to have her parents back. Their loss had left her completely alone in the world. Until Paige had come along. And that was why, if Paige was alive, Brook was determined to do whatever it took to get her back, whatever the risk to herself.

Nothing prepares you for the abduction of your child, but Brook was already a very resilient woman, and she hadn't been broken yet.

She walked up and down the beach for a long time, before heading into the silent majesty of the redwood forest, all the time thinking and planning. By the time she was back at the car it was late afternoon, the horizon was dotted with leaping kite-surfers – and she knew exactly what she was going to do.

20

It was gone 8 p.m. and turning to dusk when Brook got back to their home in the hills.

She drove past twice before going in, just to check that the police hadn't got there before her and discovered Logan's body in the garage. She now had ten missed calls and four messages from Angie, and she knew that if Angie didn't hear from her soon, she'd probably conclude that something had happened to her and call the cops anyway, so she needed to move fast. She didn't want to get into an argument with her, so she sent a text instead, saying she'd make a decision about going to the police by 10 p.m.

Two minutes later, while she was parking the car in the drive-way, Angie called again.

With a sigh, and knowing it was too risky to put it off any longer, Brook took the call.

Angie was clearly furious. 'What the hell's going on, Brook?' she demanded. 'Every minute you delay reporting what happened to Logan to the police, the more guilty you look. I can hire private detectives to investigate who's setting you up, if that's what you want, but you need the police to help you find Paige.'

Brook didn't think they'd be able to help at all – not if her abduction had anything to do with Tony Reyes – but she didn't tell Angie any of that. 'I'll call you at ten o'clock. Then you phone the police and we can go in together. There are some things I need to do first.'

'You're not doing anything stupid, are you, Brook?'

'No, I'm just getting my affairs in order, in case they decide to keep me in.'

'Okay. But if I don't hear from you by 10 p.m. sharp, then frankly I'm no longer willing to represent you. Do you understand? Your freedom might be on the line, but so is my professional reputation.'

'I understand. I'll be back to you by then. I promise.' Brook got out of the car and flicked on the central locking, feeling bad for deceiving Angie, but not seeing much alternative.

The house no longer felt like home, and there was no way she could ever think about setting foot in the garage again. As she mounted the stairs to their marital bedroom, Brook wondered if whoever had been watching them still had cameras in the house, or whether they'd now been removed to make her story look even less plausible.

She figured the latter, and experienced a moment of weakness at the thought of the sheer scale of the resources ranged against her, but refused to succumb to it. She didn't have time for the luxury of doubt. At the beginning of each chapter in *You Can Be the Hero* there was an inspirational quote from a major, well-known figure, and she was reminded of the one from Winston Churchill in Chapter Eight: 'Danger gathers upon our path. We cannot afford – we have no right – to look back. We must look forward.'

She pulled a suitcase out from under the bed and hurriedly packed it with enough clothes and toiletries to last a week, then headed to the bathroom with a pair of scissors and, with a real twinge of regret, cut her shoulder-length, chocolate-brown hair into a rough pageboy style. She had had a bit of practice cutting friends' hair when she was a student back in London, so the result didn't look as bad as it might have done, but it wouldn't be winning any style awards any time soon. She'd considered dyeing what remained a different colour, like platinum-blonde, but there wasn't time. Instead, she carefully placed all the cut hair in a plastic bag to take with her, not wanting to leave any clues behind for the police, when they finally got there. She'd seen enough cop shows on the TV to know how they tracked people down.

Finally, she opened the bedroom safe and took out the six thousand dollars in cash that was in there, courtesy of those of her coaching clients who preferred to pay for her services anonymously, and shoved it in a money belt under her jacket. Then she took out the most important thing: the pistol. She checked it over now. It had ten rounds in the magazine and one in the breech, and she shoved it in the back of her jeans, along with a spare magazine, comforted by the feeling of security it gave her.

And then, as she was shutting the safe, she smelled it.

Smoke.

Frowning, she pulled open the bedroom window and leaned out.

That was when she saw two things simultaneously. The first was the line of thick and rapidly growing plumes of dark smoke rising from the garage, where Logan still lay dead in the trunk. The second was a hooded figure in black running away across the lawn towards the boundary wall.

It took Brook a couple of shocked seconds to take in what was going on before she realized that the figure running away was almost certainly one of Paige's kidnappers.

Without even thinking about it, she yanked the pistol from the back of her jeans, flicked off the safety – holding it two-handed in front of her, as she'd been taught on the range – and stared down the sights at the fleeing figure. He was moving fast and was partially obscured by the smoke and lack of light, and he'd soon be hidden by the rhododendron bushes lining the back wall. She was only going to get one chance to hit him.

Brook could feel the full psychological weight of shooting a fellow human being bearing down on her and, for a long moment, she stood there at the window, her finger tense on the trigger, hands quivering. But then she thought of Paige – tiny, beautiful, gap-toothed Paige, trapped somewhere without her – and she fired.

The shot missed. It was impossible to tell by how much, but it was close enough that the intruder flinched and momentarily changed direction, before crouching down to make himself as small a target as possible. Brook tracked him with the pistol and, just as he reached the rhododendron bushes, she fired again, twice in rapid succession. But he kept running, disappearing amongst them, out of sight and out of range.

She knew she couldn't let him go. He was her best chance of finding Paige. Thrusting the gun back inside her jeans and ignoring the heat from the barrel, she sprinted down the stairs, hurriedly unlocked the back door and continued running along the lawn in the direction he'd gone. Brook was fit. She was usually in the gym five days at least, and for a five-foot-four woman of thirty-six she was a fast runner, reaching the rhododendron bushes less than thirty seconds after he had.

The back gate was locked, so Brook jumped up and scrambled over the top of it, landing on her feet and taking off through the trees and down the hill. In the near-darkness she couldn't see the intruder but, as she ran, she could make out the shape of a car parked up on the deserted back road. She picked up speed, certain it belonged to the intruder. If she could cut him off, or just get the licence number . . .

And then suddenly there was movement to her side and the hooded figure lurched at her, out of nowhere. As Brook tried to slow and turn at the same time, she heard what sounded like the stiff crackle of electricity, followed immediately by an explosion of pain and shock, and then she was falling forward, the thick grass rising up to meet her.

She hit the ground hard. Shoulder first, then head. Her whole body felt as if it was on fire as it shivered and jerked. Her eyes were open, but she couldn't seem to focus them, and she was vaguely aware, amidst the intensity of the sensations, that she'd been Tasered.

As the shock began to subside, Brook's anger and frustration came back. She couldn't believe she'd had her chance and blown it. She tried to sit up, but couldn't move. Her only view was of the long grass in which she was enveloped. A creature that looked suspiciously like a tick crept up one of the blades, barely a foot from her face as it picked up the scent of her blood. She tried to sit up again, this time managing to get halfway, before falling back onto her side away from the tick, then finally she succeeded on the third attempt.

For a few seconds she staggered around in a ragged circle, trying to get her body back to normal, aware that both the intruder and the car that had been parked at the bottom of the hill were no longer there. She felt drained and exhausted, as if she had the world's worst hangover, and when she shook her head, it felt like it was going to drop off.

Brook remembered the fire then. She had a neighbour on one side as well as across the road, and although the houses were spaced pretty far apart, it wasn't going to take long for someone to see the smoke, if they hadn't heard the gunshots already.

She forced herself to half-jog, half-stagger back towards the house. When she got to the gate, it took her three attempts to climb over it, but adrenalin was driving her on now, as self-preservation kicked in.

As she came back onto the lawn, she saw huge gouts of flame rising up from the trashcans next to the garage, followed immediately by an explosion in one of them, causing more black smoke to rise dramatically towards the sky. The effects of the Taser finally began to wear off as she ran back into the house and up the stairs, grabbing the suitcase containing her stuff, as well as the bag containing her recently chopped hair. She looked round desperately for the shell casings she'd fired, found two, couldn't find the third, then ran back down the stairs and out the front door, throwing everything into her car just as she heard the first wail of sirens coming from down in the valley.

Whoever had lit the fire by the garage knew that Logan's body was inside it, and that when the police and fire departments turned up, someone was going to find it.

And that was what was really worrying Brook because, as far as she was aware, only two people knew that Logan's body was in there.

One was her. And the other was Angie Southby.

21

It was 9.30 p.m. and Detective Tyrone Giant was watching an old rerun of *Seinfeld* at home in his cramped one-bed apartment when he took a call from Detective Joe Padilla, telling him that they had a man's body at a residential address over near Carmel, and there were definitely suspicious circumstances.

It was when Padilla told him the names of the people who lived there that he realized things were about to unravel for him very fast indeed. It was up to Giant, as the most senior detective in the department, to secure the scene. He took the address and told Padilla he'd meet him down there, before calling Jenna.

She was waiting for him on the street when he arrived at her place, dressed casually in jeans and sneakers, and he felt that twinge of attraction he always felt when he saw her. Jenna wasn't classically pretty. She was a big-boned woman with a prominent jaw, and the way she wore her dark hair back in a tight ponytail didn't really suit her, but none of that mattered. Giant liked her confidence; the fact that she had no airs and graces; and the way her big brown eyes twinkled when she smiled. He was also a little in awe of the fact that she'd twice been decorated for bravery, which was twice more than he had.

He never told her any of this, though. They got on well as partners and he didn't want to spoil that. But when she got in the car and he smelled the lime-scented body lotion she often wore, he had to turn away temporarily and take a breath. Giant hadn't had these kinds of feelings for a woman since he'd been with his fiancée – a relationship that had ended several years ago now – and he didn't much like how vulnerable they made him feel.

'So what have we got?' asked Jenna, rearranging the shoulder holster underneath her jacket as they pulled away.

Giant cleared his throat. 'A dead body at Logan Harris's place.' He'd told Jenna in confidence that Harris had been having an affair with Tony Reyes's wife, as soon as he'd found out about it, wanting to get her input on what she thought they could do with the information. Tony Reyes might have been living the life of a respectable local businessman, but there wasn't a person in the Monterey Police Department who didn't know about his reputation as a killer of whole families, and who didn't want to see him brought down. Jenna had told him that they couldn't do much with the information, because there was no way they'd be able to get a warrant to bug either Logan Harris or Mrs Reyes, as they weren't actually suspected of doing anything wrong – which had been when Giant had decided to go it alone and blackmail Harris with the photos, without telling anyone else what he was doing.

Jenna looked at him. 'Do we know whose body it is?'

'Not yet,' said Giant, 'but I'm guessing it's Logan, seeing as he's the one sleeping with a gangster's wife.'

His prediction proved correct. Half an hour later, after a fast drive down the coast on Highway One, he was holding a handkerchief dipped in Vicks to his nose while looking down at Harris's dead body, squashed into the trunk of his silver Toyota 4Runner.

Logan Harris was dressed for the outdoors in an unzipped tan leather jacket, check shirt above a white T-shirt, jeans and Caterpillar boots. The shirt was drenched in blood and a kitchen knife was buried almost to the hilt in his side at an upward angle, a wound that would almost certainly have pierced his heart, given the relative lack of blood. The jacket itself was undamaged, suggesting that someone had got very close to him to deliver the blows. When he pulled back the jacket with a gloved hand, Giant counted three stab wounds altogether, in a tight cluster.

Giant knew he couldn't let on that he recognized Logan Harris, so he leaned over and gently patted down his corpse, careful not to contaminate the scene, before removing his wallet. He opened the wallet and read his name on the driving licence, trying to ignore the smiling man in the photo staring back at him.

'This is one of the homeowners, Logan Harris,' said Giant to the man standing next him, the county pathologist Dr Gary Wallace, a tall, cheery soul in his fifties, who'd grown up in the same neighbourhood as Giant in Oakland. Wallace had a big smile and a real zest for life, which was ironic considering that he had more experience of dead bodies than virtually anyone else in a fifty-mile radius. 'Can you tell me how long he's been dead for?'

'He's definitely not fresh,' answered Wallace. 'The body temperature's already the same as the air temperature in here, but he's still in the early stages of decomposition. At a guess, I'd say he died somewhere between eighteen and twenty-four hours ago.'

Giant looked down at the body in silence for a long minute, reeling through the possibilities in his head. He was blessed with a very good memory. If he saw something once, he remembered it – even weeks later – and consequently he didn't tend to make many notes. Finally, when he'd seen all he needed for now, he went outside to escape the smell. He might have been used to seeing (and indeed smelling) dead bodies, but there was some-thing far too personal about this one, and he didn't want to be reminded of his potential part in Logan Harris's death.

The scene had been fully secured now. Patrol cars lined the street outside and more were in the driveway, alongside a fire engine and an ambulance to remove the body. There'd been a total of three 911 calls reporting a fire on the premises, and one of the callers had claimed that she'd heard a number of gunshots at the same time. Two patrol cars had arrived with the fire truck and had checked that the area was safe, before allowing the firefighters to put out the fire, which had broken out next to the garage. During a routine search of the area afterwards the cops had picked up the smell from inside the garage, forced their way in and found the body. Giant now had a dozen local officers making house-to-house enquiries and taking statements, while they waited for the Forensics team to give the house – a big, French-style villa that probably cost what it would take Giant several lifetimes to earn – a full search.

As he stood there, taking deep breaths to get the foul smell of Logan Harris out of his system, Jenna came out the front door of the house and walked over. 'The house is empty. No sign of anyone.'

'The body's definitely Logan Harris,' he told her.

'There are a lot of pictures of him, his wife and their daughter inside. I didn't realize the wife was Brook Connor.'

Giant looked at her. 'Should I know that name?' If the truth was told, he'd never really looked into Harris's wife's background. He hadn't even thought about the possibility that he was putting her and a child in danger. It made him feel sick. He'd let his obsession with bringing down Tony Reyes get the better of him, and now other people were paying for it.

'She's like this big, celebrity life-coach,' said Jenna. 'She's on cable sometimes. I think she might even have her own show, and I know she wrote one of those self-help books that sold a lot of copies.'

'Did you buy yourself a copy?'

She grunted with derision. 'Yeah, right. I get enough horseshit on this job without having to read it for pleasure. I'll tell you what else is interesting. Her parents died in suspicious circumstances. It was ruled as a murder/suicide – the father bludgeoned the mother, then shot himself – but for a while Connor was under suspicion for it. She inherited a lot of money and used it to kick-start her career in life-coaching.'

Now that was really interesting. Giant decided to look up the case notes as soon as he was able. In the meantime, he felt a little better. He looked up at the grand house. 'Logan Harris was a tennis coach, so I wonder if this was bought with her money. How old's the daughter?'

'Young. About five or six. Cute little thing.'

A picture of little Adalina Hernandez came into his mind and Giant felt even sicker. 'So the two of them could be in danger.' Or worse, he thought.

'There's no sign of any struggle inside. No obvious bloodstains. Do you think this has anything to do with Tony Reyes?'

God, I hope not, he thought. 'I don't know. Doc Wallace says Harris has been dead for between eighteen and twenty-four hours. He was stabbed three times. The knife's still sticking out of him.' Giant had noticed several things of interest and told Jenna them now. 'He was killed elsewhere and put in the trunk, and he's a big guy, so I think it would have taken a couple of people to have got him in there, which points to more than one killer. But there are no defensive wounds, either. Whoever killed him got very close – either without Harris spotting them or because he knew and trusted them. It was a very quick, clean kill. I'm a bit confused about the fire, though. Come and have a look.'

Giant switched on his flashlight and led her around to the side of the garage, where the three burned-out plastic husks that represented what was left of the trashcans were lined up against the garage's outer wall behind a separate line of police tape. They'd be taken away later for forensic examination to confirm how the fire had started, but the smell of accelerant in the air suggested it was pretty obvious.

Giant ran his flashlight over the trashcans and the smoke-blackened wall behind them. He turned to Jenna. 'This fire was started deliberately. You can smell that. But if the idea was to destroy Logan Harris's body and conceal evidence, surely it would have been far easier to have poured fuel over his body and do it that way? So it looks like someone set this up, not to conceal the crime, but to draw attention to it.'

Jenna smiled. 'Ah, the Mozzarella Man strikes again. They obviously taught you well in detective school, Ty. That's definitely the rational explanation, but it doesn't take one thing into account.'

Giant smiled back, pleased that she was making a reference to his one and only true achievement. 'And what's that?'

'Panic. People do bad things, the consequences creep up on them, then they panic and try to cover up the crime.' She shrugged. 'Happens all the time.'

Giant looked at the damaged trashcans and thought about that. He was still thinking about it when Detective Joe Padilla – the cop who'd called him at home earlier – walked over. He had a notebook in his hand and was moving too fast for it to be about anything casual.

Giant nodded a greeting and asked him what he'd got.

'A neighbour across the road' – Padilla consulted the notebook – 'a Mrs Welsh, says she saw one of the home owners, Brook Connor, driving her Mercedes convertible out of the property tonight, at about eight-twenty, in a real hurry. Apparently Mrs Welsh was the first person to dial nine-one-one. She was in her front room and saw the smoke rising up from here, so she went outside to take a closer look, and that's when she heard three distinctive cracks, about ten seconds apart, that sounded like gunshots. She said she got a bit scared then and went back inside the house, dialled nine-one-one and was watching the property through her front window when she saw Ms Connor leave.'

'Was Ms Connor being chased by anyone?' asked Jenna.

The patrolman shook his head. 'Not according to the witness. She stayed at the window, watching the place, the whole time until we arrived. In that time no other car came out. She's adamant. And she seems reliable.'

'My kind of witness,' said Giant. 'Were the security gates shut when you guys arrived?' he asked.

'No. They were open. That's why we were able to drive straight in. There was no sign of anyone here, and no sign of forced entry, either. Just the fire in the trashcans. Something else. I don't know if you're aware, but Mrs Welsh told me that four people lived here. Logan Harris, his wife Brook Connor, their daughter, Paige, and a nanny whose name she didn't know.'

'The house is definitely empty now,' said Jenna. 'And if anyone was killed in there, there's no obvious sign of it that I can see.'

'Do we know the car the nanny drives?' Giant asked Barker.

Again Padilla consulted his notebook. 'A red Honda.'

'Like that one over there.' Giant pointed to the solitary car in the driveway.

'Oh, yeah,' said Padilla. 'I guess that's hers.'

Giant tried to put together what they'd got. A dead husband; a wife leaving the house in a hurry; and a missing daughter and nanny. It wasn't easy to come up with a narrative for what might have happened, which would usually have irritated Giant, who was a man who liked order. However, this time round he couldn't help feeling relieved. Given what they knew so far, the obvious suspect was the wife.

'Okay,' he said, trying to keep the relief out of his voice. 'We need to track down Brook Connor. And fast.'

22

'Never be afraid to call in favours from those who owe you.'

The first line of Chapter Twelve of *You Can Be the Hero*, which dealt with the need for individuals to be assertive in handling day-to-day issues, had never been so apt as it was now for Brook.

She knew the police would be looking for her soon. She might have cut her hair short but, with the bruise on her jaw from where Logan had struck her still very much in evidence, even after the application of plenty of make-up, she was going to stand right out. The problem was that she didn't have too many people she could turn to. Her parents were dead, as was her husband; and, although she had made some good friends in the time she'd been back in the States, she couldn't think of one to whom she'd entrust herself now. And she'd already burned her bridges with Angie and was no longer sure she could even trust her.

So here she was, at close to midnight, parked next to a dumpster in the far corner of a motel parking lot set in the midst of the flat, sparsely populated stretch of coast that ran north of Monterey, waiting for Chris Cervantes. In the end she'd figured he'd be the best person to help, because he owed her for not warning her about Logan's affair with Maria Reyes, making him at least partly responsible for everything that had happened subsequently. So she'd turned up on his doorstep once again. He hadn't wanted to get involved, of course, but Brook could be persuasive when she wanted to be, and she knew which buttons to press with Cervantes.

She watched as he came out of the motel reception now, got in his car and then reversed into a space in front of one of the ground-floor rooms. He climbed out slowly, using his walking stick for leverage, and she saw him wince in pain as he stood upright. She felt for him, and was sorry she'd had to involve him once again.

He nodded in Brook's direction before opening the motel-room door.

Leaving her own car where it was, Brook strode quickly across the empty courtyard, keeping her head down, and followed Cervantes inside, shutting the door behind her.

The room was small and boxlike, decorated in various tasteless shades of brown, containing just a bed and a single chest of drawers with a cheap TV sitting on top of it.

Cervantes handed her the key. 'Here you go,' he said wearily. 'The proprietor's an old guy and he didn't see my car, so you can park yours here easily enough. I told him I might be joined by my girlfriend.'

Brook managed a weak smile. 'You wish! How long did you book the room for?'

'Three nights and I paid cash. It came to two hundred and ten dollars.'

She took a wad of cash from the money belt beneath her jacket and counted it out. 'Thank you.'

He looked at her with a sympathetic expression. 'I know I keep saying it, but handing yourself in to the police and telling the truth are the most effective ways to find your daughter.'

'I disagree,' she told him. 'If Tony Reyes wanted me dead, he would have sent around an assassin to kill me. But he didn't. He – or someone else – sent someone around to set fire to my garage for one reason only: to draw attention to the fact that Logan was dead inside. No one tried to touch me. Which means I'm better off to them alive.' She'd been thinking about this a lot over the past couple of hours. 'I'm the fall guy, Mr Cervantes. If I give myself up now, I'm going to be accused of Logan's murder, and possibly Paige's disappearance as well. The police won't be looking for kidnappers. They'll be looking for Paige's body. And maybe not that hard. And I can promise you this,' she concluded, putting a strength into her voice that she didn't feel, 'I'm innocent.'

Cervantes nodded slowly. He looked old and tired, as if the pressures of the world had squeezed all the life out of him. 'I know, and that's why I'm here. But please be realistic, Ms Connor.' He gave her a look that was almost paternal. 'What are you really going to be able to do now? You're on your own.'

Brook didn't see much point in keeping it a secret. Cervantes already knew enough to sink her. 'I'm going to approach Reyes's

159

wife. She's a mother. If she knows a five-year-old girl's missing, she might be able to put pressure on her husband.'

'You think she doesn't know what her husband's capable of? It's an open secret that he's made whole families disappear. It's not going to work.'

'Right now, it's all I've got. Unless you've got a better idea.'

He didn't say anything.

'I didn't think so. The point is: I believe Paige is alive. I was sent a photo of her yesterday morning, and I'm certain it was taken then. So I'm going to do everything I possibly can to find her. Is there anything you can tell me about Maria Reyes that might help?'

Cervantes shook his head. 'The make and licence plate of Maria Reyes's car are in the file you took, and I believe she and her husband live in a ranch up around Carmel Valley . . . But that's it. I've always figured the less I know about these people, the better.' He paused. 'Look, just do me a favour. Whatever happens to you, please don't mention my name. I've got family, too, you know.'

'I won't,' she told him. 'I promise.'

He nodded and limped slowly past her to the door. Then, without another word, he was gone.

Brook listened as he reversed out and drove away, then she retrieved her own car, parked it in the same spot and got her belongings out of the back. She'd rubbed dirt on the licence plate to help obscure the number, and most of the rooms around her looked empty, so she figured she'd be safe here for a short while at least.

Even so, there was no escaping the knowledge that she was a fugitive now and, as she closed the door behind her for what she hoped was the final time that night, she felt a wave of emotion engulf her and she collapsed on the bed, sobbing silently.

She cried for her mom, who'd always been the rock for her to cling for; for her dad, who'd shown her nothing but unconditional love. She cried for her childhood; for innocence; for the cool, grey, faraway shores of England where she'd been happy and had had a life; for the missing child whom she'd brought up as her own; for the collapse of all her desires for a happy, stable family life after the death of her parents; even for Logan, who'd at least been there, and whom she'd loved once, in those heady, early days.

And, most of all, she cried for the fact that right now she was all alone in the world, with enemies at every turn.

Part Three

23

Saturday

Yesterday morning

Detective Tyrone Giant was exhausted as he and Jenna went into the Chief's office for the 9 a.m. meeting. Neither he nor Jenna had left Harris's home address until gone 2 a.m., and they'd both been at the station for 7.30 a.m., managing only four hours' sleep in the meantime.

The Chief was sitting behind his desk, looking concerned. 'This is going to be a big one,' he said straight away.

He was a tall, well-groomed man, with a full head of neatly coiffed silver hair, a degree in Political Science and an eye for bigger things. In other words, exactly the kind of guy you don't want breathing down your neck on a high-pressure case like this one, because men like the Chief only have loyalty to themselves.

'I've got a press conference out front at nine-thirty,' he said, as they sat down opposite him. 'Have you seen how many media are out there?' Giant had. A lot. 'There's nothing those guys like more than an attractive murder suspect,' the Chief continued. 'So what have you got for me to give them?'

As the senior of the two detectives, it was Giant who apprised the Chief, first of all going through the bare facts of what they had, then moving on to the working theory that he and Jenna had decided upon a few minutes earlier. 'It looks as if at some point on Thursday night, Brook Connor killed her husband by stabbing him to death. The murder weapon matches a knife that's missing from a set in the family kitchen. It's been sent for testing and we should have fingerprint results back later today. At the moment her stepdaughter, Paige Harris, aged five, is missing, as is her nanny, Rosa Fernandez, aged forty-nine. The last known sighting of Paige and Fernandez was on Wednesday afternoon when Rosa picked Paige up from kindergarten.'

'I just spoke to the principal at the kindergarten,' said Jenna. 'She said everything was perfectly normal with Paige and Rosa on Wednesday. Apparently Rosa's a very reliable nanny who's been working for the family for two years, and Paige is a sweet, normal kid, popular with everyone.'

'Do you have photos of the two of them?' the Chief asked.

Giant nodded and passed across the desk two blown-up copies of photos they'd taken from the house the previous night.

'Wow! She's a beauty,' said the Chief, staring at the one of Paige, having barely glanced at the photo of Rosa. 'The public are going to want to know what's happened to her. Have you got any leads on that front?'

Giant shook his head. 'There were no obvious signs of foul play at the house, and Rosa Fernandez's car's still there, so it's unlikely she took off of her own accord.'

'The principal told me that Ms Connor, the stepmother, called the kindergarten on Thursday morning to say Paige was sick and wouldn't be in that day,' said Jenna.

The implication was obvious. Brook Connor had been buying herself time. But it still left plenty of unanswered questions, the most important of which was: if something had already happened to Paige by the time Connor contacted the kindergarten, why was it another twelve hours or so before her husband was killed? It bothered Giant, because it didn't seem like a case of a violent argument that had gone too far, which meant it was far more likely to have something to do with Tony Reyes.

The Chief put down the photo of Paige and gave him and Jenna a puzzled look. 'We've got a fire started deliberately, reports of gunshots and Brook Connor driving out the gate in a hurry, but according to what you're saying, the husband had already been dead for close to a day.'

Giant shrugged. 'It's possible Connor was trying to burn her husband's body to get rid of the evidence and the fire got out of hand, but we can't explain the gunshots. A single shell casing from a small nine-mill pistol was found by the Forensics team in her bedroom, but no bullet or bullet hole, so it wasn't a failed suicide attempt. The bedroom window was open, so Connor was probably firing at something or someone at the back of the property, but there's no sign that anyone was injured, and Forensics are still looking for the bullet.'

'I don't think we're going to know for sure what happened until we pick Connor up,' said Jenna. 'We've got an APB out for her and the car she's driving, but we're going to need to make a media appeal.'

The Chief grunted. 'We've got no problem with media interest. Brook Connor represents the perfect story. She's a minor celebrity; she's good-looking; and so's the stepdaughter. They'll love the fact that she's a life-coach who's made all her money telling other people how to improve their lives and now looks like she's screwed up hers. Even I like that angle. And, of course, there's the fact that she's come to the attention of the law before, over the deaths of her parents. So there's going to be a lot of heat. Do we have any idea of motive?'

Giant and Jenna had discussed this earlier and agreed that they couldn't let on to anyone about the affair that Logan Harris had been having with Maria Reyes, least of all the Chief, who would probably fire Giant in a minute if he thought he was deliberately – and illegally – following the spouses of people they weren't even officially chasing.

'No,' he said, in answer to the chief's question. 'We haven't got any idea of motive yet.'

'Well, do some digging. There's a reason why Brook Connor put a knife into her husband, and we need to find it.'

Giant and Jenna made the requisite affirmative noises and were about to leave the office when there was a knock on the door and Sergeant Joe Padilla thrust his head around it.

'I'm sorry to bother you, Chief,' he said, 'but I thought you guys would want to know that we've just had a call from Ralph Byfield. He's the manager at the National Bank over in Carmel. He said Brook Connor came in to see him two days ago and insisted on withdrawing a quarter of a million dollars in cash.'

The Chief raised his eyebrows.

'And he gave it to her?'

Padilla nodded. 'Said he figured he didn't have much choice. It was her money. He tried to persuade her otherwise, but she was insistent.'

'Great,' said the Chief miserably. 'Now we've got to involve the FBI and the US Marshals Service.'

Ordinarily Giant would have been hugely disappointed by this new development, because it meant losing control of what could have been the biggest case of his career, but he couldn't help feeling a sense of relief. Because whatever had happened between Brook Connor and her husband, it hadn't been caused by his decision to blackmail Logan Harris.

Or so he hoped.

24

Brook Connor had her first shock of the day when she switched on the TV in her room. It was 9.45 a.m. and she'd slept badly, but for a much longer time than she'd been anticipating.

On the TV a young, blonde reporter was standing outside a police station talking to the camera, while at the top of the screen was a professional photo of Brook, taken from her website. It was a good shot and she was smiling and not looking at all like a criminal.

However, as the reporter continued talking about how the local police had confirmed that she was wanted for questioning in connection with the murder of her husband and the disappearance of Paige – described as 'her stepdaughter' – as well as the stepdaughter's nanny, it became very clear that it didn't matter what she looked like, because the reporter's tone suggested that

Brook was very much the suspect in both crimes, and the wicked stepmom always makes a good suspect.

There were a lot of other reporters and camera crew in the background and an air of excitement in the blonde reporter's tone. This was obviously going to be a big story.

A photo of a grinning Paige, blown up from the one in their living room, suddenly filled the screen, and Brook felt her stomach lurch. She hadn't seen Paige now for a whole three days, and the thought that she was waking up somewhere out there alone, probably scared and definitely needing her mom, was becoming increasingly hard to bear. It was why she couldn't give herself up, whatever the cost of remaining on the run. In truth, she realized with a sinking feeling that there wasn't even any obvious evidence there'd ever even been any kidnappers. She had no doubt that they'd got rid of any incriminating evidence and were now long gone, leaving behind just a dead body, two missing people and an obvious suspect.

'Police are also trying to trace the family nanny, Rosa Fernandez,' continued the reporter on the TV, 'who hasn't been seen since two p.m. on Wednesday afternoon, when she collected Paige from kindergarten, and they are appealing for anyone who might have seen either of them since.'

For the first time, it occurred to Brook that Rosa might have been involved. Not willingly. She couldn't imagine that. Rosa was a genuinely kind person with a big heart, who adored Paige in a way that could not have been faked over so long a period. But what if Tony Reyes had blackmailed her? Or threatened her family back in Mexico. She tried to recall if

Rosa had been acting strangely in the run-up to the abduction, but as far as Brook could remember, she'd been her usual
friendly self. She'd made pancakes for Brook and Paige on the
morning before the kidnap. They'd had a competition to see
who could flip their pancake the highest and still have it land
back in the pan. Rosa had won easily. Everyone had laughed.
Life had been normal.

But maybe Rosa was a better actress than Brook had given her
credit for? And maybe she'd been too scared not to get involved?

She switched off the TV and went into the bathroom, staring
at herself in the dirt-stained mirror. She looked exhausted and
washed out. There were dark semicircles beneath her eyes and, in
the morning light, the haircut she'd given herself looked exactly
what it was – the work of an amateur. She looked very different
from her picture on the news, but the swelling along her jawline
made her stand out, and she imagined people in the street giving
her a second, closer look as they passed, furrowing their brows
because somehow she looked familiar, then realizing it was her:
Brook Connor – the wicked stepmom; the wanted killer. And
then the police surrounding her, taking her down, face pushed
into the dirt and cuffing her hands behind her back, like so many
other suspects she'd seen being arrested on TV reality shows.

Brook took a deep breath. In ordinary circumstances she would
have given up, but the thing was, it already felt like she'd lost
everything. Her success; her marriage; her beautiful daughter ...
They felt like a mirage, something from another, long-ago life.
And ironically enough, it was this sense of total loss that gave her
the confidence to carry on now.

She went back into the bedroom and pulled her laptop from the overnight bag. There was an information sheet attached to the back of the door containing the Wi-Fi code. Brook wasn't sure whether the cops were able to track her laptop or not, but figured she didn't have much choice but to use it, so she booted it up and then searched for everything she could online about Tony Reyes – this monster who made whole families disappear and whose cronies could be holding Paige right now.

There was almost nothing. Just one article about a financial advisor and his wife from Salinas who'd gone missing six months earlier, something she vaguely remembered Chris Cervantes mentioning when he'd been talking to her the previous morning. The advisor had been under investigation by the FBI on suspicion of laundering money on behalf of unnamed organized-crime figures. He had links to a construc-tion company and a nationwide chain of fast-food outlets, both of which were co-owned by Tony Reyes, who was described simply as a Mexican-American businessman. Nothing else was said about Reyes in the article, but it wasn't hard to work out that he was the organized-crime figure in question.

She looked up further articles on the missing couple, John and Judy Matthews. There were a handful, all alluding to Mr Mat-thews's possible links to organized crime, but they'd fizzled out, and the last one had been written a little over a month earlier in *The Salinas Californian*, stating that police still had no leads on their disappearance, but were not closing the case.

It amazed Brook that a man like Tony Reyes could act with such impunity in a civilized country like the United States.

Whoever had written the original article about the disappearance of the Matthews obviously knew to tread very carefully around this particular Mexican-American businessman.

Next, Brook turned her attention to his wife, Maria Reyes, only to find that there was nothing about her, either. She wasn't on Facebook, Instagram or any of the other social-media sites – or if she was, she was extremely well hidden. Brook was disappointed, but not surprised. Maria was the wife of an alleged high-level gangster, so it stood to reason she'd keep a low profile.

With a sigh, she put down the laptop and picked up the file Cervantes had given her containing the evidence he'd gleaned on Logan's affair, including the photos. She needed to see what Maria Reyes looked like.

There were ten photos in all. Four of them were shots of Logan and Maria inside the family Toyota 4Runner, taken from the front. Logan was in the driving seat, an attractive older woman in her late forties beside him in the passenger seat. In two of the photos they were kissing passionately, and Logan was squeezing her breast through the material of her top. In another, they were giggling together, their faces almost touching; and in the fourth, he was holding her close to him in a warm grip, while they looked into each other's eyes. This last one hurt the most. It was the intimacy of their body language, the obvious warmth of their feelings towards one another. You couldn't fake that. Brook's marriage might have been over long before Cervantes had captured Logan and Maria like this, but even so, she couldn't help remembering that Logan had looked at her like that once, and she at him. Brook could only imagine what a violent man like Tony Reyes would think if he ever saw the photos, and the kind of revenge he would want to take. After all, it wasn't as if either Logan or Maria had been particularly careful. Cervantes had found them easily enough. As well as the shots in the stationwagon, he'd photographed them talking to each other next to a sky-blue Porsche 911 convertible that Cervantes had said belonged to Maria.

Tony Reyes had far greater resources than Cervantes, so there was a very good chance that he had, indeed, found out about the affair, which meant that Maria might not be around any more, either.

Brook shook her head angrily, wondering how Logan could have been so stupid as to get involved with a gangster's wife. She wouldn't simply be able to leave her husband – not if she knew anything about his business. And it wasn't as if she was some alluring young beauty queen, either. She was an attractive woman, yes, but a good ten years older than Brook.

The prick. The fucking selfish prick! He'd put his whole family in jeopardy over a middle-aged woman.

But at least she now had a lead, because she was certain that if Maria Reyes was still alive, she could help her. Whether or not she wanted to.

25

Lou McPherson had killed twice. The first time had been three years ago. The second three days ago.

The killing of Brook Connor's nanny had been a joint effort. One person holding her down; the other – him – holding the bag over her head and keeping a hand over her mouth at the same time, so she didn't make a noise and wake the kid. They'd done the deed in the back yard next to the family swimming pool, and although the nanny had put up a pretty good fight, she'd soon lapsed into unconsciousness. The whole thing had been tense and exhilarating, and the fear of being caught had given McPherson a real adrenalin-kick.

Afterwards he'd been left with the task of slicing off the nanny's little finger, then dragging her body out to the car. He wasn't trusted with the kid. For this particular job he was just the muscle, and he didn't like it. He might have been a career crim-inal and one who'd never held down a good job (or indeed any job) in his life, but he was no fool.

And that was why he was so concerned now. Because he was no longer needed, and he knew too much. McPherson was thirty years old and was used to being the top dog in whatever group he chose to hang out with. But he wasn't the top dog here. He was working for someone else, someone who'd black-mailed him into taking part, who had stuff on him – bad stuff – that would put him in jail for a long, long time. Otherwise there was no way he'd have got involved. Sure, he'd been paid well for the work. One hundred and twenty-five in cash, which was more money than he'd ever seen in his life, and definitely enough to make the killing of a middle-aged Mexican nanny worthwhile.

Even the killing of the old man – the husband – wasn't such a problem, because it had been made to look like Connor herself had done it. The problem was the little kid. McPherson didn't feel anything for little kids – they were an irrelevance to him – but he was aware that, for whatever reason, plenty of people did, and they got very angry when anyone committed crimes against them. It meant there'd be huge pressure for the cops to solve the case.

That was why McPherson had had a backup plan. One that he'd come up with on his own, and which would double his money. One twenty-five was nice, but two-fifty was a lot better. With that kind of cash, he could disappear without a trace. Because the thing was, he knew exactly where they were keeping the little girl. They thought he hadn't got a clue about any of it, but that was where they'd been careless. He'd put two and two together. And now that he knew the location, he could sell that information back to Brook Connor. All he had to do was call her, convince her to part with more money and, when he'd got it, he'd tell her where the kid was. Simple, right?

Except that it wasn't, because suddenly Brook Connor was on the news and the cops were saying she was a fugitive. There'd been a fire at her house and they'd found the body of her old man in the trunk of the car, and now she was wanted for his murder. McPherson knew straight away who'd set that fire and had got the cops interested in Connor. He cursed himself for delaying things. He should have known that was going to happen and should have shaken down Connor for the extra money right away. Now it was too late.

McPherson turned away from the TV in disgust, no longer wanting to be reminded of his folly. He picked up his gun from the kitchen table and shoved it in the waistband of his shorts, then went down to the basement. He went everywhere with the gun at the moment, paranoid about someone coming here to take him out. He even slept with it on the pillow next to him. He didn't think they wanted to kill him. They thought he was their patsy, someone who could do them no harm. Even so, he knew better than to take any chances.

His instructions had been to sit tight in the house until he was told otherwise, but he was beginning to think now might be the time to split with the money and take his chances. The problem was, it would have to be a permanent move. If he defied his instructions, he'd be a fugitive as well. And one twenty-five wasn't going to last long when you were on the run.

The thought of food took his mind off his current predicament. He was a lean, well-built man without a hint of fat, and yet he ate like a horse. He was lucky like that. It was about the only thing he was lucky with. Everything else in his life was shit.

Right now he was so hungry he could eat a horse, but decided to go with some nice prime cow instead. He opened the chest freezer in the basement and took a sixteen-ounce rib steak from the corner basket. The nanny's head was on top of a pile of limbs and body parts, which took up most of the rest of the space inside. Her face – frozen solid – stared up at him, the eyes only half-open, looking like someone who'd just woken up, which was pretty ironic. The chopped-up nanny was the reason he wasn't supposed to leave. His job was to dump the parts upstate somewhere, but he had to wait for a call telling him when it was to be done, and that call hadn't come yet.

McPherson closed the lid and climbed back up the steps. He listened constantly for suspicious sounds, in case someone had broken in while he'd been down there. But, as usual, the house was silent except for the noise of the TV in the kitchen. They were still running a report on Brook Connor, as if it was the only story in the world that day.

He shoved the steak into the microwave, put it on defrost and decided it was time to change channels and find something slightly less depressing to watch.

And then the reporter said something that stopped him in his tracks. He kept listening, thought about what he was hearing, and that was when he realized there might be a way out of this for him after all.

It just required a little bit more planning.

He smiled. He was good at that.

26

The first thing Brook did that morning when she left the motel was to drive to a deli in the nearby coastal town of Marina and buy provisions: sandwiches, fruit, a couple of blueberry muffins and plenty of bottled water. She'd been nervous as hell going out in public. All it needed was one person to recognize her – only one – and everything would turn to shit, just like that.

There were about a dozen people eating at the tables and a couple more lining up at the cash register. Brook was wearing a beanie hat, which she kept on, but removed her sunglasses, trying to look as nonchalant as possible. She joined the line, ignoring her rapidly beating heart, and when it came to her turn, she looked the kid right in the eye and ordered her produce. He didn't bat an eyelid. Neither did anyone else. But she didn't finally relax until she was back in the car and driving again.

Brook had found the address of Tony and Maria Reyes easily enough and had fed it into Google Maps back in the motel. She'd seen that they lived up in the hills above the town of Carmel Valley, at the end of a dead-end road about a quarter of a mile long. The satellite image showed a huge house surrounded by fields backing onto the base of a high, rocky ridge. On the map there was a back road that ran up a hill a few hundred yards to the east of the property, and which looked like it afforded a good view of it.

Brook made a second stop at a photography shop in Monterey to buy a decent pair of binoculars. There were two assistants. One a chatty middle-aged man, the other a bored-looking teenage girl. Brook waited until the man was busy with a customer, then approached the girl and paid a hundred and twenty dollars for a pair displayed in a glass counter. The middle-aged man smiled at her as she counted out the cash, and then she saw something change in his expression. It was very subtle, but Brook thought he might have recognized her. She smiled back, knowing that putting up a confident front gets you out of most situations, thanked the girl who'd served her and then left as casually as was possible when you're coming close to having an anxiety attack.

Her Mercedes was parked round the corner and she got in it and drove in the opposite direction from the shop, so she didn't have to pass it. She knew they were looking for the car, and the fact that she'd covered the plates in dirt meant she risked being stopped by the police. It wasn't easy, she thought, being a fugitive whose photo was all over the news.

We Can See You

It was close to 1 p.m., and the day was beginning to heat up, when she finally reached Carmel Valley town. She took the road up towards the Reyes place and, as she passed the turning that led directly to their house, saw that it was blocked off with a high wrought-iron gate marked 'Private Property'. Next to the gate, two men in uniform sat in a car with 'Saber Security' written on the side in bright yellow, above a picture of a roaring lion. Both men looked up as she passed, but didn't pay her any heed as she continued driving further up into the hills.

After a couple of wrong turns and some vertigo-inducing bends as the road wound higher, Brook finally found the spot she was looking for, by the side of a steep, potholed single-track road near the top of the ridge. She parked the Mercedes a few yards away in a dent in the road and found a spot in the grass near the edge, where she couldn't be seen.

Through the binoculars, Brook could see that the Reyes house was a Mexican-style hacienda on two floors, built around a central courtyard. On one side were perfectly manicured gardens with a pool, while on the other was an open field containing horses and a large stable block. A high brick wall topped with razor wire, designed to keep out even the most determined intruders, surrounded the whole compound.

The only way to get into the house was through a gated entrance leading into the courtyard, which was guarded by a man in a fortified booth. Another man, with a rifle strapped to his back, patrolled the perimeter wall with a German shepherd. For a respected local businessman, Tony Reyes clearly had a lot of security.

Brook could see three cars in the courtyard, one of which was the sky-blue Porsche 911 that Maria drove, which meant she was probably either in residence or dead. Brook knew she couldn't break into the compound without coming up against armed resistance, and she wasn't going to risk that yet. Therefore the only alternative was waiting.

So she waited.

And waited.

She wasn't a patient person at the best of times. She'd tried hard to make herself one over the years by taking up meditation, and reminding herself that being impatient wasn't going to make the things that she wanted to happen, happen any faster. But it hadn't worked, and with the heavy burden of pressure adding to her sense of frustration, as well as the relentless sun, those next five hours were some of the most painful she could remember and gave her a new-found respect for cops on long surveillance jobs. In that time, aside from the two guards, she saw no one. The problem was that she only had a limited time – most likely hours, a couple of days at most – to find Paige before the cops found her. So to lie there, sweating and uncomfortable, watching the clock tick steadily down, when for all she knew Tony and Maria Reyes were on vacation in Palm Springs or Hawaii, was soul-destroying.

But if Maria Reyes was at home and unharmed, she was going to have to show herself eventually. She might have been a gangster's wife, but she obviously had a fair amount of freedom if she'd been able to embark on an affair with Logan, and she clearly didn't travel with bodyguards. And if she'd already been punished by her husband, then he too would have to show himself at one point. And as a last resort, Brook would talk to him.

Thankfully it didn't come to that because, at 6.23 p.m., with her body stiff as a board and all her food and most of her water gone, Brook's prayers were finally answered. Maria Reyes appeared out of her front door and walked towards her sky-blue Porsche. She was dressed smartly in jeans and heels, and didn't look like a woman under any kind of duress as she climbed inside and switched on the engine.

She was going out. And she was alone.

Brook ran back to her car and drove as fast as she dared along the treacherous, winding road back down towards Carmel Valley town, hoping she could remember the directions properly.

It took her eight minutes to reach the main road. By her calculations, it would have taken Maria no more than five to get to the same spot, which meant she was at least three minutes ahead. The left turning led in the same direction that she and Logan had driven for the ransom rendezvous at the nursery, two days and a thousand years ago. In other words, nowhere. Which meant that Maria had almost certainly gone right, in the direction of the coast and Carmel.

The traffic wasn't especially busy and the road was wide and well maintained, so Brook drove fast, hitting seventy most of the way. She found it hard to believe that Maria hadn't heard what had happened to Logan by now. After all, it had been all over the news. And it bugged Brook, because if Tony Reyes had killed Logan to punish him for having an affair with his wife, then why hadn't he also punished Maria? Because if he had, he was being a lot easier on her than he'd been on Brook's family. Maybe Reyes still loved her and had forgiven her, on the basis she didn't cheat again. Maybe Maria was glad, too, to be free of Logan, although the photos of them together suggested she'd had strong feelings for him. Either way, she had questions to answer, and Brook was relieved it was Maria she was going to be approaching and not Reyes himself.

She finally caught up with the Porsche at the intersection with Highway One. The road was busier here, and Brook sat ten cars back as the Porsche turned north towards Monterey.

Maria didn't drive fast. She kept close to the speed limit and overtook only when it was absolutely safe to do so, and Brook found it easy to stay well back and still keep track of her. After ten minutes Maria took the turning off to Monterey and then drove back on herself through Cannery Row, the site of the many now-defunct sardine canneries that had once made the area famous, but which was now just a tourist trap of overpriced restaurants. From there, and with Brook travelling several cars behind, Maria continued along Ocean View Boulevard, doing a steady forty miles per hour as downtown Monterey gave way to the palatial homes of Pacific Grove, with their views over the entirety of the bay, and where the real rich of central California lived. The traffic began to thin out now, as the road became open and scenic with the Pacific Ocean on their right and a fiery red sun beginning to set over the horizon.

And then, as Maria drove past the park at Lovers Point, she slowed down and turned into the parking lot of Lovers Beach restaurant, the most exclusive in the whole area, with its terrace overlooking the Pacific Ocean. It was where Logan had taken Brook for their first wedding anniversary, when things between them had still been good, and where the future had seemed full of hope. They'd shared a huge shellfish platter that had dominated the whole table, made a real mess of themselves trying to crack open all the crab claws and drunk way too much wine. But, boy, it had been a fun night, and the memory caused a deep pang of regret at the way it had all turned out.

She pushed the memories aside and turned in, a few seconds behind Maria. The lot was mostly full, but Brook saw a spot in the corner close to the restaurant entrance and drove straight into it, switching off the engine and watching in the rear-view mirror as Maria Reyes got out of her Porsche and walked up to the restaurant doors. She looked glamorous, dressed in a black leather jacket, tight jeans and heeled boots and wearing big-rimmed, Jackie Onassis-style sunglasses. It was hard to tell whether or not she was under stress. She was wearing the sort of arrogant frown that you see on some very rich people, as if they're permanently on the lookout for poor people to avoid, and straight away Brook hated her, feeling an almost perverse desire to make her suffer as she herself had suffered these past few days.

But it was too late to approach her now. It was still daylight and the tables directly inside the entrance looked straight out onto the lot. She was going to have to intercept Maria on the way out.

Brook watched as a young guy coming out the entrance held the door open for Maria, who completely ignored him as she disappeared inside.

Brook's eyes bored angrily into her back. And then, just as she sat there pondering her next move, she glanced in the rear-view mirror again and caught sight of someone she recognized walking across the parking lot towards the restaurant.

Brook's breath caught in her throat, and she could feel her heart beating faster because, even though she was having difficulty processing what and who she was seeing, she knew without a doubt that this was no coincidence.

And now it meant she was in real trouble.

27

The police interview room
Now

Brook Connor stopped telling her story for a moment, suddenly thirsty, and looked down at the empty plastic cup in front of her. 'Do you mind if I have some more water?' she asked the male detective, Giant. He was the kindest of the two cops interviewing her, but he was also the man who'd met her husband the previous week, just five days before Paige had disappeared, even though he was denying it. But Brook didn't buy this. She might have been exhausted and under huge amounts of stress, and he might have shaved off his beard, but the more she recalled that photo, the more convinced she was it was Giant.

'Sure,' said Giant. He turned in his seat, pressed an intercom button on the wall and requested a jug of water. Then turned back and faced Brook, giving her a smile. That was the thing about Giant. He seemed to be a nice, unassuming guy, the kind who, because he hadn't been too lucky with his looks, had grown up relying on kindness and personality to foster relationships. And yet it was clear to Brook that there was more to him than met the eye.

'Are you going to tell us who else you saw at the restaurant?' asked Detective Jenna King, her voice – like her face – hard. It was obvious she thought Brook was guilty and she wasn't making any bones about it. Brook had always assumed they didn't do good cop/bad cop in real life, but maybe she'd been misinformed.

A uniformed officer came in with a jug of water and laid it on the table. Giant poured Brook a glass and she thanked him, then downed half of it.

She opened her mouth to speak, suddenly feeling nervous.

'Come on, Ms Connor,' said Giant, the first hint of impatience in his voice. 'Who else did you see at the restaurant?'

Angie Southby leaned forward in her seat, looked at the two detectives in turn and took a deep breath. 'She saw me. I was the one meeting Maria Reyes.'

The room fell silent for a long moment while the two detectives stared at Angie.

'Care to tell us what you were meeting her about?' asked Giant, a frown on his face.

'I'm afraid not,' answered Angie. 'Attorney–client privilege.'

28

Saturday night

As Angie Southby locked her brand-new Tesla convertible (a gift to herself that was meant to make her happy, but hadn't) and walked into the Lovers Beach restaurant, she was carrying an almost intolerable emotional weight on her shoulders. She'd always been a tough, perhaps even ruthless, woman, and her business life had been a great success because of this. Her personal life, however, had been the exact opposite: a minefield of her own making, littered with the corpses of past relationships – quite literally, in the case of Logan Harris, the man who was now responsible for so much of her emotional weight. The man whose weakness for the opposite sex had always been his Achilles heel.

It wasn't lost on Angie that her own Achilles heel had been her weakness for Logan Harris. He'd betrayed her more times than she cared to admit, but she'd always managed to forgive him, at least until this latest disaster. Angie thought back to her meeting with Brook at their house the previous evening, and how hard it had been to keep up her usual cool, businesslike demeanour. More than once during the conversation she'd wanted to tell Brook the truth about the whole thing, but had held back. Anyways, it had been too late by then. Even if Brook had known the true extent of Logan's troubles, there would have been nothing she could have done about it. Angie hoped Brook hadn't noticed the maelstrom of conflicting emotions she'd been feeling as they'd talked. It would only just make everything more complicated.

It was going to be hard for her to keep up the cool, businesslike demeanour in this meeting as well. In truth, she'd been dreading it, and had thought more than once about not turning up. But that was the thing. Even in death, Logan Harris's hand still seemed to guide her. He'd made her promise to help, and now here she was.

'Oh, Jesus, Logan,' she whispered to herself as she walked inside the restaurant and saw the maître d' lead Maria Reyes to a private table in the corner. 'Why did you do this to me?'

29

Giant looked at the dashboard clock as he and Jenna drove down Highway One back towards Monterey: 7.30 p.m. They'd just come from Carmel, where they'd interviewed a friend of Logan Harris's, a big, cheery Norwegian guy called Stig Hansen, who used to drink with him in the bars of Carmel once a week or so. Hansen was the fifth associate of Logan's they'd interviewed that day. Three had been women whom Logan had coached at tennis, and the other had been a tennis buddy and the owner of the courts where Logan played and taught. All five had said pretty much the same thing about him. That Logan was a decent, friendly guy, but one who, in recent weeks, had seemed distracted, as if something was on his mind. Hansen had been the only one of the interviewees who admitted to asking Logan what the problem was.

'And what was it?' Giant asked him.

'He said it was women trouble,' Hansen told them. 'But he wouldn't tell me any more than that. I figured it was his wife.'

That was another thing they were getting, wherever they went. The fact – sometimes only hinted at – that it wasn't a happy marriage, but it was clear that none of them had known Logan that well, and that only one of them – Hansen – had ever met Brook, and in his case only once (he'd described her as 'a cool chick, but one you wouldn't want to fool around on').

They'd asked all five interviewees whether, to their knowledge, Logan had been having an affair, and they'd all said no, they didn't think so. Everyone expressed shock about what had happened, and it was clear none of them could shed any light on it.

They were still tracking down Brook Connor's friends, and not having that much luck. It didn't sound like she had that many, which was interesting in itself. They had a list of moms with kids Paige's age at the kindergarten to talk to, but that could wait until tomorrow. Giant was tired. He guessed Jenna was, too. It had been a long twenty-four hours, and now that the US Marshals Service had taken over the search for Connor, he was feeling increasingly pushed out of his own investigation and reduced to the basic legwork, while all the glamorous stuff was left to the marshals, who'd arrived en masse earlier that afternoon (forty of them altogether, including support staff) and, according to one of Giant's junior detectives, had overrun the whole station, pissing off even the Chief.

Giant had no desire to head back and get involved with all the hoo-ha surrounding the hunt for Brook Connor, which, if the lack of noise on the radio was anything to go by, hadn't got much further than it had done this morning.

He looked at Jenna. They'd been together all day, and every time they were alone, Giant felt like he had ants in his pants. He was attracted to her in a way he had almost forgotten existed, and it was getting worse. Sometime soon something was going to have to give. 'You know, I think we might as well knock off for the day,' he said. 'I'll call in what we've got to the Chief.'

Jenna yawned. 'Good move. I'm pooped.'

Giant had a sudden thought and spoke it before he could stop himself. 'Would you like to grab a beer, a drink, or something? You know, now. On the way back ...' The sentence trailed off and he immediately felt stupid.

Jenna raised an eyebrow, an amused look on her face. 'Are you asking me on a date?'

Giant felt himself going red. He cursed himself for his stupidity and his pathetic lack of confidence. 'Well, you know – no, of course not. It's just ...'

Jenna laughed. 'I'm only ribbing you, Ty. Sure. Let's go pick up my car and we can get a beer downtown somewhere.'

'Sounds good,' he said, trying to regain control of the situation while simultaneously reviewing Jenna's exact words, for clues as to whether this was a date of sorts or simply a drink with a work colleague.

He still hadn't come to a conclusion when the radio crackled into life. 'All available units, we have reports of a possible two-one-five in the parking lot of the Lovers Beach restaurant at Lovers Point, Pacific Grove. We need urgent response now.'

Giant and Jenna exchanged puzzled looks. People didn't tend to get carjacked in Pacific Grove, especially not at eight o'clock in the evening. The Pacific Grove turn-off was coming up just ahead. They were ten minutes away from the restaurant at most, and Giant was never going to ignore an emergency.

Neither, it seemed, could Jenna. 'I guess that's us,' she said.

'I guess it is, but I'm holding you to that drink,' he answered, taking the turning as Jenna picked up the radio and told the dispatcher they were on their way.

30

Brook watched through her rear-view mirror as, a little over forty-five minutes after she'd walked into the Lovers Beach restaurant, her lawyer and former friend Angie Southby came walking back out again, fishing her car keys out of a Hermes purse as she strode towards her car. She was dressed for business in a tailored black pantsuit and court shoes with three-inch heels, and Brook toyed with the idea of confronting her and demanding to know what she was doing, meeting the woman that her husband had been having an affair with, but she held back, figuring she'd do better to wait for Maria Reyes's appearance.

Brook watched as Angie got into her black Tesla and drove quickly out of the lot. She'd known Angie for three years and had considered her a friend but, since she'd split up with her boyfriend, Bruce, Brook had hardly seen or heard from her.

And now, sitting here, she asked herself why it was that things had tailed off. Had Logan and Angie been having an affair? If so, who'd finished it? If it was Angie, then no problem – Logan would have accepted it and moved on to his next victim, as he clearly had. But if Logan had been the one who'd broken it off, that put a different slant on things. Angie was a hard woman, a ball-breaker, some men would call her. Brook had always admired that about her character. She was the kind of woman who could take on men at their own game and win. She was aggressive and almost impossible to intimidate – both essential traits for a successful criminal lawyer – but she was also pretty damned scary, and Brook couldn't imagine her taking rejection very well at all. In a rare candid moment, Angie had once told Brook that she had a hard exterior but was soft inside, and Brook remembered looking into her eyes and thinking she really didn't believe that.

But was she capable of killing Logan and setting Brook up for the rap? To do that required a ruthlessness that sat far better with a cartel gangster like Tony Reyes and, in the end, what was in it for Angie? It didn't make sense. But then nothing did any more.

Brook was just trying to work out exactly how many enemies she might have when Maria Reyes walked out of the restaurant and headed towards her car, looking round a little too furtively as she did so.

This was it. Brook's one chance for answers and, now that it came to it, she was scared stiff. But as she'd learned a long time ago, the longer you think about taking an important step, the harder it becomes, and the easier it is to convince yourself you can't do it. Sometimes everything in life comes down to one important lesson. Don't think. Act.

Taking a deep breath, Brook got out of the Mercedes and started to follow Maria, pretending to look for something in her purse. It was almost dark now and, although there were still people in the parking lot and cars driving past on the coastal road, no one was paying her any heed.

Two girls in their early twenties walked past her without a second glance. Both were talking and looking at their cellphones at the same time, like so many people these days. No one notices anything any more, thought Brook. It was an insidious development that she'd covered in her new book, but right then it suited her just fine because, as Maria unlocked the Porsche, she too removed her cell to check it and was staring at the screen as she got inside.

Brook was still five yards away from the car, so she moved rapidly, keeping her head down, and, already going for the gun in her jeans as she yanked open the Porsche's passenger door before Maria had a chance to start the engine and reactivate the central locking,

'What's going on? Get the fuck out of my car!' demanded Maria as Brook sat down beside her and pulled the door shut. There was a look of utter fury on her face, as if she couldn't believe someone would have the temerity to confront her like this, but she stopped dead when she saw Brook's gun pointed straight at her midriff.

'Start the car and drive out of here as if you're going home,' Brook told her, surprised both at the coldness in her own voice and at the intense excitement she was feeling.

'Do you not know who I am? Or who my husband is?' Maria's accent was pure California, which for some reason surprised Brook.

'Of course I do,' she answered. 'Now I'm not going to ask you a second time. Start the engine and drive the car or I will shoot you.'

'You wouldn't dare. There are too many people around.' Maria made a play of looking in her rear-view mirror.

'Do you want to try me? This is a small gun. It won't make much noise. And if I shoot you in the right spot, you'll still be able to answer my questions. Now drive. I'm not going to ask again.'

Maria Reyes actually snarled and her nostrils flared, but she started the engine and reversed out of the parking spot, before driving out of the lot and turning back towards Monterey. 'I recognize you now,' she said. 'You're that woman who's on the run.'

'You know exactly who I am,' said Brook. 'You knew the second I got in this car. And that's because you're the woman who's been having an affair with my husband.'

'I don't know what you're talking about,' said Maria, staring straight ahead.

'Don't give me that shit. I know. That's why I'm here.'

There was a silence in the car. Brook let it linger. Maria's expression tightened, revealing a faint frown line between her eyes. She took a deep breath, let it out. Then finally she spoke. 'Is that what's this is about? Logan? If it is, then I'm sorry.'

'Sorry for what?' demanded Brook, still keeping the gun trained on Maria's stomach.

'For everything that's happened. How did you find out about us? Did Logan tell you?'

Brook suddenly got the gist of what she was saying. 'Jesus! You think I killed Logan, don't you?'

Maria looked at her, confused. 'Didn't you? That's what they're saying all over the TV. That they're looking for you in connection with his murder.'

'No,' Brook said firmly. 'I didn't kill him.'

'Well, I didn't do it, either. You may not believe this, but I loved Logan.'

'You don't look especially upset that he's dead.'

'Why? Because I'm not sitting here, crying about it to his wife?' Maria paused for a moment and took a deep breath. 'I've been torn up ever since I heard the news. It's like I've lost a limb. But I'm trying to keep my emotions under control. You, of all people, should understand that, being the celebrity life-coach. Isn't that what you say in your book? That it's essential to keep a lid on your emotions and not let them overcome you?'

It was exactly what Brook had said and she was almost flattered that this woman might have read one of her books, but she didn't need a lecture from her about it now. 'What were you doing in the restaurant with Angie Southby?'

The question surprised Maria. She opened her mouth to say something, possibly thought better of it and turned her gaze back towards the road. 'I'm sorry, I can't say.'

'That's not going to wash, Maria. I want answers, and you're going to give them to me. Because if you don't, I swear to God I will put a bullet in you. I want to know who killed my husband;

who cut off my daughter's nanny's finger; and, most importantly of all, I want to know what they've done with my daughter, who is only five years old and has been missing for the past three days. So bear this in mind. I have nothing left to lose. I have a gun. And it's pointed at you. So it's very much in your interests to tell me what I want to know. Now I repeat: why were you meeting Angie Southby?'

Maria's knuckles went white as she gripped the steering wheel. 'Please don't make me say this.'

'I have to.'

'Okay,' she said at last. 'I was in love with your husband. I'm not proud to say it, but I think he was in love with me, too.'

Hearing the words felt like a punch to the gut, because Brook knew Maria was right. In the photos they'd looked like two people in love.

'We were going to run away together,' continued Maria. 'Logan knew what a good mother you were – are – to Paige, so our plan was to disappear and leave the two of you together.'

'Logan would never have deserted Paige.'

'But he wouldn't have been deserting her, would he? He was leaving Paige in the care of someone who loved her more than anything else. And he believed that she'd be better off with you than with him.' She sighed. 'But we couldn't just run away. You know who my husband is, right?'

Brook nodded. 'I do.'

'Then you know that he would have hunted us down, whatever it took, because I'd always be a threat to him and his business partners. I've been married for over twenty-five years to a man who's a monster. Do you have any idea what that's like? I'll tell you – it's like a continuous death sentence, knowing that Tony has the power to kill me at any time, if I displease him; and then having to watch my two sons, as they've been growing up, for any sign that they might take after him. And do you know what really hurts? They do. They're bullies. Just like he is.'

Maria took a deep breath. 'So when I met Logan and fell in love with him, I knew there was only one way out. We had to disappear completely, and the only people who could guarantee that happening were the authorities. I was planning to go to the FBI and testify against my husband, but I wanted legal advice first. Logan knew of Angie Southby and spoke very highly of her as a lawyer. Our plan was to meet her and discuss our options. But then, before we had a chance to ...' She paused. 'All this happened, and now Logan's ... he's gone. The one fucking good thing that ever happened to me.' Her face crumpled with emotion and Brook thought she might cry.

'So why meet Angie today? And why at the Lovers Beach, right on your own doorstep? Isn't that a tad stupid, if you're so scared of your husband?'

Maria gave Brook a withering look. 'Logan might be gone, but I still want to leave my husband, and the authorities are still my only option. But you want to know why I chose to meet her on my own doorstep? Since Logan's death I've been out of my mind with worry, because I wasn't sure if Tony had anything to do with it or not. It wouldn't surprise me if he killed Logan without saying a word about it, just to torment me. It's the sort of thing he likes doing. But then, when I heard you were on the run,

I thought you'd killed him. Even so, I'm not taking any chances. If my husband's got anyone tailing me, then all they would have seen is me driving to meet a friend at a restaurant. What *does* look suspicious is someone like you appearing out of nowhere and jumping into my car. So if there *was* someone following me, they're going to be wondering what's happening now.'

'No one was following you,' said Brook, hoping she was right. 'I was watching. So has your husband acted any differently since the murder?'

'No. He's been exactly the same as he always is. Distant. Cold. He's not the jealous type. The only reason he would have killed Logan would be out of male pride. I don't think it's him, because he wouldn't have done it that way. He would have made Logan disappear, so it didn't rebound on him.'

'But that's the thing,' Brook said. 'It hasn't rebounded on him. Someone's set me up to take the rap. And as far as I'm concerned, your husband is the prime suspect.'

'Even if he is, there's nothing you can do about it. He's got security everywhere. You won't be able to get within a hundred feet of him.'

Brook took a deep breath. This was it – the moment she'd been waiting for. 'That's where you come in,' she said. 'You're going to get me inside your home.'

Maria shook her head emphatically. 'No way. If I help you, I'll be signing my own death warrant. All I want to do is start a new life, and you're not going to deny me that.'

She pulled over to the side of the road, ignoring the blast of a horn from the car behind.

'What the hell are you doing?' snapped Brook.

Maria gave her a defiant look. 'I'm sorry about your husband. And I'm sorry about your daughter, I really am. But I'm not prepared to die at the hands of a sadistic monster like my husband, for either you or her. So either shoot me now or get out.'

Brook had had plenty of time to think and she'd planned for exactly this reaction. Still keeping the gun trained on Maria, she reached into her purse, pulling out an envelope containing two of the photos of Maria and Logan that she'd got from Chris Cervantes's file and threw it onto her lap.

Maria looked at Brook, then at the envelope. Finally, reluctantly, she slipped out the first photo, saw herself in an embrace with Logan and took a sharp intake of breath.

Brook didn't like doing this to her. Against all her instincts, she actually had some sympathy for Maria's plight. Here was a woman who, like Brook, was being backed into an ever smaller corner. 'Those are copies,' she said quietly. 'The originals are even better-quality. And there are plenty more of them.'

'You bitch,' whispered Maria, still staring at the photos. She looked shell-shocked.

'I won't shoot you, Maria, but if you make me get out of this car, your husband will be getting these photos in the mail tomorrow, along with a letter telling him about your plan to turn state's evidence against him. And don't think you can go running to Angie tonight. I know how she works. She'll be reviewing her options, working out if helping you is too big a risk or not. You know as well as I do that, if she was that keen, she'd have taken you with her tonight.'

Maria stared at her, the hatred, hurt and frustration written all over her smooth, beautifully made-up face. 'Please,' she said, changing tack. 'Don't sentence me to death.'

Brook looked her straight in the eye and laid her cards on the table. 'If you do what I say, I guarantee I'll get both of us through this unscathed. But if you try to double-cross me, we'll both be going down together. Now start driving again.'

Maria took a deep breath, then pulled the Porsche back out onto the road, and Brook felt a looming sense of dread as they headed towards the lion's den.

31

The Lovers Beach restaurant was the kind of place reserved for rich tourists and the beautiful people of Monterey, where if you were someone like Giant – not so beautiful, twenty pounds overweight and wearing a suit that cost less than one round of the famously overpriced cocktails – the young, cool staff would give you that down-their-nose look that said: this isn't your kind of place. And they'd be right. Giant wouldn't have eaten there if they'd paid him, and if he wanted a view out over the Pacific Ocean he'd go to the beach.

There was a patrol car already there when they pulled into the parking lot, and two officers – a male and a female – were questioning a young blonde woman near the front entrance, while a staff member hovered nearby.

The male officer peeled away as Giant and Jenna walked over. Giant recognized him by face, but not by name.

'The young lady here thinks she witnessed some kind of carjacking,' the male officer said, not sounding too convinced.

'What's "some kind of carjacking"?' asked Jenna. 'Either there was one or there wasn't.'

'Why don't you talk to her? You'll see what I mean.'

They both went over and introduced themselves, and Giant asked the girl if she could tell them what she'd seen. She was only young – probably no more than twenty-one – and worryingly underdressed for the chill in the air and the wind coming off the ocean, although that wasn't his business.

However, she'd hardly even opened her mouth when the staff member who was hanging around butted in. 'I'm sorry to interrupt, Detective, but I'm the manager here, Klaus Wilding. Would it be possible to conduct this interview a little bit away from the restaurant? I don't want to scare our customers.'

It was hard for Giant to take seriously a man named Klaus who wasn't German, especially when he was dressed in a burgundy waistcoat and a miniature matching bow tie, but he made an effort. 'We'll be finished as soon as we can, sir, and can you stay here, please? We may need you.'

Klaus didn't look too happy, but he didn't argue, either, and Giant turned back to the girl. 'Go on.'

'Look, it may be nothing, but I was getting out my car earlier, just as this older woman was getting into hers a few yards away, and I saw this other woman in a hat and sunglasses come out of nowhere, walking real fast and reaching for something in the back of her jeans. She pulled open the door on the passenger side – but real fast, you know – and it looked, you know …' She paused for a couple of seconds. 'It looked like she was pulling out a gun.'

Giant nodded slowly. 'Okay. Then what happened?'

'The other woman yelled something like "What the fuck are you doing?" and then the door shut and I couldn't hear any more. They looked like they were talking in there for a bit, then the car reversed out and I moved out of the way, because I wasn't sure what was going on, and I watched them as they drove out. The driver looked pretty scared.'

'Could you be mistaken about the gun?' Jenna asked her gently. 'I mean, the light's not that good, is it?'

The girl nodded. 'Yeah, I'm not totally sure it was a gun, but the whole thing looked weird. And the woman in the hat looked really intense, like she was worked up about something. I called you guys because it didn't look right.'

'I have to say, we've never had a carjacking – or anything remotely similar – at this restaurant in all the five years I've been here,' said Klaus.

Giant ignored him. 'You did the right thing,' he told the girl. 'Can you describe the car's driver?'

'She was black-haired, quite a bit older, Hispanic-looking.'

'And what car was she driving?'

'A blue Porsche nine-eleven. It looked brand new.'

Maria Reyes was older, black-haired and Hispanic-looking, and she drove a brand-new blue Porsche 911. It wasn't likely to be a coincidence, especially if she'd been carjacked by a woman.

Giant looked at Jenna and she raised her eyebrows, obviously thinking what he was thinking. That Brook Connor, rather than making a run for it, was hell-bent on taking revenge for Maria having an affair with her husband.

Giant turned to the maître d'. 'We need to see the security-camera footage from seven-thirty till eight p.m. tonight. I'm assuming you've got the parking lot covered.'

Klaus nodded. 'I can get it for you in the next hour. We've got a full house in there right now, but we'll be easing off soon.'

All his life Giant had been the kind of man who wasn't taken that seriously by people when they met him, even when they knew he was a cop. Maybe it was the fact that he wasn't that tall, and carried too much weight, by California standards; or maybe it was because he'd got what his mom had always described as a non-cop face (which she meant as being too kindly-looking for law enforcement). Whatever it was, it never failed to piss him off. He glared at Klaus, irritatingly conscious that he wanted to appear a tough guy in front of Jenna. 'This is an abduction, sir. Not someone leaving without paying their bar bill. We want to see the footage right now.'

Klaus didn't look happy, but he didn't argue, either. 'This way, please,' he said curtly, and they followed him inside and through the restaurant. Most of the customers turned and looked their way with interest, and Giant felt strangely important as they were led into an office at the back. Klaus sat down at a desk, pressed a few buttons on a keyboard and brought up a split screen containing two different views of the restaurant parking lot. He clicked on the right-hand one and began rewinding the footage, which Giant was pleased to note was HD-quality, keeping it at a steady speed as the two detectives looked on.

It didn't take long for the sky-blue Porsche to appear on the screen as it reversed out of a space.

Giant told Klaus to slow down the rewind and they watched as the passenger door opened and a woman in a black beanie hat appeared in the shot, definitely pulling something from beneath the back of her jacket.

Giant let him rewind further, then told him to play the footage forward at half-speed. Now they watched as a woman he immediately recognized as Maria Reyes came into view from the right of the screen, taking out her keys and unlocking her car, while simultaneously checking her phone. As she climbed inside, the woman in the beanie hat came into shot, her head down, moving quickly, until she too reached the car. It was impossible to tell from the camera angle whether she was pulling a gun from her waistband, because she was angling her body slightly away from the camera as she reached round, and then she was yanking open the door and getting in. The Porsche's windows were tinted, so they couldn't see what was going on inside, but there was a pause of thirty-seven seconds before the Porsche reversed out and then drove out of shot.

Giant asked Klaus to get a close-up of the woman in the beanie hat. The image was slightly blurred as he focused in, but even so, she still looked a lot like Brook Connor.

The other camera showed the Porsche coming out of the parking lot and turning right towards Monterey. The time in the corner said 7.58 p.m., just over twenty minutes ago.

'Do you recognize either of those two women?' Giant asked Klaus.

He looked conflicted, and Giant could tell he didn't want to say, but eventually he nodded. 'The dark-haired woman is quite a regular client of ours. Her name's Maria, I believe.'

'Maria what?'

'Maria Reyes,' Klaus said reluctantly, as if mentioning her name would hex him. 'The other woman I don't recognize. She wasn't in the restaurant tonight.'

Giant thanked him and walked outside with Jenna. He announced to the uniforms who the likely victim and suspect were and put in a call to the dispatcher, ordering her to get an urgent APB out for Maria's Porsche Carrera, then he put a second call in to the Chief.

'Are you sure it's Brook Connor?' demanded the Chief.

'As sure as I can be.'

'What on earth is she doing carjacking Tony Reyes's wife?'

'I honestly don't know, sir,' he lied, 'but it's definitely Maria Reyes, and I'm 95 per cent sure the 'jacker's Connor.'

'I'll take those odds. Good work, Tyrone.'

When he was off the phone, Jenna looked at him. 'Where do you think they've gone?'

'I don't know, and they've got twenty minutes' head start on us, so the chances of you and me finding them are pretty slim. But there's one person we can talk to who might be able to shed some light on things.'

She raised an eyebrow. 'Who?'

'Maria's husband. Tony Reyes.'

32

Brook was lying on her side in the space behind the front seats of the Porsche. The space was tight, and Brook's back hurt like crazy, but unless someone poked their head through the window and looked very closely, they weren't going to see her. Brook still had the gun trained on Maria and had already informed her more than once that she could hit her very easily from the angle she was at.

Maria was talking to her husband on the phone, saying they needed to talk about Peter, their youngest son, and that she'd be home shortly.

'Okay, Tony's at home,' she said, coming off the cell. 'And I don't think he's suspicious. Peter's been having some issues at college, so it's not a big surprise that I want to talk about it. But I'm just setting this up for you, okay? Then I'm out of there.'

'No,' said Brook. 'We need to leave together. Otherwise I'll be stuck here high and dry without a car.'

'There's a back way out of the house,' said Maria, as she drove up the hill to the house. 'It's an emergency exit, in case the police ever come for Tony. You reach it through the out-building directly behind the house, next to the back wall. The code to get inside is nine-nine-nine-nine, and there's a trapdoor in the middle of the floor, underneath a rug. It leads to a tunnel that takes you out the back of the property and up into a copse of trees at the base of the mountain. You can get out that way.'

'It's still no use to me. I'll need a car.'

'There's a car there, hidden in some bushes with a full tank of gas, and the keys are under the front seat. The track next to it will take you back down to the highway.'

'Okay,' said Brook. 'But first you need to lead me to your husband, remain there while I question him, then we leave together. After that, you can go straight to Angie's place or to the police, and I'll be on my way.'

'Let me go into the house and confirm where he is, while you stay in the car,' said Maria. 'Then he and I will talk for a few minutes, I'll make an excuse – like I need the bathroom – and then I'll come back out to you, let you know how to find him. You go in, do what you have to do and I'll leave. There should only be two men up here tonight. One will be on the gate, the other's usually patrolling the grounds and won't be in the house.'

'It's too risky.'

'It's the only way I'm doing it.'

'I'm the one pointing a gun at you.'

'Then fucking shoot, but that way you'll never get through the gate and you'll never get answers out of my husband.'

Brook knew she had no choice. There was no way she could pull the trigger on Maria. Not now.

Maria took a deep breath. 'We're coming to the main entrance now. I need to stop talking.'

Brook tensed, keeping her finger firmly on the trigger, knowing that this was the moment when things could go spectacularly wrong.

The car stopped and Maria waved at someone Brook couldn't see and said something in Spanish. A few seconds later the car started moving again and they drove inside the gates, turned a corner and eventually stopped.

'Okay,' said Maria quietly. 'I'm going into the house now. I will be back soon, I promise. Stay where you are.'

She got out of the car, shutting the door behind her, leaving Brook feeling vulnerable and alone. Brook stayed as still as possible, only moving enough so that she could see the time on her watch. It was 8.30 p.m. and darkness had finally fallen. Her heart was pounding with anxiety. The minutes passed, each one seeming to move interminably slowly; 8.30 became 8.35; 8.35 became 8.40. Maria could easily have betrayed her to save herself, and Brook wondered if, even now, men with guns were creeping up on the car, ready to put a bullet through her head. Her imagination played tricks on her. She thought she could sense movement, hear the scrape of a foot on gravel; feel the weight of a body leaning against the trunk.

A shadow moved across the front of the car and Brook almost pulled the trigger by mistake, such was the tension running through her, but then the door opened and Maria got inside, looking just as tense. 'All right, you need to go now,' she hissed in the darkness. 'Go in the front door, turn right down the corridor and take the second door on the left. Tony's in there, waiting for me to come back, and there's no one else around.' She started the engine to demonstrate that this conversation was over and, moving as fast as she could manage, having lain in the same uncomfortable position for the past twenty minutes, Brook lifted the passenger seat and climbed out the door without a word.

The car reversed immediately and Maria turned it round, before driving around the corner towards the gate, leaving Brook standing in the shadows of the house, feeling horribly exposed.

There were lights on inside, but nobody around as Brook crept quickly across the courtyard to the front door, opening it slowly while holding the gun in front of her.

She found herself in a large ranch-style entrance hall with whitewashed stone walls, a large wooden staircase and corridors running off on both sides. She could hear the faint sounds of classical music coming from the right-hand corridor, and she suddenly felt as if she was in some kind of strange dream and this wasn't really happening to her.

She took a deep breath and took the right-hand corridor, creeping on tiptoes. Grand, very expensive-looking paintings of landscapes, many of them featuring horses, adorned the walls, and Brook found it hard to believe that someone with such a fine appreciation of art could be the monster that both Chris Cervantes and Tony Reyes's own wife had made him out to be. And yet it was very probable that this man, with his classical music and his incredible paintings, had arranged Paige's abduction and Logan's murder.

The second door on the left loomed up in front of her and she swallowed. The music was coming from behind it. This was it. Taking a single deep breath, she pushed open the door and stepped inside.

She saw him immediately: a surprisingly handsome man of about fifty, with a fine head of curly silver-black hair and a beard of the same colour, sitting in a comfortable-looking armchair next to a huge open fireplace. He was wearing suit pants and a dark suit jacket with silver cufflinks. In his hand was a glass of red wine, and when he looked Brook's way and saw a strange woman in a beanie hat pointing a gun at him, he looked surprised, but not exactly scared.

'What can I do for you?' he asked, in a very slight Mexican accent.

'You're Tony Reyes,' said Brook. It wasn't a question.

'That's right,' he said. The beginnings of a smile played around his lips. It was disconcerting. 'What do you want?'

'My husband is Logan Harris, and my daughter is Paige Harris. She's five years old, and I know you've kidnapped her. If you don't tell me where she is, I'll kill you. Right here. Right now.' She took a step forward, trying to look a lot more confident than she was feeling.

'You're the woman I saw on the news today. You killed your husband, didn't you? That's what they're saying on the TV.'

'I didn't kill him,' said Brook. 'You did.'

Reyes looked towards the door. 'How did you get in here?'

217

'Your security isn't as good as you think it is.'

'Did you use my wife? Because it seems coincidental that she arrives back home, visits the bathroom and then you appear five minutes later.'

His voice was calm and melodic, and Brook couldn't help feeling that she was losing control of this conversation.

'Tell me where my daughter is.'

The gun wobbled slightly in Brook's hands. There was so much adrenalin pumping through her now that it felt like she was about to explode, but in reality she was confused. Here she was, facing the man she needed answers from, but he wasn't playing ball. Instead he was staring at her with a look in his eyes that was almost playful.

'Why do you think I know?'

Brook didn't want to tell him, for fear of compromising Maria. She owed his wife that much. 'Just answer the question.'

Reyes took a sip of his wine and started to get to his feet.

'Do not move,' hissed Brook. 'Stay exactly where you are.'

He ignored her and stood up. She followed him with the gun, pointing it at his chest. They were in a big room and a good twenty feet separated them, so she took two steps forward, trying to show Reyes she wasn't intimidated as she planned her next move. A warning shot might alert one of his men, but she knew she had to show him that she was serious. A vision of herself and Paige laughing at the beach came to her, followed by the image of Paige that the kidnappers had sent them, dressed in different clothes and looking all alone. If Tony Reyes knew anything, then she had to get it out of him.

'I'm going to give you five seconds to tell me where my daughter is, Mr Reyes. And if you don't tell me, I'll put a bullet in your belly and ask again. Soon enough, you'll tell me.'

The playful look in his eyes disappeared and they became hard. 'You're out of your depth, I'm afraid, Mrs Harris.'

'It's Ms Connor, and I've been out of my depth for the past three days, but do you know what? I'm still here, and right now I'm the one with the gun. Remember that.'

The music was coming from a speaker on a corner table and Brook walked over to it now, still keeping the gun trained on him. She was about to turn up the volume, to mask the noise of the pistol firing, when the door opposite her opened and Maria Reyes appeared in the doorway, a terrified expression on her face. She was being held in a head-lock from behind by a hard-faced Hispanic man who also had a gun to her temple.

As Brook turned towards them, the door she'd come in from opened behind her and another Hispanic man stood there, armed with a machine gun, which he was pointing straight at her.

'As I said,' continued Tony Reyes, slowly pulling out a pistol from under his jacket, 'I'm afraid you're out of your depth. Now put the gun on the floor. Slowly.'

For a moment Brook didn't move, as she realized, almost with a deep regret rather than fear, that she wasn't going to recover from this. There were now two weapons pointed at her. She was still pointing her own pistol roughly in Reyes's direction, but there was no guarantee she'd even get off a shot before she was torn apart by machine-gun fire.

Out of the corner of her eye she could see the terror on Maria's face. If Maria was that scared of what her husband would do to her, then what would he be prepared to do to Brook herself?

In the end, it's human instinct to try and delay something bad for as long as possible, so she slowly crouched down and placed the gun on the floor, before standing back up and taking a deep breath to prevent herself from hyperventilating.

'Take three steps backwards, away from the gun,' demanded Reyes, his voice calm and authoritative, just like a cop's.

Brook obeyed and he walked over and picked up the gun, placing it in the waistband of his pants.

Reyes then looked at Maria and shook his head. 'So, it seems the two of you have been having a nice little conversation about me in the car. So I'm a monster, am I? The man who's given you everything – money, a beautiful home, two beautiful sons ...'

Maria made a small whining sound. 'Please, I ...'

'Shut up!' The words were like a slap. 'I heard everything you said, you treacherous bitch. Everything. And do you know the real irony here? The only reason I put a listening device in your car is because you've been acting so strangely these past few days. I knew something was wrong. But until it came on the news today, I had no idea who this Logan Harris even was, let alone that you've been sleeping with him and planning to betray me.'

'Please, Tony, it wasn't like that ...'

'I told you, shut up. You no longer have the right to speak. And you.' Reyes turned to Brook, all the coolness gone. 'You come into my home and threaten me? Me?' He struck his chest in a pure alpha-male gesture. 'Nobody does that, least of all a loud-mouthed whore like you.' He said something in Spanish to the man with the machine gun. The man slipped away with a nod and Reyes waved his pistol at Brook. 'We're going to find somewhere a little quieter,' he said. 'Move!'

He directed her down the corridor until she came to a door at the end, and told her to go inside.

She opened the door and walked into near-pitch darkness, and a second later a series of strobe lights came on overhead, temporarily dazzling her.

She was in a large, square room with with two floor-to-ceiling windows that looked out into the darkness. Half the room was completely empty, while the other half was filled with various pieces of brand-new gym equipment. It was cold in there and she shivered, turning round as Maria was also led into the room, a gun still held to her head. Reyes pressed a button on the wall and shutters came down on the windows, then he said something in Spanish to the other guy, who immediately let Maria go. Reyes grabbed her and manhandled her further into the room.

A few seconds later the guy with the machine gun came in as well, except that this time the machine gun was slung over his shoulder and he was carrying something under each arm.

Brook's heart sank as she realized what they were. Rolls of tarpaulin.

Reyes said something in Spanish to the man and he walked to an empty part of the room and laid each sheet out, so they made a square strip on the floor about ten feet across. He then produced a roll of tape and taped them down.

'Go stand in the middle of the tarpaulin,' Reyes said to Brook, his face cold and hard.

Brook hesitated because she knew that if she stood on it, it would be the place where she died.

'Go,' he demanded through clenched teeth, 'or I'll shoot you in your fucking pussy.'

The urbane middle-aged gentleman listening to classical music, with a glass of wine, was long gone now, and Brook knew there would be no mercy from Reyes.

Slowly, with her legs feeling like they might buckle at any time, she walked over to the tarpaulin, listening to it crinkle under her feet as she turned round to face them: three hard-faced men with guns, all of whom were now donning clear plastic gloves, while off to one side Maria stood alone, crying and literally shaking with fear – a far cry from the confident, attractive woman who'd walked out of the restaurant barely an hour earlier. It hurt Brook to know that it had been her own actions that had got Maria into this position. But it hurt far more to know that she'd also failed Paige.

Reyes turned to his wife. 'Now, go over there and stand next to your friend.'

'Please don't do this,' sobbed Maria.

Reyes stepped forward and struck her hard around the face.

Maria staggered backwards, putting up her hands to defend herself.

'Do it, you whore!' he roared, his voice echoing around the room.

With her head down, Maria crossed the floor and stood on the tarpaulin a few feet away from Brook, refusing to make eye contact.

Now Reyes came over, swaggering as he walked, and Brook realized he was revelling in the power he had over them. She'd never seen a true sadist at work before, and it was taking all her self-discipline to stay calm and not give up entirely. *Never lose hope*, she kept repeating to herself. *While you're still breathing, there's a chance.*

'Face each other,' Reyes snapped.

They did as they were told, standing barely four feet apart.

Reyes placed the barrel of his pistol against the side of his wife's head. 'You've betrayed me, you bitch. And even worse, you've betrayed our sons, too. You were going to walk away and desert them. You sicken me.'

Tears ran freely down Maria's face and her legs quivered and shook. . 'Please, Tony, it wasn't like that.'

'Then what was it like? Tell me. Because maybe my ears were deceiving me but I'm certain I heard you tell this whore here that you were going to go to the authorities and testify against me. After everything – everything I've done for you.'

'Forgive me, please. For the sake of Peter and Michael. I'm still their mother. I swear I'll never even think of leaving you again.'

Brook stood there in silence. It felt like she was watching a TV drama that was being acted out especially for her, but her eyes were fixated on Reyes's tensed trigger finger. He was serious. A tiny bit of added pressure and the gun would go off.

'Please, baby,' continued Maria, keeping her eyes fixed on the floor. 'Give me one last chance. I'll do anything. Please.'

That same little half-smile he'd been wearing earlier appeared on Tony Reyes's face. 'Anything?' he asked, looking towards Brook.

'Yes, yes,' Maria said hurriedly, nodding her head frantically as a tiny chink of hope appeared for her, just as it disappeared for Brook.

'Good, because I can be a merciful man. I'm going to spare your life, Maria, even though you don't deserve it.'

'Thank you, baby. Thank you.'

'But there's a condition.' He puffed out his chest, clearly enjoying this. 'My worry is that you know too much about my business to be trusted. But of course, if you do something that makes you a part of it, that will go a long way to allaying my concerns.'

'What do you want me to do?'

'Very simple,' he said, motioning towards Brook with a contemptuous nod. 'Kill Ms Connor here.' He pulled Brook's own gun from the waistband of his slacks and placed it in Maria's hand. 'Kill her and you can leave. You can go wherever you want. I no longer want you as a wife. You've betrayed me once. You'll only do it again.'

He took a step back, still keeping his gun on her and, with his free hand, took out a cell, pressed a few buttons on it through his plastic gloves and pointed it at the two of them. A few yards behind him, the two gunmen stood, watching impassively.

'You're on film now, baby,' continued Reyes. 'Kill her and you can be free.'

And then, as Brook watched, Maria's grip on the gun tightened perceptibly and she slowly raised it so that it was pointed at Brook's face, their eyes meeting for the first time since they'd been in the car.

Brook's whole body stiffened as she waited for what was to come. She held Maria's gaze and saw all kinds of emotions crossing her face: fear, regret, anger, determination, confusion.

'Please don't kill me,' Brook said to her. 'You know your husband killed Logan, the man you loved. Think about his little girl. She's five years old. All I want to do is find her.'

Maria's gun hand shook slightly.

'See, that's your problem, Ms Connor,' said Reyes. 'You've been so convinced I had your husband killed that you've ceased to think straight. If I wanted him dead, no one would ever have seen him again and I wouldn't have bothered involving either you or his daughter. Someone else targeted your family, Ms Connor, and it may not have been your husband they were after. I think they were after you. The problem you have right now is you're never going to know.'

'She's five years old,' said Brook, turning towards him. 'Have a heart. I'm her only chance.'

Reyes shook his head. 'It's not my problem. In a few moments it won't be yours either. Finish her, Maria, and then you can start your new life. There'll be no Logan Harris, but I'm sure there'll be someone else for you to fuck.'

Brook turned back towards the gun, begging now. 'Don't kill me, Maria. Please. Not for my sake, but for a little girl who's all alone.'

Maria's face contorted with all kinds of emotion. 'You fucked me, you bitch,' she hissed. 'You put me in this position. You!'

Two feet separated Brook's forehead from the end of the gun barrel, and now she could see Maria's gun hand steadying as she prepared to take the shot.

Brook could no longer speak. It was as if all the words were stuck in her throat. She felt terror like she'd never experienced before. There was no fight left. It had gone. She prayed there was a heaven and that she would be going there, to be reunited with her mom and dad, Logan, maybe even Paige. *We could start again, it would be all right . . .*

She shut her eyes.

A second passed. Then another. And another.

The wait seemed to last an age.

And then the shot erupted in the room and it was all over.

33

Brook fell backwards to the floor, conscious of the warm, sticky liquid that had splattered onto her face, realizing with shock and confusion that she was still alive and not in any kind of obvious pain.

She opened her eyes and sat up, blinking away the blood, which was when she saw Maria lying on her back on the tarpaulin, her left leg jutting out at an odd angle, the gun she'd been about to shoot Brook with lying a few feet away from her. A tiny pall of black smoke rose up from her temple where the bullet had entered, and blood pooled around her ear. As Brook watched, her body twitched wildly, then stopped just as suddenly, as if announcing her death.

It took her a couple of seconds to realize that Maria had turned the gun on herself.

Tony Reyes was standing a few yards away, his gun by his side, staring at her body as if he couldn't quite believe that his wife of close to a quarter of a century could defy him in such a way, while the two other gunmen looked on nervously, seemingly unsure what to do.

'What the fuck?' shouted Reyes at no one in particular. 'What the fuck?' Then he gave Brook a look of such hatred that she thought he was going to pull the trigger then and there. 'You!' he demanded, waving his gun at her. 'Stand up and step off the tarpaulin. Now!'

For the tiniest moment Brook thought about going for the gun that Maria had shot herself with. After all, it was her own pistol and she knew how to use it. But there were still three men pointing their weapons at her, so she got to her feet, hands in the air, and stepped off the tarpaulin.

Reyes shouted to his men in Spanish and they temporarily put away their weapons and hurried over to the tarpaulin, wrapping Maria's body in one of the sheets, but leaving the gun that she'd killed herself with lying on the other one.

'You're going to die fucking slowly for this,' Reyes snarled at Brook as he stalked over to the tarpaulin and leaned down to pick up the gun.

And that was when he made a mistake. Maybe it was the shock of his wife's death, maybe it was simple complacency, but Reyes had turned away from Brook as he leaned down and was only pointing the gun loosely in her direction. At the same time his men were both occupied wrapping up Maria's body. Barely three yards separated Brook and Reyes and, in that single moment, she knew this was going to be her only chance.

Still full of adrenalin, she charged at him.

He just had time to register what she was doing but, even as he was swinging his gun around to face her, she was on him, jumping onto his back and grabbing him in a chokehold, while at the same time wrapping her legs around his and grabbing his gun hand at the wrist. They both stumbled to one side together while Reyes desperately tried to keep his balance.

The two other men went for their weapons as Brook tried to get control of Reyes's gun hand while simultaneously staying on his back, but now that he'd got over the shock of her initial assault, Reyes was trying to shake her off. He was strong, too, and angry, but she was holding fast and he was weakening.

The other two were manoeuvring around so that they could get a clean shot at her, but then, as Reyes suddenly yanked his gun hand free of her grip, the gun went off, hitting the guy with the machine gun in the leg. He fell backwards, crying out in pain, and the machine gun opened up in an explosion of noise.

Instinctively Brook loosened her grip on Reyes, and both of them dived for cover in different directions. Brook rolled onto the remaining strip of tarpaulin, immediately scrambling for the gun that Maria had killed herself with. It was the one she'd practised with at the range plenty of times, and she grabbed it and rolled over onto her back, just as Reyes and the other gunman were stumbling to their feet. Reyes was going for his gun on the floor, and so was temporarily the lesser of the two threats, so Brook fired at the other man – two shots without hesitation, exactly as she'd been taught. She hit him somewhere in the body, because he went down and his gun went off as well, a single shot that seemed to ricochet around the room, but thankfully didn't come anywhere near her. Reyes had now picked up his own gun and fired a shot at her, but it was a wild one as he was already trying to jump out of the way as Brook sat up and swung round, holding her gun two-handed as she took aim and squeezed the trigger twice more, both shots missing him.

Out of the corner of her eye, Brook saw the machine gunner sit back up, his face scrunched up in pain but still holding onto his weapon. He was trying to rest it on his knee with the barrel pointing her way, ready to fire. But before he did so, an intensely loud alarm started up all around the house, which momentarily stopped everyone in their tracks.

Taking advantage of this sudden interruption, which seemed to disorient Reyes and the machine gunner more than it did her, Brook brought her gun round in a sudden movement and shot at the machine gunner. He fell or dived backwards – she couldn't tell which – but the machine gun clattered to the floor. And then she was swinging the gun back to aim at Reyes, who was now running for the door, firing wildly in her direction, the bullets whizzing around the room.

Brook flattened herself on the floor, desperate not to get hit by a stray round, and then, as Reyes reached the door, she took rapid aim at him and pulled the trigger to loose off a final shot, before the slide extended to signify that she was out of ammunition.

The alarm was going crazy now, sounding like it was coming from every room, and if Reyes had decided to make a run for it, Brook knew it could only mean one thing: the property's security had been breached. Panting with adrenalin, she rolled over and jumped to her feet, took a last look back at the two gunmen – both of whom were writhing on the floor, but no longer representing any immediate threat – and ran.

As Brook came out into the corridor there was no sign of Reyes, so she kept going back through the house the way she'd just come, looking for a route out and feeling a heady mix of panic and elation. But as she approached the living room where she'd first confronted Reyes, she saw flashing blue lights reflecting off the whitewashed walls in the entrance hall, followed by banging on the front door, which was loud enough to be heard above the alarm.

She turned back round, pulled open the nearest door and found herself in a study bathed in silver-blue moonlight, with a large, bay window at the far end, looking out onto trees. The window was open and she ran over to it, tripping over a chair she didn't see en route, and saw the figure of Tony Reyes sprinting along a tree-lined path that ran between two stretches of perfectly manicured lawn. He was no longer holding the gun. Brook remembered what Maria had told her about the emergency escape route. It looked like that was where he was heading. Somewhere off to the left she could hear the sound of dogs barking wildly above the din of the alarm.

She scrambled out of the window, banging her head on the frame, and took off after Reyes along the flagstones. He had about thirty yards on her, but Brook was a fast runner and, even after what had just happened, she still had enough energy and adrenalin to sprint, and soon she was gaining fast.

Reyes must have heard her pursuit, because he glanced back over his shoulder, saw her coming up behind him, and redoubled his pace.

As the path curved around, she could see a shed at the end of it, in front of the high, wire-topped wall marking the border of the property, and by the time Reyes reached it, the thirty yards had reduced to ten.

Hurriedly he typed some numbers onto a keypad, took a last glance at Brook, then yanked opened the door and went inside, slamming it shut behind him.

The door was a self-locking heavy steel model, designed to be secure, and doubtless Reyes thought there was no way Brook was going to get to him now and so, knowing that surprise was on her side, she punched in the 9999 code that Maria had given her and rushed in after him.

He was on his knees in the middle of the floor, a roughly rolled-up rug to one side, just about to pull open the trapdoor. His gun was on the floor next to him.

Reyes looked shocked to see her and immediately went for the gun. But Brook was already running forward and, as he grabbed hold of it, she launched a flying kick, which hit him full in the face with an immensely satisfying smack. The gun flew out of his hand and he toppled over backwards, lying sprawled across the floor.

Brook landed on her feet, stabilized herself, and leaped on top of him, sitting on his chest and pinning his arms down by his side with her knees. His face was bleeding and he looked dazed, but she wasn't going to give this bastard an inch of slack. She drove her fist into his face three times, putting all her power into the blows, wanting to really hurt this man for all that he'd done. He cried out in pain and turned his head to one side, spitting out blood.

'Where's my daughter?' hissed Brook, still not convinced that he'd been telling the truth earlier. 'Tell me, or I'll kill you.'

He looked up at her, a raging anger in his eyes. 'Fuck you!'

She rained punches down on him then, knocking his head from side to side, splattering his blood on the floor, hatred fuelling her like a poison, before leaning over and grabbing his gun. She thrust it into his face, holding his chin in her other hand, forcing him to look up at her.

She could still hear the incessant barking of the dogs and knew that pursuers wouldn't be far behind. She had to move fast. 'You have five seconds to tell me where Paige is or, so help me God, I will pull this trigger.'

That was when his expression changed to one of fear, because he could see that she was deadly serious.

'I keep telling you, I don't know,' he said. 'I never had anything to do with what happened.'

'Last chance,' she said through clenched teeth.

'I'm telling the truth, by God!' he shouted.

She got up, still keeping the gun trained on him. 'Stand up. Now!'

Reluctantly Reyes got unsteadily to his feet and, as soon as he was upright, Brook delivered a front snap-kick to his groin, putting all her force into it.

He went down to his knees, his mouth open, suddenly very pale and now completely incapacitated. She would have liked to make him suffer more, but she now knew she'd been wasting her time here. Whatever else Tony Reyes was guilty of, there was no way he knew Paige was. He wasn't that brave. He would have told her.

She unloaded his gun, scattered the bullets on the floor, then threw it across the room. The next second she was on her hands and knees and scrabbling around in the darkness for the trapdoor handle, pulling it open and climbing inside, feet first.

Her feet found the rung of a metal stepladder, and she took a further couple of steps down it and shut the lid behind her, turning the world pitch-black. Brook hated dark, enclosed spaces. She always had. On a trip to Mexico once with a former boyfriend he'd persuaded her to visit a cave complex and she'd barely got ten yards inside before she'd broken into a cold sweat. But as she clambered down the steps to the bottom and felt her way through the narrow black tunnel, all she could think about was putting as much distance as possible between herself and the Reyes house.

She walked quickly, with her hands straight out in front of her, until she reached another stepladder. With a sigh of relief she climbed it, fumbled around for a slightly panicky thirty seconds until she found the latch and then, with a big shove, pushed open another trapdoor and clambered out into a tangle of thick brush. Looking back towards the house, she thought she could see figures moving down the path towards the shed.

For a moment she thought about giving herself up to the police, but dismissed the notion just as quickly. What could she say? That she'd entered a private residence by stealth to interrogate the home owner at gunpoint, to find out the location of her kidnapped stepdaughter, whom it seemed he hadn't actually taken? No one would believe a word of it, especially given her current fugitive status. In hindsight, she'd made her situation a whole lot worse by coming here tonight, but the time to worry about that had already been and gone. Now she needed to keep moving.

She fought her way through the bushes, trying to remember where Maria had said the getaway car was parked. It had only been forty-five minutes since she'd given Brook that information, but now Maria was dead and the conversation seemed like something from another, more innocent life.

Once again, Brook felt panic building as she stumbled aimlessly through the thick wall of undergrowth and trees, remembering all those TV shows in which a police helicopter arrives at the scene of a crime with heat-seeking equipment that can track fugitives, however well they're hidden.

She couldn't let them get her. Not yet. Not before she'd found Paige.

In the end she literally ran into the car, bouncing off its bodywork with a loud grunt before she realized what it was.

It was small, khaki-coloured Rav4. The driver's door was unlocked and she got in and quickly found the keys under the seat, as Maria had told her she would.

The engine started first time. Brook didn't switch on the lights, but she could see a rough trail cutting through the undergrowth and she threw the car into Drive and drove down it, weaving through the trees, suddenly feeling an incredible exhilaration. She'd faced death – been inches away from it – and survived. For a few moments she felt invincible, and when a fence appeared up ahead with a hole just about big enough to drive the car through, and what looked like a drop beyond, she kept going, clenching her teeth as she went through the hole and the car suddenly hurtled down a steep, near vertical incline, before levelling out with a bump that almost ripped off the hood.

Brook was now on the track that she'd driven up earlier in the day. Still keeping the lights switched off, she drove as fast as she dared, braking suddenly as she came to the bends, before the track joined another and then suddenly there it was, up ahead: the highway.

She looked in the mirror and felt the kind of relief that had been completely alien to her these past three days. No one seemed to be following her. With a sharp exhalation, she turned on the headlamps, slowed up for a car to come past and then turned back in the direction of Carmel, passing two patrol cars coming fast in the opposite direction, sirens blaring as they headed towards the Reyes house.

Only then did the questions start to nag at Brook. If Tony Reyes had nothing to do with Logan's murder and Paige's kidnapping, then who on earth lay behind it? And was Reyes right? Was it her, and not Logan, who'd been the target?

34

When it happened, it happened fast.

Giant had actually been standing at the locked front gates to the Reyes hacienda – an irritatingly tasteful-looking place up on the hill – about to ring the buzzer on the wall, since there was no one in the gatehouse, when he'd heard a single faint pop that could have been a gunshot, coming from inside. At the time he'd spotted Maria Reyes's Porsche 911 parked at an odd angle in the courtyard a few yards away, facing the gates, and had still been trying to process what that meant when there was another pop, followed immediately by a burst of what was unmistakably automatic weapon fire.

'What's going on?' Jenna called out from the car as Giant sprinted back to it. 'Did I just hear shots?' She looked tense but, unlike Giant, she'd been in an active shooter situation before.

Three years ago she'd become something of a legend in the police department when she'd shot dead two suspects during a bungled robbery, so she'd proved herself under pressure.

'Yeah, you did,' he said, jumping inside. 'From at least three different weapons. One automatic. And Maria's car's here. Call for backup. We're going in.'

As Jenna pulled out her gun and reached for the radio, Giant drove straight at the front gates and, although they were pretty sturdy-looking, they burst open, immediately setting off an incredibly loud alarm that reverberated around the courtyard. Giant continued on, past Maria's Porsche, keeping his head low in case anyone opened up from inside the house, and stopped a few yards away from the front door, throwing on the lights and the siren so that anyone inside would know who they were.

In truth, he was terrified. His guts were churning and he prayed the shooting was over and that no one was going to want to continue the fight with them. But he also knew that he had to step up to the plate. The rules on active shooters had changed. No longer could law-enforcement officers wait for the arrival of a SWAT team. If they believed lives were in danger, it was their duty to confront the shooter.

He fumbled for his gun, almost dropping it in the process, and looked across at Jenna, hoping she hadn't seen him do that. Her expression was tense, but in control. 'Ready?' he whispered.

'Let's go.'

They exited the car, using the doors as cover. It was hard to hear anything above the sound of the alarm, but Giant was pretty sure there was no further shooting from inside. They stayed where they were for a good thirty seconds, checking out the courtyard, which had now been illuminated by spotlights, in case someone was targeting them. But there was no movement, nor was there any sign of backup. They were close to fifteen miles from Monterey here, so it was going to be a while before anyone showed up. They were on their own.

'You ready to approach?' shouted Jenna above the noise of the alarm.

Giant was never going to be ready, but he replied in the affirmative, pleased that his voice betrayed none of the fear he was experiencing. They moved to the front door and he tried the handle. Locked. 'Police. Open up!' he yelled, his voice drowned out by the noise of the alarm, before banging hard on the door and standing off to one side opposite Jenna.

There was no reaction from inside.

Giant wasn't sure what to do. He could hardly kick the door in. And suddenly, in one of those nightmare moments straight out of childhood, his mind went completely blank.

It was Jenna who saved him. 'We need to find if there's a way in around the back,' she said.

He nodded and they crept quickly around the side of the house, keeping low, with Giant in the lead, because he didn't want Jenna thinking he was scared. Nor did he want her seeing that his gun hand was shaking.

The side gate was open and led onto a vast back yard with a huge swimming pool shaped in a figure of eight, with a water slide at one end, beyond which a lawn ran down to a line of trees that were rustling in the cool night breeze at the foot of the mountain. A pair of French doors led out onto the pool, but a curtain was across them, preventing any view of inside, and they were both locked.

And who said crime didn't pay? thought Giant. It sickened him to think that a murderous thug like Tony Reyes was living in this kind of luxury, while an honest cop like him lived in a cramped apartment with a view of the block next door.

Dogs were barking wildly from somewhere off to the left, but it was clear they were shut away in a kennel. Giant tried to ignore all the noise as they circumnavigated the house along a flagstone path lined with potted plants. Whenever they came to a window, he held up a hand and they'd both pause while he peered inside, knowing that every time he did so, he might find himself staring down a gun barrel. But every time the windows were either shuttered or the curtains were drawn, with no lights on inside.

It was as he approached yet another window that he saw it – a beanie hat lying on the path directly beneath it. The window was open and the hat was black, the same colour as the one Brook Connor had been wearing in the restaurant camera footage. As he leaned down to pick it up, he saw a figure staggering towards them up another path that led to the back of the property.

Giant moved away from the window, as Jenna joined him. They both held their guns in front of them and began moving towards the figure, who didn't look as if he'd seen them.

As they got closer, Giant could see that it was a man in a sports jacket. His face was bloodied and he was holding one side of it with his hand.

He looked unarmed, but they weren't taking any chances.

'Police! Stay where you are, and put your hands up!' shouted Giant, relieved that the man didn't appear to be a threat.

The man fell to his knees and raised his hands. That was when Giant recognized him in the moonlight, and he felt a warm glow inside as he realized the scale of the beating Tony Reyes had received. Even in the near-darkness Giant could see that his nose was twisted and broken, and one eye was badly swollen.

'This is my house,' Reyes called back.

Giant felt an urge to shoot him, then and there, but he held back. 'I know who you are,' he said, not quite managing to keep the contempt out of his voice.

'I want to report a homicide,' Reyes continued. 'That fugitive you're after on the news, Brook Connor? She just murdered my wife.'

35

Brook staggered back inside the motel room, locking the door behind her.

All the exhilaration and relief she'd felt earlier had long since disappeared. Now she felt exhausted, scared and, most of all, confused.

Tony Reyes was innocent. She knew that now. Which meant that someone else was behind Logan's murder and Paige and Rosa's disappearance – someone who'd put huge effort into planning the destruction of her family, while simultaneously setting her up for it. And it wasn't about money. A quarter of a million dollars in cash was never going to be enough to justify all this. So who hated her that much?

It was a hard question to have to ask herself. Brook wasn't perfect, she knew that. She had faults, and plenty of them, but overall she considered herself a good person. Even her private clients, though occasionally they were not the most pleasant of people, were generally pretty harmless. One – a married guy in his fifties, high up in IT – had made a very clumsy and pretty aggressive pass at her once, as he was leaving her office a couple of years back, grabbing her in a bear hug and trying to plant a kiss on her lips. When she'd kneed him straight in the groin, causing him to collapse to his knees and throw up all over her carpet, he'd threatened to sue her for assault and – believe it or not – 'testicular injury'. He'd even gone so far as to send her a lawyer's letter and issue proceedings, although he had soon pulled back when Angie Southby had written back, informing him that the camera in Brook's office had filmed everything. Brook hadn't heard another word from him after that, but she'd read a few months ago that he'd been fired from the company he'd founded, after a string of sex allegations against him, a well-deserved victim of the 'Me Too' movement, so she figured he'd have far bigger fish to fry than coming after her after all this time.

Brook poured herself a glass of water and lay on the bed, with the pistol that had saved her life beside her, along with the cellphone that the kidnappers had first contacted Logan on. She wasn't sure what to do with the gun. She'd shot two men with it tonight, so in many ways it was just another thing to incriminate her with, but she was still loath to part company with it. Being armed somehow made her feel less vulnerable.

She lay there for a long time, staring up at the ceiling, trying to work out who could possibly hate her this much. And who could have the sheer ruthlessness to kidnap a child. The thing was,

Brook remained certain Paige wasn't dead. It was the photo she'd been sent that convinced her. Paige was wearing clothes that had clearly been bought for her, and although she looked confused, there was no evidence that she'd been mistreated in any way. If the kidnappers had simply intended to kill her, they wouldn't have bothered buying her new clothes. But if they intended to release her, surely she would have been freed by now. So who had her – and why?

Paige's maternal grandparents would have been the obvious suspects, except that the grandfather was dead, and the grandmother lived in Costa Rica and had made no move to keep in touch with her granddaughter. Logan's parents weren't much interested, either, and anyway they would never have killed their own son.

Brook's thoughts turned to her lawyer and friend, Angie Southby. Maria Reyes had given Brook a good reason why she'd been meeting Angie, and it seemed logical that Logan would have recommended her as a lawyer, since he'd known her for so long and knew how capable she was. But Brook didn't like the fact that it was only Angie who knew that Logan's body was in the trunk of the car in her garage. Angie wouldn't have set the fire herself, but then she wouldn't have needed to. She was a criminal lawyer. She had access to plenty of would-be accomplices. She also, it seemed, had known about the affair between Logan and Maria Reyes, and yet she hadn't mentioned it when they'd talked two nights ago.

There was something else, too. Brook remembered Angie telling her long ago in a rare, unguarded moment, after a couple of drinks, that she longed to have children, but had always put her career first and now realized she'd left it too late. What if she'd had an affair with Logan and had killed him out of revenge? What if she'd taken Paige as her own, now that she'd split up from Bruce and was alone? Angie lived in a big house. She could hire a Mexican nanny like Rosa, who didn't ask too many questions, and live happily ever after.

For a good few minutes Brook ran with this idea in her head. At one point she was even contemplating driving up to Angie's house in Half Moon Bay to see if Paige was there. Then slowly it dawned on her what a ludicrous theory this was. If Angie really wanted a child that badly, she could simply have adopted one. It wouldn't have been hard for a career woman like her to do, and was far, far easier than setting up a conspiracy to murder Logan, kidnap Paige and set Brook up for both crimes. And there was no way she'd have been able to hide Paige away with a nanny, while the news was constantly showing photos of her. It would have been way too risky.

But someone was holding Paige.

For the first time in awhile Brook thought back to the deaths of her parents. She'd never believed her dad had killed her mom. He simply wasn't that kind of man. Brook knew that a lot of people say that about their loved ones, because they don't want to believe they're capable of the horrific crimes they're accused of, but where her dad was concerned, she was sure she was being objective.

Brook had been to visit them three weeks before they died. It had been just after she'd discovered that the guy she'd been seeing for six months had been cheating on her with a woman at work, and she'd been feeling sorry for herself. She and her parents had gone for a long walk around the lake near their house; and afterwards Mom and Dad had comforted her – Dad by putting his arm around Brook's shoulder, hugging her close, and saying that the guy didn't deserve her; and Mom by cooking her favourite childhood meal of beef and bacon meatloaf with roast potatoes. They'd sat by the fire that night, not really saying too much, happy in each other's company – a family once again. When Brook left the next day after lunch she'd been feeling a lot better, and she remembered promising to herself that she was going to visit them every month without fail from then on.

It had been the last time she'd seen them, and she'd been dismayed when the police eventually concluded that it was a murder/suicide, and that no one else had been involved.

Rather than cry tears of hopelessness, Brook had got on with her life and had used the money they'd left her to better herself. Whenever the subject of her parents came up in interviews, she always said she didn't believe the official theory, but she hadn't shown her grief on air. She didn't break down; instead she talked about her mom and dad with genuine fondness, but kept her emotions from running too free, which, looking back, had probably been a mistake. Maybe she should have wept publically, but that wasn't her. She was a private person. What she did do was get Angie to petition the Modesto police department to reopen the case two years ago, but they'd refused, on the basis that there was no new evidence contradicting their findings.

And that was the thing. Brook had moved on. She didn't blindly pursue her parents' killer. In hindsight, maybe she should have hired a PI like Cervantes to look into the murders. But she hadn't. And more and more, that was looking like a mistake, too, because her parents had been targeted for a reason, just like Brook herself had. And now, lying there on the bed in the shitty motel room, she couldn't help thinking that perhaps the same person had targeted them all. Seven years might have passed since her parents had died, but she now thought it was no coincidence. Find who had killed her parents and she might find who'd set her up.

Exhausted she might have been, but Brook wasn't ready to give up yet and, as she lay there thinking about her next move, she realized there was one person who might be able to help. She'd only seen him once since she was a child – and that had been at her parents' joint funeral. She didn't even know if he was still alive, and it was a long shot. Jesus, it was a long shot.

But right then, he represented pretty much her last option.

Part Four

36

This Morning
12.30 a.m.

For Tyrone Giant, one of the most frustrating things about police work was when you knew the person sitting opposite you was a crook of the lowest order, but the evidence to prove it remained as elusive as ever.

Tony Reyes had become an obsession to Giant and now, for the first time in his career, he had the guy in front of him, alongside one of his hotshot lawyers. Giant had been questioning Reyes about exactly what had happened at his house that night. And it wasn't exactly going according to plan.

He leaned forward on the interview-room chair, conscious of it creaking. 'Mr Reyes, you're saying that Brook Connor turned up at your house tonight, accompanied by your wife, whom she'd kidnapped, and threatened you at gunpoint.'

Reyes nodded, meeting Giant's gaze. 'That's right.' He might have had a badly bruised face, the beginnings of a black eye and a fat lip, but his manner was calm and authoritative.

'Do you have any idea why Brook Connor would kidnap your wife?' Giant asked him.

'Ms Connor said that my wife Maria was having an affair with her husband, which was something I was unaware of.'

Giant looked at Jenna as if this was news to them, too, and scribbled something in his notebook. Now, finally, this information could be made public. 'Did she say how she found out about this?' Giant asked, knowing that if Brook had found the photos that he, Giant, had given to Logan, then he was complicit in this whole thing.

Reyes shook his head. 'No, she didn't. She – Ms Connor – said she'd killed her husband and now she had nothing left to live for.' He paused and adopted a pained expression. 'She had the gun against my wife's head at the time. And then she just ... pulled the trigger. I couldn't believe it.' He shook his head. 'Then she turned the gun on me. I thought she was going to shoot me, too. She had madness in her eyes. Thankfully, the sound of the gunshot alerted two of my staff and they both came in, armed with licensed firearms. They managed to get her to drop the gun, and I asked them to get some tarpaulin to wrap my wife's body in.'

Giant frowned. 'Why would you do that? Your wife had just been murdered. You call the police; you don't wrap her in tarpaulin. That's tampering with evidence.'

Reyes made a confused hand gesture. 'But I'm not a police officer. I don't know about evidence. I thought it was the best thing … I'm sorry. I was going to call the police straight away, but, as my staff members were wrapping Maria's body, Ms Connor attacked me, got hold of her gun and shot both my men. Are they both all right, by the way?'

'They're being treated for gunshot wounds,' said Jenna. 'But the conditions of both men are stable. They'll live.'

'Thank God for that small mercy at least,' said Reyes. 'I was very lucky not to get shot myself. I fled into the back yard and Ms Connor chased me.'

'Why would she chase you?' asked Giant. 'Had you done something to cause her to act in that way?'

'Not at all. I was simply trying to escape. She caught up with me, there was an altercation …'

'And she beat you up?'

For the first time there was a flash of anger in Reyes's eyes and he gave Giant a cold stare. 'I don't hit women. So when they attack me, I try to calm them down. Unfortunately there was no way of calming down this woman. She kicked me in the groin and, naturally, I was incapacitated for a few moments. I thought she might shoot me, but instead she ran off. I assume you haven't caught her yet?'

'Not yet, no,' said Jenna. 'We have a major search going on around your property, but so far there's no sign of her.'

'You need to track her down – she's dangerous,' said Reyes, without a hint of irony. 'She killed my wife.'

'We're putting all our resources into finding her,' said Jenna.

'Good. I want to see her go on trial for murder.'

'I still can't work out why she targeted you,' said Giant. 'It was your wife having the affair, not you.'

'Who can tell with these people?' Reyes said with an exaggerated sigh.

The way he was talking annoyed the hell out of Giant. Reyes knew Giant didn't believe his story, and he didn't care. It was as if he couldn't even be bothered to take Giant and Jenna seriously.

'You don't seem that upset about the death of your wife,' Giant said.

'I assure you I am. But I prefer to grieve in private. Now, I've told you everything that happened, so I'm assuming I can go.' He looked at his lawyer.

The lawyer, a big, silver-haired guy in his sixties – one of a number whom Tony Reyes kept on his books – nodded firmly. 'Absolutely. There's no reason to hold my client any longer, is there?' He gave both detectives a bored, patronizing look.

'No, there isn't,' said Giant reluctantly. Reyes's story might have had holes in it, but it was plausible enough to convince most observers, which meant they'd just get in trouble for holding him. 'We may need to talk to you again, though, Mr Reyes, so please don't leave town.'

'I absolutely expect to talk to you again, Detective. If nothing else, I need to be kept abreast of the investigation into my wife's murder. And I want Brook Connor caught, before she harms anyone else. Now if that's all …?' Reyes and his lawyer stood up. 'Thank you for your time, Detectives.'

He put out a hand and Giant thought of the Hernandez family, torn to pieces on that living-room floor, and of all Reyes's other victims over the years. Lives that he'd snuffed out without a second thought. Giant wanted to punch him, but he held back. He didn't take the proffered hand, though. He looked at it, then back at the man holding it out, the beginnings of a smile on his face. 'You'd better go get that face looked at. She really did a number on you back there.'

Reyes's expression darkened and he stared at Giant. 'I think you need to talk to ordinary citizens with more respect, Detective,' he said icily.

'I do,' said Giant. 'I'm always respectful to ordinary citizens. It's lying killers I tend not to be so polite to.'

The lawyer took Reyes by the arm. 'Okay,' he said, 'I think we're finished here. Come on, Tony. And, Detective, at least make an attempt at being professional.'

'You want to watch yourself,' said Reyes as he passed.

A familiar voice, deep down, told Giant to get a grip and not say anything that he might later regret, but for once he found himself ignoring it. He took a step forward. 'Are you threatening me?'

He felt Jenna take his arm. 'Easy, Ty. Let's leave it.'

'That's right, said Reyes, glaring at him. 'Leave it, Ty. And try to remember you're not some big hotshot. You're just a small-town, hick detective.'

The truth in the words stung Giant, but before it could go any further, Jenna gave him a pull, and Reyes's lawyer gave Reyes a push, and both men were separated.

As the lawyer manoeuvred Reyes out of the door, he gave Giant a withering look. 'I'll be making a formal complaint about this. You cannot talk to my client like that.'

'Come with me,' said Jenna and, still holding Giant's arm, she led him down the corridor to the canteen. It was empty. Most of the marshals were up in the Carmel Valley, either crawling over Reyes's house or trying to track down Brook Connor in the area around it, and the Chief was fast asleep at home, so thankfully no one had been around to witness Giant's near-meltdown with Reyes.

'What the hell was that about?' demanded Jenna when they were alone at one of the corner tables. 'His lawyer's right. You can't go talking to Tony Reyes like that, especially when his wife's just been murdered and it looks, for once, like he's actually a victim.'

Giant sighed and looked down at his hands. They were shaking. He'd come close to losing it completely, and the thought scared him.

Jenna leaned forward and touched his arm, more gently this time. 'Look, I know it's hard, having to let a lowlife like Reyes go, but those are the breaks – you've got to live with it, Ty. We'll get him another day.'

He forced a smile. 'I know. I don't usually get that irate. Did you believe his story?'

Jenna thought about it for a second. 'It makes sense. We know Brook Connor abducted Maria Reyes, and that the car they were both in made it to the Reyes household, so it seems a fair assumption that Brook wanted to harm Maria. So yeah, I believe him.'

Giant still wasn't convinced. 'But if she just wanted revenge on Maria, why not take her some place isolated and kill her? Why get her to drive all the way to her home when, as far as we know,

Tony Reyes has got nothing to do with the affair, and where there'd be armed security?'

Jenna shrugged. 'Connor is an angry, violent woman, probably with some kind of death wish. It doesn't surprise me that she's not acting rationally.'

'But she managed to escape, so she's not being that irrational.' Something else struck him. 'You know, when Reyes was confronted by Brook Connor, he told us she said – and I quote – "she'd killed her husband and now she had nothing left to live for".'

'And?'

'All our witness statements suggest Brook was very close to her stepdaughter, Paige. And yet, according to Reyes, when she came to his house hell-bent on revenge, she never once mentioned anything about Paige. It seems strange. As is the fact that we can't find any trace of Paige anywhere. Or of the nanny. No sightings, no bodies. No nothing. So what else are we not seeing?'

'I don't know,' said Jenna. 'The only person who can give us some answers is Brook Connor.'

Giant sighed. 'And for a mad, irrational woman, she's damned good at hiding.'

37

Brook's mom had grown up in Iowa, but her dad had been a California native. He was brought up near Sacramento before moving first to San Francisco, then to England when Brook was five, the same age as Paige was now. Her mom had been an only child, but her dad had been the eldest of two boys. He and his brother Charles, who was two years younger, hadn't been especially close. Apparently Brook had met Charles a couple of times as a very young child, before they moved to England, but after that she'd only seen him once, and that had been at her parents' joint funeral. Charles had come alone, even though he was married, and he'd said little, beyond offering his condolences and saying he couldn't believe that his brother could have done such a thing (but, interestingly, he didn't say that he *didn't* believe it), and telling Brook that she'd grown into a beautiful young woman. He'd left immediately after the service.

At the time Brook had been so shell-shocked by her parents' deaths that she hadn't paid too much attention to Charles, and had simply put his indifference down to the fact that he and her dad weren't close. But looking back now, his behaviour hadn't seemed natural. Something had gone wrong between the two brothers, and it was for this reason that Brook was looking up Charles now. She wanted to find out more about the side of Dad that she'd never known. The one where he didn't talk to his brother, and where he'd allegedly beaten his wife to death, before putting a bullet in his own head.

What Brook was going to do with this information was anyone's guess. Once again, she'd been all over the news that morning. The reports were talking about the altercation at the Reyes house the previous night. There was no mention of Tony Reyes's gangster credentials. Instead, the report said that a woman believed to be Maria Reyes had been shot dead and two other men shot and wounded, and that Brook was the main suspect.

It was incredible how everything in her life had been turned upside down in such a short space of time. Last Wednesday she'd been on San Francisco radio promoting her new book, and the world – if not exactly at her feet – was at least giving her a pretty easy ride. Now, on Sunday, she was a fugitive being hunted by every law-enforcement official in the state, with a one-hundred-thousand-dollar bounty on her head. She also knew that the moment she gave herself up, she would never see Paige again. She would probably never see the outside of a jail cell, either. She might even end up on death row. Things were looking that bad.

Her uncle Charles still lived in the place that he and her dad had grown up in. She'd looked him up online this morning and, having registered with one of those websites that sell you individual addresses, had located his.

Knights Landing was a pretty little town on the Sacramento River, and Charles's home was situated in the middle of a new development of small, neat houses on its northern edge. A red Hyundai stood in the driveway and Brook parked behind it. She checked the rear-view mirror to see if there was anyone around (there wasn't, the place was deserted) and then, taking a deep breath, and knowing this was her last hope, she got out of the car and walked up to the front door. A sticker on the window next to it stated that the occupants of the house didn't buy from door-to-door salesmen. A sticker below that one announced that the occupants were also members of the NRA and for burglars to beware.

Brook rang the doorbell and waited for what felt like a long time, before she saw someone moving slowly towards the door through the frosted window glass.

She took a step back as the door opened and found herself staring at a handsome blonde-haired woman in her mid-sixties, dressed in an unflattering pantsuit. Either way, it wasn't Uncle Charles.

'Yes?' said the woman, looking at Brook suspiciously.

'I'm looking for Charles Connor,' Brook said. 'I'm related to him.'

'Not very closely,' the woman replied. 'Otherwise you'd know he died earlier this year.' Then she looked at Brook more closely and something seemed to click. 'Oh, my goodness, you're his niece – the woman they're after ...'

Her eyes widened and she tried to shut the door, but Brook put her hand in the way and stepped over the threshold, pushing the woman aside. She was in enough trouble already. A little more wasn't going to make any difference.

'I'm not going to hurt you, I promise,' she said, shutting the door behind her and putting her hands up in a semi-passive stance as the woman retreated down the hall and into the kitchen. 'Please. I just need to talk.'

Brook followed her into the kitchen, then stopped as the woman – who she now realized was her Uncle Charles's wife – reached into a drawer, removed a handgun and pointed it at her. 'Don't come a step closer or I'll shoot,' she said, her grip on the gun steady. 'You're a wanted woman. You need to hand yourself in while you still have the chance.'

Brook stood still, keeping her hands where the woman could see them. 'I know this is difficult to believe, but I'm innocent. My husband was murdered and my stepdaughter has been kidnapped. Someone is trying to destroy me.'

The woman eyed her coolly. 'They're doing a good job.'

'I know. And the only reason I haven't surrendered is that Paige, my stepdaughter, is still missing and I need to find her. She was abducted four days ago.'

'I've seen her photo on the news. She's a beautiful little girl.'

'She's everything to me.'

'But they're making out you killed her.'

'I've never harmed a hair on that child's head. I know they're saying some terrible things about me on the news, but I've never been in trouble before. I've never done anything I'm truly ashamed of, and I've never killed anyone. Ever. Look, I'm unarmed.' Very slowly Brook opened up her jacket so that the woman could see there wasn't a gun underneath. She then turned round and lifted up the back. 'Please. I just need to ask you a few questions.'

'I don't see how I can help you.'

'You're Charles's wife, aren't you? Annie?'

'I am.'

'I think the person who's doing this to me is the same person who killed my parents. I'm certain Dad never killed Mom. I've been certain about it ever since it happened.'

Annie sighed and seemed to relax a little. 'I never believed it, either. If anything, it would have been the other way around.'

Her comment surprised Brook. 'What do you mean?'

Annie stared at her for a few seconds, as if she was working out what to do. Brook didn't say anything and eventually she seemed to come to a decision. 'You'd better come in and sit down,' she said, lowering the gun, but keeping hold of it.

'Can I have a cup of coffee and a drink of water?' asked Brook. The thought of a coffee made her almost deliriously excited.

'Sure,' said Annie, taking pity on her and putting the gun down on the worktop next to her.

Brook waited while she used a machine to make her a strong black Americano and poured a glass of water from a bottle in the fridge, then followed her through to a small lounge that looked over a paved back yard with a fence at the end. Annie sat down in an armchair and put the gun on the coffee table next to her, so it was still within reach. Brook sat down in a chair facing her.

They didn't say anything for a few seconds and then finally Annie spoke. 'I don't know how much I can help you. I haven't seen your parents in over thirty years, so anything I tell you about them is old, old news. My best advice to you would be to give yourself up to the authorities and tell the truth. They'll find your little girl.'

'And I will. I know I can't keep running much longer. But while I'm here, would you mind telling me why you said that you could understand if my mom killed my dad, but not the other way around?'

Annie sighed again and gave her a sympathetic look. There was something about her that Brook trusted, and it made her yearn for her own mom.

'Are you sure you want to hear this?' she asked. 'Because I don't see how it's even relevant.'

Brook took a sip from the coffee. It tasted delicious. 'Tell me anything you can. Please.'

'Your father was a charmer. In his day he was very handsome and he had a way about him that was very attractive, I have to admit. He was also' – she paused – 'and I'm sorry to have to say this, he was also a philanderer, at least when I knew him.'

'How do you know?' Brook asked tightly.

Annie crossed and uncrossed her hands. 'Because I had an affair with him.'

Brook felt sick. Her dad had meant so much to her. It was a huge jump for her to believe that he'd ever cheated on Mom, and yet somehow she knew that what she was being told was true.

'I'm not proud to have to admit that,' Annie continued. 'I remember being attracted to him the very first time we met. Your father was very different from Charles. There was so much more about him, and I think I got swept up in his charm. At the time I was working in Oakland, not far from where your dad was lecturing at Berkeley. We met a couple of times – just for coffee, he said, but I could tell he liked me.' She paused, looking up at the ceiling and then back at Brook. 'One thing led to another and we began a liaison. I knew it was wrong and I kept telling myself to stop, but I couldn't seem to help myself. I was young and in a dull marriage with a man who I thought, at the time, was dull, too. Your father represented a way out for me, and I'll be completely honest with you here, I wanted him to leave your mother and you for me.'

She must have seen the look of shock on Brook's face because she quickly continued. 'But your dad made it clear that he would never leave the two of you. I was devastated. I thought he loved me, but unfortunately I found out the hard way that he didn't.'

'What do you mean?' asked Brook, detecting a change in her tone.

Annie continued to cross and uncross her hands on her lap, clearly uncomfortable. 'I'm ashamed of what happened,' she said. 'You have to know that.'

We Can See You

'I understand,' said Brook, although she wasn't sure she did.

'One time you and your mom were away somewhere, and Charles was away, too. I stayed the night at your house with your father. We hadn't seen each other for some time, I remember that. I also remember thinking that our affair couldn't continue like it was for much longer, because it was hurting me too much.' She frowned at the memory. 'Anyways, we were there drinking wine. It was evening. And there was a knock on the door. Naturally your father was concerned. He wasn't expecting anyone, and obviously I was there. He told me to stay where I was and checked who it was through the window. Straight away he came back into the room, looking like he'd seen a ghost. I thought it must be your mom, but he told me to stay absolutely silent, and that the woman at the door was a crazy lady who was after him for something that he didn't seem to want to talk about.

'But this lady didn't go away. She kept banging on the door. I could hear her shouting and yelling outside, saying that she knew your dad was in there. I kept asking him who she was, but he didn't want to say, and I guess it dawned on me then that I wasn't the only woman, apart from your mom, that he was seeing.

'I was furious, but scared too, because this lady really wasn't giving up. I remember she found a rock or something in the yard and threw it through one of the front windows. That was when your dad went out to confront her. He told me to stay where I was, but I wanted to make sure he was going to be okay, so I followed him over to the door. He left it open when he went outside, so I saw and heard it all. She was screaming at him, telling that she couldn't believe he'd left her, that he was going to pay for it – and all the while your dad was trying to calm her down. But then she just started hitting and kicking him, saying she thought he loved her, and that was when your father hit her.'

'Dad hit a woman? I can't believe he'd do that.' Brook's tone was defensive. 'I never saw him raise a hand to anyone. Ever.'

'Well, he hit her hard. Round the face. And she went down on her back like a sack of potatoes.' Annie had been speaking fast as she recounted the story, but now she paused, as if she wasn't sure how to continue.

'What happened then?' asked Brook.

'You sure you want to hear?'

'Tell me everything. I can't feel any worse than I do right now.' She took another sip of the coffee, wondering what coffee tasted like in jail.

'I remember this as if it was yesterday, because it damned near floored me, too. She burst into tears and said, "How can you do this to the woman who's carrying your baby?"'

'She said that?' Brook felt like throwing up.

'Those were her exact words.'

'What did Dad say?'

'He accused her of lying, saying there was no way he could have made her pregnant, and that he hardly knew her. But he didn't sound certain, so it was obvious to me that he had slept with her.

'Anyways, this lady got to her feet, a lot calmer now, looked your father in the eye and said she'd make him pay for what he'd just done. Then she saw me in the doorway and gave this kind of dark look and said I'd pay for it, too. That we'd all pay. And then she turned tail and left. Your father saw that I'd seen everything and tried to gloss over it, making out she was this crazy lady stalking him for no reason.' Annie slowly shook her head. 'But that was it, for me. I felt such a fool. I told your father I never wanted to see him again, grabbed my things and left.'

The room fell silent. Brook had been wrong about not being able to feel any worse than she did already. She was feeling far worse now. All she had left of her family were memories. If they were tarnished, she had nothing

'I know what you're thinking, honey,' said Annie quietly. 'That's why I didn't want to tell you. It was a long, long time ago, and three months later you guys moved to England. I remember that Charles wanted to come and say goodbye to you all, but I couldn't face seeing your father again, I was that devastated. And angry. I was very angry. So I said I didn't want to go. Charles was shocked and demanded to know why. Eventually I told him.' There was a long pause. 'Charles never spoke to your father again. Neither did I. It took a long time, but Charles forgave me and I was never unfaithful to him again.'

'Is that why you didn't come to the funeral?' said Brook, as it dawned on her that all this made perfect sense.

She nodded. 'I'm sorry. I should have done. But even after all that time it still hurt, and Charles didn't want me to attend it.'

'You don't think Charles had anything to do with what happened to my parents, do you? I mean there was no sign of forced entry when they were killed. I think that's why I was suspected.'

'No,' she said emphatically. 'Charles would never have done that. He didn't want anything to do with your father, but he

267

wouldn't have killed him. Not all those years after everything had happened.'

Brook thought back to the pregnant woman. 'And do you have any idea who this crazy lady was? And how my father met her?'

Annie shook her head. 'I haven't a clue. I can't really remember anything about her, except that she wasn't pretty or your father's type. She was in her twenties, I think, very skinny with long, dark hair. She kind of reminded me of a bird. That's all I can tell you.'

Brook knew from experience that memories can play all kinds of tricks on people, and this was probably the best description she was going to get of this mysterious woman. She wondered if the woman had indeed been pregnant or was just trying to scare her father. Brook had been five years old when they'd moved to England, so if there had indeed been a child, he or she would be around thirty now, and the mother would be somewhere in her fifties.

But in the end she knew she was clutching at straws, hoping that a crazy lady from more than thirty years ago could provide clues as to what had happened to her parents seven years earlier, and indeed, what was happening to her now And even if she could, there was no way of finding her before the police closed in on Brook herself.

She finished the coffee. It was over.

The two women stood up together and Brook surprised herself by stepping forward and hugging Annie. Annie hugged her back, and Brook had to stop herself from crying. She'd always preached that you should never suppress your emotions –

that was unnatural – but right now she had to stay strong. There were things she had to organize before she gave herself up. She didn't trust the police to find Paige, especially as it seemed they thought she was dead, but someone else could continue to search.

'Thank you for talking to me,' she said as Annie led her back to the front door, not carrying the gun with her this time.

'Stay safe,' said Annie, moving aside as Brook stepped into the bright sunlight.

The street was still empty as she reversed the Rav4 out of the driveway and drove away. She still had close to six thousand dollars in cash. Her plan was to deliver that money to Chris Cervantes, tell him what she knew, ask him to do whatever he could to find Paige, then call 911 and let the cops know she was ready to come in.

In many ways, it was a relief that journey's end was near. The stress of the last four days had been so much that it had only been a matter of time before she hit burnout, and she knew she was hitting it now.

But fate, it seems, has a way of delivering the most left-field blows, because she'd only been driving for about twenty minutes when she heard an unfamiliar ringing sound.

And then she realized it wasn't unfamiliar. It was the ringtone of the cellphone that the kidnappers had left for them four days earlier.

Brook was on a quiet stretch of road surrounded by fields and she pulled over and hurriedly took the cell from her purse. The words 'No caller ID' appeared on the screen.

She fumbled in the purse for the tape-recorder she'd borrowed from Angie, trying to remember where the hell it was. She had to record this call, so people would know she wasn't making up the whole thing.

The cell rang a third time, then a fourth as she rifled through the purse. She couldn't let it go to message. They might never call back.

And then she saw the tape-recorder in an inside pocket. As the cell rang for a fifth time, she powered it up and switched the cell to loudspeaker.

'We can see you,' said the man on the other end of the line.

38

'Where's my daughter?' demanded Brook.

'She's safe,' said the man. He had a Californian accent and sounded white. Twenties or thirties. Very likely the man Logan had been speaking to before he was killed.

Brook took a deep breath, concentrating on remaining focused. She was certain he couldn't see her. He was bluffing to throw her off guard. 'You were given the ransom you asked for. So why haven't you given her back?'

'We wanted to make sure you hadn't involved the police.'

In spite of herself, Brook was filled with hope. Nothing else mattered, if she could just get Paige back. There were a hundred questions she needed to ask, but in the end she settled for the most important one. 'When can I see her?'

'Tonight. How much money do you have in cash?'

'Six thousand dollars. That's it.'

'It's not enough, if you want to see your daughter again.'

'You must have seen the news. I'm on the run, for Christ's sakes. I can't get hold of any more money. Look, I'll give you six thousand cash, plus I've got a diamond wedding ring and a diamond necklace, which are worth at least ten thousand together. You can have them, too. But you've got to let me have Paige back.'

There was a pause. 'All right. Six thousand dollars, with the ring and the necklace. Come to the place where you and your husband came before. The nursery. Be there at midnight. I'll be there with Paige.'

Brook swallowed. 'Why should I trust you? The last time I came to the nursery you took the ransom money and murdered my husband.'

'Your husband was a fool. He tried to rip us off.'

Brook remembered the way Logan had punched her. If she'd fallen on her head, the blow could have killed her. Had he really been trying to double-cross the kidnappers?

'My husband might have been a fool, but I'm not. I need proof that Paige is still alive. I want a photo of her that you can prove was taken today. And don't try to doctor it.'

'I'm offering you your kid back,' the man snapped. 'Don't start setting conditions.'

Brook couldn't be seen to be weak. 'You want me there tonight with the money and the jewellery, then you need to send me a photo. Otherwise there's no deal.'

'This is what happens when you threaten me,' he said and abruptly ended the call.

Brook sat staring at the phone, willing him to call back.

Five minutes passed. Then ten. No one called. She wondered if he was trying to get hold of a photo.

But as the minutes passed, it slowly dawned on her that she'd probably nixed the best chance she had of getting Paige back. She'd overplayed her hand.

She was suddenly filled with a terrible impotent rage. She screamed out loud, filling the car with noise, and threw the phone across the car. And as the stress of the past four days finally overwhelmed her, she put her head in her hands and let the tears come, no longer caring how she looked to anyone who might be driving past. It was over. All of it.

The buzz of the cellphone receiving a text brought her back to reality.

She took a handkerchief from her bag and used it to wipe the tears away, before reaching down to pick the cell off the floor. The screen was filled with an image of a little girl in a pretty white dress, standing on a patch of lawn with pine trees in the background, looking down at a bright-pink soccer ball on the grass. It had obviously been taken from a distance and the girl was unaware of the cameraman's presence. As Brook zoomed in, she saw that the girl was indeed Paige, and that the dress, like the pink sandals she was wearing, was unfamiliar. As she zoomed back out, she saw a date and time stamp in the top right-hand corner: 05/06/18 14.26. The photo had been taken barely an hour ago.

A wave of relief washed over her, and she smiled for the first time in what felt like months. Paige was alive and well. She looked reasonably happy and well cared for. Clothes had been bought for her. So had toys. They all looked new. It meant that whoever had abducted her didn't mean her any harm. But it suggested something else, too.

That the people who had her might not want to give her back.

The cellphone rang again, interrupting Brook's thoughts. She picked it up straight away, almost dropping it in the process.

'That's the best photo you're going to get,' said the man. 'Now the instructions remain: be at the nursery at midnight. Come alone or the whole thing's off. Understand?'

'Okay, but answer me this. If you're serious about giving Paige back to me, why did you set fire to my house? Because it looked like you were doing it to frame me.'

'Well, that's the thing,' the man said. 'I didn't set it.'

And with that, he ended the call, leaving Brook staring at the phone.

39

Lou McPherson leaned back in the driver's seat of his pickup and smiled. Brook Connor had fallen for the ruse, like he knew she would. It had taken a long time to get that photo. Three hours in all, sitting in undergrowth, watching the house where he knew they were keeping the kid, waiting for them to appear outside, knowing that this photo would be his meal ticket. And then, just as he'd been beginning to think he might have to think of something else, the back door had opened and out they'd come.

He'd already got the photo when he'd first called Connor, but he knew enough about women not to give them what they want immediately. Treat them rough. Get them begging. Then cut them a little slack, so they think you care. It was like fishing: you throw out your line, tantalize them with the bait. And then reel them in, ready to devour.

The fact that his actions had ruined Brook Connor's life didn't overly bother McPherson. Connor had never given a shit about people like him. She'd profited from her parents' death, peddling a load of New Age shit to gullible rich people and housewives on antidepressants, made a heap of money and lived her perfect little life in her big house with her perfect family, like nothing else in the world mattered. She'd got what was coming to her, although he had to admire the way she'd turned up at the house of Tony Reyes and shot his wife in front of him. That took some cajones. And Connor was pretty hot, too. Under different circumstances, he'd have enjoyed fucking her. But this was business.

The number of the police hotline was on the seat next to him and he punched the digits into the burner phone he'd just used to call Connor. It rang for a while before it was answered, but that didn't surprise McPherson. He imagined there were plenty of people calling today.

'US Marshals Service, how can I help?' said the guy on the other end.

McPherson suddenly felt nervous. 'The hundred-thousand-dollar reward for information leading to the arrest of Brook Connor, how long would I have to wait for it?'

'Do you have information, sir?'

'I do. But I need to know I'm going to get that money. And I need it in cash. Is that possible?'

'Yes, it's possible to give you the reward in cash, if your information's correct. It would take several days, though.'

McPherson needed it sooner than that. But he also knew not to push things. 'And can it be paid anonymously, so only you guys – the Marshals Service – know about it?'

'Yes, it can. So do you know where she is, sir?'

'Not right now. But I can tell you exactly where she'll be at midnight tonight.'

40

It had been another day of doing all the low-profile legwork that the marshals weren't interested in for Giant and the rest of his small team of detectives.

And now, at 6.30 p.m., things suddenly got interesting again. He and Jenna were sitting across the desk from Dr Gary Wallace, the county pathologist, who had just completed the autopsy on Maria Reyes. Wallace gave them one of his cheery smiles, knitted his unfeasibly thick eyebrows and stroked his chin, as he looked at the blown-up autopsy photos of Maria Reyes.

'If I was a betting man, I'd say the victim here – Maria Reyes – shot herself. Everything points to that. The gun was probably a nine-millimetre pistol or revolver.'

'There were nine-millimetre shells found at the scene,' Giant told him. 'They matched a shell found at Brook Connor's house, so it was probably Connor's gun that was used.'

'Interesting. The shot went into the temple at point-blank range – you can see that from the burn mark there,' and he tapped his finger on one of the photos and passed it over to them. Jenna had a good look. Giant gave it a cursory glance. 'And the angle of the bullet was slightly upwards, which almost always suggests suicide. What really gives it away, though, is the fact that the victim has traces of powder residue from unburned carbon on her left hand, which means that hand was holding the gun when it was fired; and that would tally with the fact that the bullet entered her left temple.'

Giant and Jenna exchanged looks. Neither of them had been expecting this. 'And is there are no other explanation for how that residue ended up there?' Jenna asked him.

The doc shook his head. 'None that I can think of.'

Jenna raised her eyebrows. 'That doesn't tally with Mrs Reyes's husband's account of what happened.'

'I'm aware of that,' said the doc. 'I've been watching the news, like everyone else. And I'm also aware of who her husband is.'

'You know him?' Giant asked.

This time Wallace's smile was devoid of humour. 'By reputa-tion. He's not a man I'd like to cross. But I wouldn't be doing my job if I didn't tell you what I think.'

'And is there any way you could be mistaken?' asked Jenna.

He shrugged. 'I guess it's possible. But I don't see how, unless Mrs Reyes had taken hold of the gun at some point and then it was snatched from her, placed against her head and the shot fired. Which seems highly unlikely. She doesn't have any obvious defensive injuries to suggest that a struggle took place, and my understanding is that you guys were on the scene very quickly. How was she positioned when you found her?'

'She was lying on a tarpaulin sheet. According to her husband, he and a couple of his security people were trying to move her body, so it didn't make a mess . . .' Giant didn't bother keeping the scepticism out of his voice.

Wallace raised his eyebrows. 'I'd have thought a man with Tony Reyes's reputation would have known that you should never move a body from a murder scene.'

'Yes,' said Giant, 'so would we.' He stood up and Jenna followed suit. 'Thanks for your time, Gary. I'd appreciate it if you could keep what I've told you to yourself. And I'll keep your name out of any media briefing.'

'I'd appreciate that,' Wallace said, shaking hands with both of them. 'If it's all the same to you, I'd rather not be in Tony Reyes's black book.'

Giant knew that he himself was already in it, and in truth the thought unnerved him. But it also bugged him hugely that it was common knowledge amongst those within, and connected to, the law-enforcement community that Tony Reyes was a murderous thug whom you went out of your way not to cross. Giant had always thought America had got rid of the era of untouchable gangsters like Al Capone and John Gotti – that they'd finally been tamed. But the truth was they'd been replaced by men who knew that adopting a high profile is dangerous. The gangsters of today worked around the clock to keep themselves as far away as possible from the crimes carried out on their behalf, and they'd turned out to be just as untouchable.

'This case, Ty, it gets stranger and stranger,' said Jenna when they were back outside in the sunshine.

'The Chief's not going to like it,' he said.

'What do you think's going on?'

Giant would have loved to come up with a solid, workable theory, not least because he knew it would be a good way to impress Jenna, but right now he couldn't think of one, so he was honest. 'I really don't have a clue. We know Tony Reyes's security guys were also shot with a nine-mill, so probably with the same weapon. Maybe it was Reyes's wife who shot them, and he's protecting her memory.' He shrugged. 'The point is, we may never know for sure. Tony Reyes will stick with his story that Connor shot Maria, and there'll be no way we can disprove it. You heard what Gary Wallace said in there – if he was a betting man, he'd say Maria killed herself. That's not proof, it's opinion, and it's not going to be enough to sway a jury. And Reyes's men aren't cooperating, either.' He and Jenna had tried to question them earlier at the hospital and had been referred to their lawyers. Giant know that by the time they gave official statements – if they ever did – they'd be giving exactly the same story as their boss.

'Brook Connor will probably give us her side of the story,' he said, 'but it's going to be her word against theirs. And right now, her word doesn't count for much.'

'So Tony Reyes walks free, even though we found his wife wrapped in tarpaulin? It doesn't seem right.'

'I know, but for once it seems he hasn't done anything. Nothing we can prove, anyways.'

Jenna looked at him. 'You should have been more careful – the way you talked to him last night.'

There was a tenderness in her voice that Giant hadn't heard before. She actually cares about me, he thought. 'Reyes won't hurt a cop,' he replied, with more confidence than he felt. 'He's not that stupid.'

'Just be careful next time.'

'I will be,' he said, conscious that they were still looking at each other.

'Your phone's ringing,' she said with a smile, and he realized with surprise that it was.

It was Detective Joe Padilla. 'I've been tracking further back through Brook Connor's phone records,' he said, 'and there are two calls in the week running up to the murders to a cellphone that we've ID'd as belonging to Chris Cervantes.'

'I know that name,' said Giant, although he couldn't recall where from.

'He used to be on the squad, long before your time,' said Padilla. 'He was invalided out of the Force three years ago, after he got shot in the hip during a raid. He's a private detective now, still based in Monterey. Do you want me to go see him?'

'No. Leave it with us. We'll go there now.' Giant took down the address and ended the call, before telling Jenna what Padilla had just told him.

Her expression became serious. 'Chris Cervantes? Oh yeah, I can tell you a story about him.'

'Tell me on the way over to his place,' said Giant, getting in the car.

41

Sunday

6.40 p.m.

The Rav4 was close to running on fumes by the time Brook parked on Chris Cervantes's driveway next to his Dodge Avenger. But she had a plan of action and, if all went well, she wouldn't need it again anyway. She knew Cervantes wouldn't want to see her, which was why, once again, she didn't ring the front doorbell.

Cervantes was in his study. He tried to duck down, but he wasn't quick enough. Their eyes met and he gave her an exasperated look.

'Please,' Brook mouthed at him through the window.

With an angry shake of his head, he got up from his chair and motioned her round to the back door. It was locked this time (she guessed he'd learned, after her last visit) and she waited while he walked slowly down the hall, leaning heavily on his stick, and unlocked it for her.

He didn't stand aside to let her in, but stood motionless in the doorway. He was wearing cheap suit-pants, socks with no shoes and a dress shirt that was greying around the collar. It was obvious that he wasn't seeing clients today, and Brook wondered how many he actually had.

'What are you doing here?' he demanded. 'You need to give yourself up before they kill you.'

'Paige's kidnappers have been back in touch,' she said.

Cervantes looked at Brook like she was making up the whole thing.

'I put the phone on loudspeaker and I taped the call. It's all on here.' She held up the tape-recorder.

'What did they want?' he asked, still making no move to let her in.

'They said they're prepared to give me Paige back tonight if I turn up at the same place as last time with all the money I've got, plus some jewellery. Please. Listen to it, if you don't believe me. All I want to do is make sure Paige is safe.'

This time he finally moved aside and she went in.

'Are you okay?' she asked Cervantes as they walked back through to his study. His limp seemed a lot more pronounced.

'With this leg, I have good days and I have bad days. Today's one of the bad ones.'

He motioned for her to sit down, and Brook faced him across the desk. 'This doesn't seem right, Ms Connor.'

'Just call me Brook,' she said wearily. 'And what do you mean?'

'Why are they calling you now? If they'd wanted more money, either they would have asked for it in the first place or – if they wanted to extort more from you – they would have done it the next day, before you were on the run and while you still had access to cash. And if they were interested in handing Paige back to you, why did they set fire to your house?'

'I asked them that, too, and the man on the phone said they weren't the ones who set fire to it.'

Cervantes frowned. 'That doesn't make sense.'

Brook could see that she was losing him. 'Look, they even sent a photo of Paige. And check the date on it. It was taken today.' She rifled through her bag and pulled out the phone, bringing the photo back onto the screen. She paused to take a look at it, feeling a mixture of despair and hope, then handed the phone to Cervantes. 'It's definitely her,' she said. 'And those clothes have been bought by someone else for her.'

'The date could have been doctored – it's not that hard to do,' he said and handed the phone back, giving her a sympathetic look.

When a man who looks as beaten by the world as Chris Cervantes feels sorry for you, you know things really are bad.

He folded his hands on the desk and leaned forward. 'You said the kidnapper who called you told you to go to the same place you went before, right?'

Brook nodded. 'Tonight at midnight.'

'I'd put a bet on it that if you turn up there tonight, you'll be met by the police.'

'Why so?'

'Because that way the kidnapper – or kidnappers – can collect the reward that's out on your head. You know it's two hundred grand, right?'

'I thought it was a hundred.'

Cervantes shook his head. 'Tony Reyes doubled it this afternoon. What happened at his house, by the way?'

She gave him the short version.

When she'd finished, he gave her a grim smile. 'You've got balls, Brook. I'll give you that.'

'I'm going to give myself up anyway, so will you come with me if I go to the rendezvous tonight, in case they do have Paige? I've got six thousand dollars in cash on me. If they're not there, you can keep that money, as long as you promise to try to find her after I've been taken into custody.'

He shook his head. 'I've discharged my debt to you, Brook. You can call the police from here and wait here until they come for you, if you want, but that's the full extent of my involvement.'

All the earlier hope Brook had been feeling vanished now. What Cervantes was saying about the kidnappers made sense, and she suddenly felt foolish for believing they'd risk a handover for the sake of six thousand dollars and some jewellery. But she was determined to go to the rendezvous. Just in case.

'At least listen to the tape of the kidnapper's phone call,' she said. 'You might get a better idea of who I'm dealing with. Please.' She leaned across the table with the tape-recorder.

Cervantes sighed impatiently, but he took it and pressed Play.

There was a slight pause and then Brook's own voice came out of the tinny little speaker, clearly enough to hear the fear in her voice.

'Where's my daughter?'

'She's safe,' said the kidnapper.

On the tape, the tension in Brook's voice was obvious as she asked why the kidnappers hadn't given Paige back and, as she sat there in Cervantes's cramped little study, she could feel the hairs on her arms stand up as the man spoke again. 'We wanted to make sure you hadn't involved the police.'

She looked across at Cervantes as the tape continued, and straight away she could see that something was wrong. His eyes were wide with shock, his mouth hanging open.

'What is it?' she asked.

He stopped the tape and slammed the tape-recorder on the desk as if it was white-hot, then sat staring at it for at least ten seconds before he finally spoke, his voice shaking with disbelief. 'That man who phoned you about Paige ...' He paused.

'What about him?' she said urgently.

Cervantes stared at her and it looked as if he might cry. 'He's my son.'

42

'I used to work pretty closely with Chris Cervantes,' said Jenna as they drove towards his house. 'We're a small department, right. He'd probably been with us ten years at least when I joined, but originally he came up from LA, where he'd been with Robbery Homicide. People used to like him. I did. He was one of the boys. A good cop. Not afraid to get his hands dirty or to take on suspects.'

Giant flinched inside when she said this, because he didn't like to get his hands dirty or take on suspects. The previous night's incident with Tony Reyes had been an aberration. In truth, Giant was a run-of-the-mill cop just trying to do his job and, for whatever reason, that made him feel inadequate around the rest of the department, and particularly around Jenna.

'But he was also a bit of a fuck-up,' continued Jenna. 'He liked a drink too much, and the word was that he had a bit of a thing for hookers. And his son was a real bad seed. Cervantes never talked about him, but I know he'd served some serious time for drug dealing, robbery – that kind of thing. Anyways, although Cervantes had way more experience than me, we ended up getting partnered together.'

Giant smiled. 'Lucky him.'

She shrugged. 'He didn't see it that way. He thought he was going to end up being Chief of us detectives.' She paused. 'And then one day he got shot.'

Giant looked at her. 'What happened?'

'We were going to arrest a suspect who lived in an isolated place out in Moss Landing. The guy was a meth- and coke-dealer called Billy Harvey. But he was strictly small-time – a stick-thin little white guy with no history of violence – which was why there were only the two of us going around there. In hindsight, we should have taken backup, but that's what I meant about Chris. He preferred to go in and make the arrests himself. I think it was because he came from Robbery Homicide, where he was used to a bit more action.

'We parked some distance away, because we wanted to surprise Harvey. The place he lived in wasn't much more than a tumbledown shack set at the edge of a wood, which you could only reach down a long track, so it was well out of the way of the neighbours. We approached on foot, and we could tell he was in, because his car was out front. Chris reckoned that if we both knocked on the front door, Billy would run out the back and disappear into the woods, and Chris wanted to be the one to take him down. So he headed around to cover the back door and told me to give it a minute before I knocked on the front. I remember Chris was pretty pumped up, considering Billy was so small-time, whereas for me it was just a routine bust.'

She paused and screwed up her face in concentration. Giant thought it made her look cute. 'I remember everything about what happened next, like it was a couple of hours ago. I hammered on the door, but there was no answer. All the curtains at the front were pulled, so I couldn't see inside. I hammered again, shouted that it was the police, but again there was nothing. I didn't hear any commotion out the back, either, so I guessed Billy was hiding in there somewhere, hoping we'd go away. We had a warrant and the door was unlocked, so I drew my gun and went inside.

'It was silent in there, and very hot. We were right in the middle of a hot spell at the time, and the place stank of sweat and fried food. And straight away I started to get this bad feeling. I called out Billy's name again. And that was when I heard it. This kind of low whimper, coming from down the hallway. It was definitely human, and it sounded like someone was in pain. I went towards where it was coming from. There was this narrow little hallway with a door on either side that led down to the back of the shack.'

She paused again. The car was silent. Giant was completely wrapped up in her story. 'Both doors were open,' Jenna continued, 'but I didn't know from which one the sound had come. But then it came again, from behind the door on the right, except this time it was different. It was like a gasp. A sharp intake of breath. And then nothing.' She sighed. 'Jesus, this is tough for me talk about, you know. I've never really spoken about it to anyone before.'

Giant knew all too well how hard it was to put into words those grim experiences that fill your nightmares. Experiences like seeing the small, tortured bodies of the Hernandez children. 'Listen,' he said, 'you don't have to tell me, if you don't want to.'

She continued as if she hadn't heard him. 'I stood there in the hallway for two, three seconds. I had both hands on the gun, because that sharp intake of breath, it was like the sound of someone dying, and I was scared to go inside and find out who or what it was. I was alone in that house. I couldn't see or hear Chris. I called out again, something lame like "Billy, is that you? Are you okay?" Like they do in those teen horror movies I used to watch when I was a kid.

'And then, just like that, I saw a shadow appear in the opposite doorway and this figure, dressed all in black, came rushing out of it. He was a blur. Then there was this loud bang. I knew he was shooting at me. It was weird. We were only a few feet apart, and I didn't think – I just pulled the trigger, again and again. At the same time, because he was firing at me, I fell backwards and landed on the floor, and immediately I thought I'd been hit. I'd hit him, though, and he was stumbling all over the place, but he was still upright and holding the gun. He had a scarf pulled up over his face and was wearing a thick jacket, even though it was a boiling hot day, and I realized he probably had a Kevlar vest on, so I kept shooting, aiming at the head now. At the same time, two other guys came running out of the other room and one of them also had a gun pointed at me. I remember shooting him, and him going straight down like he'd been poleaxed, falling over the other guy I'd shot and landing face-first at my feet.

'The whole thing happened that fast. Three, four seconds at most, from the moment the first shooter came out, to the two of them dying in front of me. And I was in a complete state of shock, because nothing like this had ever happened to me before. You've never shot someone, have you?'

They were stopped at an intersection in a residential area not far from Cervantes's place. There was no traffic about. Giant looked at her and shook his head. 'No,' he said, trying to sound nonchalant, as if he needed to let her know that, if it came down to it, he definitely could. 'I've been lucky.'

She let out a long breath. 'It's a strange feeling. You're exhilarated, spaced out, frightened, ecstatic, depressed – all at the same time. And then suddenly you've got to drag yourself back to the present, because there's another suspect making a run for it. I got up as fast as I could and changed magazines on my gun, because I knew I'd let off a lot of shots. It turned out later that I'd fired nine, and six of them had hit their targets. The first guy had fired three as well, but they'd all missed. My ears were ringing from the gunfire, but even so I still heard the back door swing open as the third guy made a bolt for it. Then there was a delay of a couple of seconds. I always remember that, because I'd already taken off down the hall towards the back door, and then there was a single shot. I kept running out into the yard and saw Chris lying on the ground, holding his hip, while the suspect was running off into the trees. I checked to see that Chris was okay. He was in a bad way, but conscious and, typical of him, was telling me to get after the suspect. So I radioed it in, told Chris I'd be right back and took off after the guy. The problem was that he was fast and had a head start, so I lost him.

'We never found him, and the other two suspects were dead. So was Billy Harvey. They'd tied him to a chair and tortured him to death. We never really uncovered what had happened, whether it was a robbery gone wrong or something else, but we recovered a couple of pounds of dope and a whole pile of coke from the property, so maybe the gunmen were after that. Either way, the hip-shot that Chris took meant he was going to walk with a limp for the rest of his life and he was invalided out of the Force. He'd done close to his thirty years, so he got most of his pension, but the whole incident pretty much broke him. I think it was the shame of it, knowing that he – this old-school Robbery Homicide cop from the big city – froze under pressure when it came to it and couldn't pull the trigger. It didn't make it any easier for him that I could.'

Giant knew exactly how Cervantes must have felt, but it filled him with renewed admiration for Jenna.

'Anyways, that's the story,' she said. 'Chris left the Force under a cloud of his own making and didn't really keep in touch with anybody, least of all me. I haven't seen him since I visited him in hospital afterwards, and he didn't say a lot then. It'll be strange seeing him now, after all this time. I don't know how he'll react.'

'He's going to be the one under pressure,' Giant told her, 'especially if Brook Connor hired him for something, and Cervantes hasn't seen fit to tell us.'

43

Brook found it almost impossible to believe what Chris Cervantes had just told her about his son.

'Are you absolutely sure?' she asked him, but she could see from the stricken expression on his face that he was.

'I'm positive,' he said wearily.

Brook felt for him – she really did – but at the same time she was ecstatic at the prospect of this new, and potentially ground-breaking, lead. If they could get Paige back, then she finally had a chance of proving her innocence. 'We've got to find him, Chris. Do you know where he is?'

Cervantes placed his chin in his hands and stared down at the desk. 'I haven't seen him in a long time. We've been estranged for years.'

'Could he have done something like this? Kidnapped a little girl and committed murder?'

'I'd dearly love to say no, but sadly, I think that yes, he is capable of that. Especially if there's money involved. He's not a good man. He never has been.'

'Can you track him down for me?' Brook didn't attempt to keep the desperation out of her voice.

Cervantes pondered this for a moment. 'I think maybe I can. I know he was in jail for burglary until a few months ago, and that probably means he's still on probation. I could call one of my contacts in the department and see if I can get an address for him.' He hunted around the desk for his phone.

Brook could see it, partially covered by some paperwork, and she handed it to Cervantes and waited while he looked up the number and made the call, working hard to keep her excitement in check.

'Joe, how you doing?' said Cervantes, when the call was picked up at the other end. He sounded and looked happier now and was even smiling, and it struck her that human beings can be very good actors.

Brook listened impatiently as they made awkward small talk, before Cervantes slipped his son's name into the conversation, asking if Joe knew how to track him down.

After a few seconds Cervantes thanked him and wrote something down. He was just about to come off the phone when Joe must have said something else, because Cervantes suddenly frowned. 'That's right,' he said uneasily. 'I talked to her a few weeks ago. She wanted some work done – she didn't say what exactly – and she was meant to come and see me, but she never turned up. Then she left a couple of messages for me last week. If I'm truthful, I didn't think it was worth reporting.'

As they talked, Cervantes looked at Brook intensely, the smile gone. It was clear that she'd been connected to him, probably through her cellphone records, although Cervantes was doing a good job of making the connection sound as tenuous as possible.

There was a pause while Joe talked at the other end, then Cervantes apologized for holding him up from going home, said something about grabbing a beer sometime and ended the call.

'Where's your car?' he demanded.

'Out on your driveway. It's not mine. It belongs to Tony Reyes. The police don't know about it.'

'It doesn't matter. The police are on their way here now. You've got to get out of here, fast.'

'But we need to sort this out.'

'We will. Text me from the phone you're using, and I'll text you back when they've been and gone. Now go!'

Brook ran out of the front door and across the courtyard, shoving on her sunglasses and forcing herself to slow down to a casual walk as she made for the Rav4.

The street was quiet, but as she reversed out of the driveway she saw a car driving slowly down the street. It was barely thirty yards away, and there were two people in the front. It looked as if they trying to find a house. Conscious of her heart beating in her chest, Brook drove as slowly as she dared away from them, watching in the rear-view mirror as the car stopped directly outside Cervantes's house.

A man and a woman – both obviously cops, by their dress and demeanour – started to get out, but Brook kept her cool, saw a right turn ahead and took it, remembering to signal and thanking whoever was up there, watching over her, that once again she'd got away by the skin of her teeth.

Now all she needed was for Cervantes to keep his nerve with the cops and then lead her to his son.

After that, she'd do the rest.

44

When Chris Cervantes answered the door to Giant and Jenna, Giant saw immediately that he didn't look pleased to see her.

'How are you doing, Chris?' she asked him with a tight smile.

He gave her a nod in return. 'Jenna. Long time no speak. To what do I owe the pleasure?'

'It's official business. This is my partner, Detective Giant. Do you mind if we come in?'

Giant gave him a nod. Cervantes wasn't what he'd been expecting. He was on the short side – about five eight – with Latino features and a narrow, lined face flushed with booze-veins. He leaned heavily on a walking stick and, although he could only have been about fifty, it was the type of fifty that didn't much look like it was going to make sixty. Giant felt an immediate sense of superiority. He had nothing to prove to a man like this.

Cervantes stepped aside and let them in, limping down the narrow hallway into his kitchen, his stick banging heavily on the wooden floor. 'I guess you're here about Brook Connor,' he said, leaning back against a work counter that looked like it could do with a clean. He didn't seem unduly nervous.

He obviously wasn't going to offer them a seat, so they stood opposite him a few feet away. 'That's right,' answered Jenna. 'What were you and she in contact about?'

'Nothing,' he said, looking at Giant rather than Jenna. Giant could sense an atmosphere between the two of them, but that was no real surprise, in light of what she'd told him. 'Well, what I mean by nothing,' he continued, 'is that she – Brook Connor – contacted me a few weeks back. She said she wanted to hire me to do some work for her.'

'What kind of work?' asked Giant.

'She never actually said. She made an appointment to see me, but never turned up, so I let it go.'

Giant frowned. 'You didn't try to find out why Connor didn't come?' It didn't sound to him like the action of a private detective not to be curious.

'No.'

'You must be doing very well not to have to chase clients,' said Giant, looking around the dilapidated kitchen.

Cervantes shrugged, not rising to the bait. 'Busy enough that I don't have to put up with people who miss appointments. She also phoned and left messages a couple of times last week, apologizing for the missed appointment, and said she wanted to see me and that this time she'd definitely turn up.'

'Can we listen to them? The messages?' asked Giant.

'Sorry. I wiped them.'

Giant didn't believe him, and wondered why Cervantes was lying.

'Did Brook Connor say why she wanted to see you this time?' Jenna asked him.

Cervantes looked at her and there was something dismissive in his gaze that Giant didn't like. It was clear he'd have far preferred someone else coming here to question him, rather than Jenna. He shook his head. 'No. And I didn't call her back, either. Like I said, I don't enjoy being stood up; and I'm an ex-cop, so I don't tend to believe in second chances, either. If someone lets you down once, they'll do it again.'

'And you never thought to call and tell us this?' said Giant 'You must have known Connor was a wanted murder suspect. She's been all over the news for the past thirty-six hours,'

'Point taken,' said Cervantes, leaning hard on his walking stick. 'I should have done, but because I only spoke to her for about a minute and there was nothing useful in the conversation, I figured it wasn't worth clogging up your phone lines for.'

'Well, according to our phone records, it was four and a half minutes,' Giant told him.

Cervantes made a gesture with his free hand. 'Well, either way – one minute or four – Ms Connor didn't tell me what it was she wanted me for. So I had no information for you guys. I'm guessing you haven't been able to track her down yet?'

'We'll get her soon,' said Jenna.

'Well, good luck,' said Cervantes, signalling that as far as he was concerned, it was the end of the interview.

Giant didn't move. 'Who was that who just left your place in the Toyota Rav4?' he asked.

Cervantes didn't hesitate. 'A client.'

Giant sighed. There wasn't much else that he could ask. Cervantes had answered their questions. His story made sense, too, at least on the surface, and his account of the number of phone conversations he'd had with Brook Connor tied in with what they'd found in her records. But he found Cervantes's lack of curiosity as a PI hard to swallow; and his lack of desire – as an ex-cop fallen on hard times – to want to be a part of the manhunt for a quadruple murder suspect even harder. Cervantes might have been projecting an air of confidence while he'd been talking to them, but it was the work of an understudy rather than a first-night actor. And there was a tension about him that he couldn't quite hide. And wiping the messages, too ...

'Thanks for your help, Chris,' said Jenna after a pause. 'It's good to see you again. I hope you're doing all right.'

'I'm doing fine,' he said tightly. 'Thanks for asking.'

She gave him an awkward smile and asked him to get in touch with them if he heard anything from Ms Connor, then they left.

When they were back in the car, Jenna turned to Giant. 'Did he seem agitated to you? He did to me.'

Giant told her his own thoughts. 'Yeah, a little. He might be protecting Connor, although I can't think why. There's no evidence he even knew her. I'll let the marshals make the decision about whether it's worth putting him under surveillance.'

'It was weird seeing him like that,' said Jenna. 'All wizened and small, with that limp. He used to have so much confidence. You know, all the time I was talking to him in there, I kept thinking that it could have been me. All it would have taken was for one of those bullets fired at me to have hit its target and I'd have been dead or, even worse, a cripple with a pension, hanging around some shitty house and dying slowly day by day.' A shadow passed over her face, and Giant could see there was a lot of pent-up emotion there. 'That's why I don't like talking about it. It brings all the memories back.'

Giant wasn't sure what to say. He wasn't good at talking in depth with women. With anybody, really. It embarrassed him and he was always afraid of saying the wrong thing. In the end, he was saved by the crackle of the radio.

'All units. Be aware. We've had a reported sighting of Brook Connor driving a silver Toyota Rav4, heading north on Del Monte Avenue north Monterey, no more than five minutes ago. We've got a partial licence plate – seven LH.'

It was the car they'd seen leaving Cervantes's place earlier. Giant turned around and they drove back fast, lights flashing, but his white Dodge was no longer on the driveway.

The bastard had tricked them.

45

It was 8 p.m. and dusk, and Brook was sitting in the Rav4 on a deserted piece of waste ground just outside Monterey when Chris Cervantes pulled up beside her in the Dodge. She watched as he got out and limped over to the Rav's passenger side, leaning on his stick and carrying a pizza box under one arm. 'I got you this,' he said, climbing inside and putting the box on her lap, as well as a bottle of water.

Now that she knew Paige was alive and well, Brook's appetite had returned and, with her mouth already watering, she attacked the pizza, revelling in the smell of the pepperoni and fat, and eating the whole thing without so much as a word. When she'd finished, she downed the water in one go and wiped her face with the paper towel provided.

'I guess you needed that,' he said.

'Totally. Thank you.' She put the pizza box in the back seat and looked at him. 'What did the detectives say?'

'It was what I suspected. They were fishing. I told them we'd never actually met, and I think they bought it. They definitely didn't follow me here.'

'Are you sure they didn't put on a tracking device on your car?'

His face broke into a smile for the first time. 'You'll make a detective yet. I checked for that. They didn't. They'd need a subpoena for it anyways.'

'So what's the plan now?'

'According to the records, Luis, my son, lives just south of Salinas. It's a twenty-minute ride from here. Our best bet is to go there now and see if that's where he's holding Paige.'

'And if she's there, we call the police, right?'

He nodded. 'That's right. Then we call the police.'

Brook could see the doubt in his eyes. This had to be incredibly hard for Cervantes, knowing that his own son was a kidnapper and a murderer. There'd also be the huge shame he'd have to carry, if the crimes his son had committed ever came to light.

And that worried her.

'I'm putting all my trust in you, Chris. And so would Paige be, if she knew we were coming to get her. I know this is hard, but please don't weaken.'

'Look, if my son is something to do with this, then I want him to suffer the consequences. But I don't want us to do anything stupid, either, so if you're still armed, leave the gun here.'

'But what if he's got a gun?'

'I'm armed.' Cervantes lifted his jacket to reveal a shoulder holster containing a revolver with a scuffed handle.

'There's no way you'll shoot your own son.'

'No one's shooting anybody – least of all you. But we'll get the answers we need, and if Luis has your daughter, we'll find her. Have you still got the tape-recorder with his voice on it?'

She nodded.

'Then let's go. Where's your gun?'

Brook didn't want to be parted from it. She had no desire to shoot anyone else, but she'd put a bullet in Cervantes's son if she had to. The problem was that Cervantes probably knew it, and right now she needed his cooperation more than she needed the gun. 'It's in the glove compartment.'

He checked, saw it was there and climbed slowly out of the car.

'Are you sure you're okay?' she asked, watching him leaning hard on his stick as he limped heavily back to the Dodge.

'No,' he said without turning round. 'I haven't been okay in a long, long time.'

46

As Chris Cervantes drove, he told Brook about his son. It seemed he needed to unload everything to a sympathetic listener. He explained how he and his wife, June, had met when he'd been a cop in uniform and she was under investigation for assaulting an ex-boyfriend. Apparently the boyfriend had had it coming, and Cervantes himself, who'd been one of the arresting officers, thought she had real spunk and had been immediately attracted to her. 'I was always impulsive,' was his reasoning behind it. They'd started dating soon afterwards and although it had been a stormy relationship, they'd loved each other enough that when June became pregnant, they'd both been happy. 'It should have been the start of something amazing,' he said, 'but it was the beginning of the end. Of everything.'

The birth of their son, Luis, coincided with Cervantes's promotion to detective in LA's Robbery Homicide division. He was working long hours, drinking too much, by his own admission, and keeping out of the way of home, where a screaming baby wasn't much of a relief from the stresses of the job. This had infuriated June, who left him a number of times – sometimes taking Luis with her, sometimes not. On those occasions when she didn't take him (which became more and more frequent), Cervantes palmed off his son on whichever relative he could find to look after him.

Eventually, when Luis was about seven or eight (Cervantes couldn't remember exactly), June left for good, and without leaving a forwarding address. Cervantes tried to look after Luis, but failed and eventually he went to live with his paternal grandparents out in Pasadena, with Cervantes visiting whenever he could.

With a cold predictability, Luis began to go off the rails. He was caught dealing drugs at school, then charged with burglary and eventually ended up in juvie, where he remained for several years, after a series of assaults on staff and other prisoners. By the time he was released he was in his late teens (Cervantes seemed vague on all the dates) and his mom, who was now living way to the north in Salinas with a new husband, had reappeared in his life. Luis immediately left to live with June, not even bothering to say goodbye to his father, whom he'd seen little of in the previous years, and quickly changing his last name to McPherson, after June's new husband.

'I failed Luis, I think,' said Cervantes, staring out into the growing darkness.

Brook raised an eyebrow. 'You think?'

'Okay, I *did* fail him. June and I both did. I tried to reconnect with him, even transferring up here so I wasn't far away, but he didn't want to know. I could tell he hated me. I think Luis hated the whole world. He didn't last long at his mom's. From what I heard, he stole from her, got into trouble and eventually ended up in jail again. I've kept an eye on what's been happening to him over the years, but none of it's been good, and I stopped trying to make contact with him a long time ago.'

It was a classic story. Both parents too busy or self-absorbed to look after their child. Child feels unloved and insecure. Does everything he can to get attention, including acting very destructively. Eventually grows up into a dysfunctional adult. Even so, Brook thought it took a special kind of badness to do what Cervantes's son had done. A lot of people have bad upbringings. A lot go off the rails. Most of them eventually get back on them and make something of their lives. So her sympathy, both for Cervantes and his son, was limited.

'How old's he now?' she asked.

He had to think about that. 'We had him when I was twenty-one. I'm fifty-one now, so I guess he'd be thirty.'

Brook thought back to what Annie had told her earlier in the day about the woman who'd confronted her dad all those years ago, claiming to be pregnant with his child. Was it possible that one of June Cervantes's infidelities had been with Brook's own father, and that Luis was *his* son, not Cervantes's? Was Luis doing this out of some kind of revenge against her? It was tenuous, but it made sense.

'What are you going to do if Paige isn't there and your son doesn't want to cooperate?' she asked Cervantes.

'Then we call the police and Luis has to explain the tape to them. The recording's enough to get a warrant to search his house and car. They may even be able to link him to the cellphone he gave you. He definitely won't want us to involve the police.'

'But what's his incentive to cooperate? Because if Luis leads us to Paige, I'm still going to have to involve the police to clear my own name.'

Cervantes was silent for a moment. Brook tried to read his expression, but it was blank, inscrutable, although a single bead of sweat ran from his temple to his cheek. 'He'll have an incentive because I'll be pointing a gun at him,' he said at last.

'You're his father. He knows you won't shoot him.'

'I made a mistake last time. I won't make it again.'

Brook stared at him. 'What do you mean?'

'I mean,' Cervantes said, still staring out into the night, 'that this limp that I carry – this shitty, godforsaken life that I lead – is all down to Luis.' He turned to Brook and the anger was visible all over his face as he spoke. 'My son was the man who pulled the trigger and ended my career.'

47

The man now officially leading the hunt for Brook Connor was a short, squat US marshal with a buzz-cut and a swagger, who was straight out of central casting, called Seamark Jeffs. He'd done nothing to conceal his irritation when Giant had reported back that he and Jenna had been within a few yards of Connor and had somehow managed to avoid apprehending her. The fact that they hadn't known it was her – nor could they have known what car she was driving at the time – was irrelevant, as far as Jeffs was concerned. He was pissed because they'd taken Chris Cervantes's word as fact and had not done more to get the truth out of him. But most of all he was pissed because he'd been in charge for more than twenty-four hours and had still not been able to bring his fugitive to justice. And so he took it out on Giant.

Giant had taken the shit that Jeffs had thrown at him without resisting too much, thankful at least that he'd done so in the Chief's office, with only the Chief as witness, and not Jenna, who'd finished for the night. The Chief hadn't tried to intervene on Giant's behalf. It was clear that he also thought Giant and Jenna should have done better somehow, although quite how he didn't actually say.

Giant had left the station feeling like a kid who'd been chastised by the principal, wishing he'd stood up for himself more. It was a familiar feeling and it made him think – not for the first time – that his mom and his former boss had been right. Maybe he would have been better in a different job.

Whenever he felt sorry for himself, Giant ate, and fifteen minutes later he was at home frying succulent pieces of breaded chicken in oil, using a recipe that his mom had perfected many years ago, when his cellphone rang.

He almost let the call go. His mouth was watering so much at the prospect of a decent meal that he didn't think he'd be able to hold back, but when he saw that the caller was one of his detectives, Joe Padilla, who never rang at this time unless it was important, he was curious enough to pick up. 'What's up?' he said, removing the chicken from the pan piece by piece and putting it onto a plate covered with absorbent towels.

'I've got a bit of a problem, Boss. You know I told you about the phone records showing that Brook Connor had been in contact with Chris Cervantes? I'm hearing now that we're looking for Cervantes in connection with the Logan Harris murder. Is that right?'

'It is. He met with Connor today and didn't report it to us. No one can quite work out why. You used to work with him, didn't you? What was he like?'

'He liked a drink, and he could be pretty tough, but he was straight as an arrow. I can't see how he'd be mixed up in this. But the reason I'm calling you now is that Chris phoned me earlier, before I left for the night. He wanted to track down his son, Luis McPherson. The kid's bad news. He's been behind bars for most of the past three years for robbery, and now he's out on probation. Chris wanted to know if I had an address for him.' Padilla paused for a moment. 'I know it's against policy to give out information to a civilian, but because Chris is an ex-cop and a friend, and I didn't think he was involved in any of this, I gave him the address. I'm sorry, Boss, I know I made a mistake, but will you be able to cover my back with the marshals and the Chief?'

'I'll sort it somehow,' said Giant, pleased to be able to do his colleague a favour. He wasn't angry at Padilla. These things happened, and Padilla wasn't to know that Cervantes could be involved in all this. 'What time did he call?'

'I left work at seven, so it would have been just before that.'

Giant glanced at his watch. A little over an hour ago would have been about the time Brook Connor's car had been leaving Cervantes's place. Was she going to see his son for some reason? Giant took Luis McPherson's address from Padilla, told him he'd take care of everything and then called Jenna.

When she answered, it sounded like she was outside and Giant felt an immediate flash of disappointment – wondering if she was doing something fun without him? 'I've got some news,' he told her. 'Where are you?'

'Out shopping for some food. What is it?'

He told her about the call from Joe Padilla. 'I want to get over there now, see if the son can throw any light on what his old man or Brook Connor want with him. The timing's all very coincidental. Do you want to come with me?'

'Sure. Do you think we need to call in reinforcements?'

Giant thought of Seamark Jeffs bawling him out in the Chief's office, as if he was some snot-nosed intern rather than a senior detective. 'No. It's not a raid. We're just going to talk to the guy. If things look suspicious, we'll call in backup then. He lives over near Salinas. Do you want me to come and get you en route?'

'No, from where I am, it'll be easier to meet you over there. I'll park close by and wait for you to arrive.'

Giant gave her the address, ate a piece of the chicken and then, unable to stop himself, ate the rest, before finally hurrying out the door, hoping to put one over on the US Marshals Service by bringing in Brook Connor before anyone else did.

48

'Why did you never report your son for what he did to you?' Brook asked Cervantes as they drove along a quiet stretch of road towards his son's house.

She was angry with him. She'd been angry with him ever since he'd told her that Luis had been the man who'd shot him. Because if Cervantes had done something about it then, her own life would still be intact, and Paige would be sleeping softly in her bed surrounded by her toy animals, and Luis McPherson would be rotting in jail.

'I didn't hand him in because he was my son, and I guess I knew that I'd let him down and was responsible for what he'd become. I thought about confronting him afterwards, but when he ended up in jail for something else a few weeks later, I figured it was best to let him be If it's any consolation to you, I regret that decision now.'

'It's not,' she said, staring out of the window. Night had fallen and trees lined both sides of the road now, with signs containing house names and numbers or mailboxes nailed to the occasional one, and narrow driveways disappearing off into the woods. According to the satnav on the dashboard, they were almost there.

Cervantes slowed the car. 'That's it,' he said, as they passed a narrow turning on the left and he pulled over to the side of the road just beyond it.

'How are we going to do this?' asked Brook as they walked along the edge of the road, back to the turning.

'Carefully,' he said. 'And I'll do the talking.'

He didn't cut a particularly impressive figure, with his cheap suit and painful-looking limp, and she wondered if she was making a big mistake letting him take the lead.

A car came past, its headlights temporarily blinding her, and she stepped into the undergrowth, keeping her head down and a hand over her face to prevent herself being recognized. The car slowed down as it passed them, then immediately picked up speed again.

Brook cut in behind Cervantes as they walked down the track towards the house where, according to the probation service, Luis McPherson was currently residing. It was a ramshackle wooden property, with a dark-coloured pickup in front. The lights were on inside and the curtains were drawn.

A security light came on as they approached and Cervantes stopped. 'Let's have a look around the back,' he whispered, and they made their way around the side of the house, keeping in tight to the undergrowth. There was a small yard at the back and, although it backed onto pine trees, the grass was long and unkempt, and it was clear that the photo of Paige earlier that day hadn't been taken there.

The curtains were drawn at the back of the house as well, making it impossible to see who, if anyone, was inside.

Cervantes tried the back door, but it was locked. He mouthed the words 'Don't worry', then leaned on his stick and took a small cloth package from inside his jacket. Next, he placed the stick against the door and got very slowly and stiffly down onto one knee. That was when Brook saw that the package contained a set of picks and, as she watched, Cervantes carefully picked the lock until the handle turned with a satisfying click.

She put her hands under his shoulders and helped him back to his feet, her finger brushing against his shoulder holster. Cervantes was light and only a couple of steps away from frail, and it occurred to Brook that she could take the gun from him right then and there. She knew she'd have no problem getting Luis Cervantes to talk, no matter how tough he thought he was. She'd fired a gun in anger on two occasions now, and she'd shot two men. The fact that both of those incidents had happened in the past forty-eight hours had hardened her considerably.

Cervantes must have guessed what she was thinking because he turned his body away and gave her a sharp look, before slipping the gun from its holster. 'Don't do anything stupid, Brook,' he whispered. 'This is dangerous enough without me having to worry about you.'

She nodded and stood to one side, out of sight of whoever might be behind the door, as Cervantes opened it and stepped inside. She gave it a couple of seconds and followed him into a narrow, unlit hallway that ran the length of the house. Light spilled out from a room up ahead, and Brook could hear the sound of someone moving about inside.

Cervantes led the way. He was moving at an almost glacial pace, his gun in one hand, his stick in the other, trying not to make it tap on the floor. As she walked behind him, Brook looked around for any sign that she was in the same place where the first photo of Paige had been taken, or indeed for any sign that she'd been here, like kid's toys, but the place was largely empty and there was nothing familiar about it.

Cervantes stopped at the open door and then, taking the revolver from its holster, stepped into the light.

'Hello, Luis,' he said, and Brook felt a potent mix of fear and relief as she moved around behind Cervantes, still keeping in the shadows, and saw for the first time the man who'd kidnapped her daughter.

He was a good three inches taller than his father, lean and rangy and surprisingly good-looking, with well-defined features, long dark hair and golden skin – more like a surfer than the hardened criminal she'd been expecting. He was standing in a large kitchen wearing jeans and a hooded jacket, and holding a half-eaten sandwich in one hand. Next to him, on the table, was an open holdall and a gun that was a few feet out of his reach.

He looked at Cervantes in surprise, and then his lips formed into a thin smile. 'Well, well, well. Long time no see, Dad. What brings you here?'

Brook immediately recognized his voice from the earlier phone call and she felt her whole body tighten as the adrenalin surged through her.

'Why are you pointing a gun at me, Dad?' he continued. 'And who's that behind you?' He saw Brook, and his expression tightened. 'So it's not a social call, then?'

'We're way beyond social calls,' said Cervantes, his voice trembling with emotion. 'You know why I'm here. I heard the tape of your call to Brook. The one where you demanded ransom money for the return of her daughter.'

'Sorry, Dad,' MacPherson said. 'I don't know what you're talking about.' There was something mocking in his tone that made Brook seethe with anger.

'You know exactly what he's talking about,' she said, stepping into the light. 'I've got you on tape, telling me that you know where my daughter is and demanding more money from me. I've also got the photo you sent of Paige.'

'You must have the wrong person, bitch,' he said, the handsome face now twisted in a sneer. 'But what I do know is that, even with your hair cut short like that, you're the woman the cops are looking for about all those killings.'

'Well, maybe it's time for us to call the cops then and play them the tape,' she said. 'Perhaps I'll use the cellphone you left for me.'

She could see him tense. He was scared. But the tape on its own wasn't going to convict him of anything, or the photo – even an amateur like her realized that. So there was something else worrying him.

'Where is she, Luis?' said Cervantes.

'It's Lou. I haven't been Luis since I was a kid.'

'She's a little girl. She's five. Please tell me you haven't hurt her. We just need to know where she is.'

'Why don't you stop pointing that gun at me, Dad?'

'Not until you tell us where that little girl is. Is she here?'

'I don't know what you're talking about.'

'What's in the bag, Son? It looks like you're going away somewhere.'

'You don't get to ask me questions, Dad. You haven't earned that right.'

Brook could see McPherson looking towards the gun on the table next to the bag, only feet away from his left hand. She would have run in and grabbed it herself, but Cervantes was blocking her path.

'Tell us, you cowardly asshole!' she hissed from behind him, the frustration at this impasse getting the better of her. 'Is my daughter here?'

'I don't know shit about no little girl,' said McPherson. 'You're insane, coming here like this, making accusations. Dad, you might want to calm this woman down. And you might want to be careful about the company you keep. She's wanted for mass murder.'

Brook wanted to kill him then. To rip the arrogant bastard apart, piece by piece, until he told her where Paige was. Because right now McPherson might have been tense, but he was nowhere near scared enough. He needed to experience the kind of fear that Brook had had to endure these past four days.

She considered grabbing the gun from Cervantes, but it was too risky with the other gun still on the kitchen table. She didn't like the expression on Cervantes's face, either. He looked torn and indecisive.

'Don't let this bastard move,' she whispered in his ear. 'If Paige is here, I'm going to find her.'

She looked round hurriedly, shouting Paige's name and ignoring McPherson's shout to get the fuck out of his house, and almost immediately she saw a door that led down to the basement. If you were going to hide someone, that was where you'd do it.

She unbolted the door and opened it, staring into the darkness. 'Paige. Are you in there?'

No answer. No movement.

She stepped inside, fumbling on the wall until she found the light switch. A short flight of wooden steps led down into a gloomy, windowless space lit by a single naked bulb hanging from the ceiling. Leaving the door open behind her, she descended the steps, noticing the strong smell of disinfectant.

A workbench with a buzz-saw took up a chunk of space, and a large, well-used hacksaw hung from the wall behind it. On one side of the bench were a couple of boxes, one of which contained more DIY tools and other assorted junk, while on the other side there was a washing machine and large chest freezer. There was nothing to suggest that Paige had ever been here.

Brook approached the bench. The smell of disinfectant was stronger here, and she could see that the wooden surface and the razor-sharp saw-blade had both recently been cleaned meticulously. Even so, there were still a string of dark flecks on the woodwork beneath the base of the blade, with more dotted about on other parts of the bench.

She felt her breathing get faster, not liking the feeling she was getting, then turned towards the chest freezer, staring at it for several seconds before finally pulling open the lid.

She let out a cry when she saw what was in there.

'Oh, Jesus!' she whispered, her voice cracking. 'Jesus, no.'

Slamming the lid shut, she raced back up the stairs and back into the hallway.

Cervantes was still standing a few yards away, pointing his gun into the kitchen, but he looked scared. 'Don't pick that gun up, Luis!' he called out, the fear in his voice obvious.

'What are you going to do, Dad? Shoot your own son?' McPherson demanded inside the kitchen.

'I should have done it last time. It would have saved the world a lot of trouble.'

'There are body parts in the freezer in the basement!' Brook called out, still reeling from the shock of what she'd just seen, but knowing that she needed to steel Cervantes's resolve. 'It's Paige's nanny – Rosa. Your son's a killer!'

'I know he is,' said Cervantes. 'He murdered a drug dealer three years ago. You still have to answer for that, Luis.' His face tightened. 'Do not pick up that gun. I will shoot you, and I won't miss.' But as he spoke the words his hands were shaking, and Brook already knew what was going to happen.

'Dad, no!' McPherson shouted.

Cervantes opened his mouth to say something and his eyes widened. At the same time, his finger tightened on the trigger.

'Don't kill him!' Brook screamed. 'He's my only—'

The shot exploded around the house with a deafening blast, and Brook's eyes reflexively shut.

A second shot followed a moment later and, as her eyes opened again, she saw Cervantes stagger backwards and fall to the floor, his gun, and then his stick, clattering after him. He rolled over onto his side so that he was facing her, his eyes wide and uncomprehending, one hand clutching at his rapidly reddening shirt, the other reaching out towards her in a last desperate gesture. Then the hand dropped and he lay still.

Cervantes's gun was no more than five yards away from her, and Brook was moving towards it, but had barely put one foot in front of the other when McPherson appeared in the doorway, pointing the smoking pistol at her.

She stopped dead. She and McPherson faced each other. Adrenalin pumped through her, fuelled by anger. But she was trapped. The gun was too far away, and she'd never make it to the back door before McPherson put a bullet in her.

McPherson glared at her. 'You really fucked things up, bitch.'

'Just tell me where my daughter is and I won't say a word about any of this, or come after you in any way,' Brook said quietly.

'You might not have noticed but you're not exactly in a position to make demands.' He aimed the gun at her chest. 'So you taped my call, did you? That was the cleverest move you've made all week. Give me the tape, and the cell I called you on.'

'I haven't got them.'

But she did. In the pocket of the hoodie she was wearing. And although she was putting on her best poker face, it was obvious he didn't believe her.

'Either you can hand them over or I can search your corpse for them. You choose. But be quick about it.'

Book took out the tape-recorder and slid it across the floor to him, then hesitated for a second before taking out the cell, knowing it was the only proof she had that her whole story was true. She cursed herself for not leaving it somewhere else, but everything had happened so fast. Reluctantly, she slid it across the floor.

McPherson picked up both items and placed them in the front pocket of his jeans, so that the top of the phone was sticking out of it. He smiled at her, making no effort to lower the gun.

'I've sent another copy of the tape to my lawyer,' she told him, playing for time, 'naming you as the man in the call. It's not going to take the police long to track you down, especially as your father called one of his former colleagues to get your address. If you kill me, it's another homicide against your name, but all I care about is getting my daughter back. Just tell me where she is and, as far as I'm concerned, I never saw any of this.'

McPherson looked confused as he tried to work out what to do with this new information. 'You're bullshitting me.'

'Why would I? I was always going to make backups.' Her voice sounded surprisingly calm. She was still terrified, but not as much as she had been the previous night, when Maria Reyes had been pointing the gun at her. Maybe, in some bizarre way, she was simply adapting to this violent new life of hers.

'I can't let you go,' he said at last.

'All I want is my daughter.'

'You don't get any of this, do you? Right from the beginning, you were never going to see her again.'

'Why not, for Christ's sakes? What have I ever done to you?'

'Sorry, bitch, but you were just in the wrong place at the wrong time.' He raised the gun and shut one eye, and Brook realized he was aiming at her.

The whole world fell silent.

And then, without warning, his father's body juddered and it sounded like he actually groaned.

McPherson frowned and tried to look back over his shoulder to see what was going on.

Four days ago Brook would have stayed frozen to the spot, waiting for the inevitable, but now she took her chance and dived to one side and straight through the open basement door, as two shots rang out in quick succession and glass shattered.

She lay sprawled on her front on the wooden steps and, in one movement, leaped back up and slammed the door shut behind her, then ran halfway down the steps before jumping through the air, yanking the light bulb and the cable holding it from the ceiling and plunging the room into darkness. Landing on her feet, she crept over to the workbench and felt about in the box of tools for a weapon – anything that she could use to defend herself against McPherson's attack – quickly locating a large spanner. It would probably be useful only as a missile, but it was better than nothing.

Then she crouched down to wait in the darkness.

A minute passed. Then two.

She heard McPherson moving about outside and tried to calm her breathing as she prepared for the inevitable. She might die, but she'd die fighting.

And then she heard the sound of the bolt being pulled across the door and footsteps walking away, and it struck her, with a sinking heart, that he didn't need to come in here to kill her because, right now, she was crouching in her very own tomb.

49

McPherson cursed his luck. He didn't know how the hell his old man and Brook Connor had found him, but if they'd just come ten minutes later he would have missed them. He'd already packed and cleaned the place up before they'd arrived, but then, typically, he'd got hungry. And now, because of that fucking appetite of his, he'd been completely caught out.

He walked back into the kitchen, ignoring the corpse of his father, who, as far as he was concerned, had been dead to him for years anyhow, and put down the gun, thinking through his options while he finished the remainder of his ham-and-cheese sandwich. The most effective option would be to go into the basement and kill Connor. That way, at least he'd have a chance to get rid of all three bodies and clean up afterwards. He'd still have to go on the run and with a lot less money now, but there was nothing that could be done about that.

The problem with this first option, though, was obvious. Brook Connor might have been a rich bitch living the easy life, but the fact that she'd come this far showed she was no pushover, and he risked getting injured or even killed if he went into the basement after her. McPherson would never admit to himself that he was a coward, but he wasn't prepared to take that risk.

A second option was to burn the place down and get rid of all the evidence that way, but McPherson had enough knowledge of forensics to know that the cops would quickly be able to tell that it was arson, and even if the fire burned for hours, there'd be traces of all three corpses, and then he really would be heading for the chair.

In the end he decided on the third option, which was to leave Connor down there for now. There was no way she could get out, and it bought him time to get as far away as possible from here with his hundred and twenty-five grand.

He put down the sandwich, grabbed the solitary Coors that was in the fridge and drank it quickly. He was certain Connor and his old man wouldn't have called the cops before they came here, but there was no point hanging around. The sooner he was gone, the better. Then he could think things through and come up with a better plan.

But as he put down the empty beer can, he caught sight of the figure reflected in the glass.

He turned round, saw the gun and knew that on this occasion his time really was up.

50

Time passed in the darkness and Brook waited, spanner in hand, feeling increasingly claustrophobic, conscious that she was only feet away from the frozen body parts of the woman who'd shared her home for the past two years, knowing that she could end up in exactly the same situation – murdered and dismembered – if McPherson chose to come down here.

And yet he didn't. Brook had no idea how long had passed since she'd been there. It could have been five minutes. It could even have been ten.

And then she heard voices coming from beyond the door. They were very faint, but she knew wasn't mistaken.

Slowly she stood up and felt her way over to the staircase, wanting to hear more. But the voices had already stopped. And then, just as silence began to descend again, a shot rang out that made her start.

Brook stayed perfectly still, trying to work out what this meant. Had the police arrived? Had McPherson shot himself?

She heard the faint sound of footfalls in the hallway, followed a second later by the bolt being pulled back across the door to unlock it. Someone was coming inside.

As silently as possible, she slunk back further back into the darkness, raising the spanner above her head, ready to throw it.

Giant and Jenna moved quickly down the track towards the house where, according to the probation services, Luis McPherson lived. Their guns were drawn and Giant was tense. Chris Cervantes's car was on the road outside, but there was no sign of the Rav4 that Brook Connor was supposedly driving.

As they reached the door, Giant peered through the strip of frosted glass and saw the body. The walking stick down by its side suggested it was probably Chris Cervantes. Giant felt his whole body tighten. He'd seen too many corpses in the last forty-eight hours.

He knew he should definitely call for backup, but something stopped him. It was the memory of his dad coming home from work in his pristine uniform when Giant was a little kid and was always pleased to see him. All his life, Giant had wanted to make his old man proud, and yet somehow he'd always fallen short. This time he wasn't going to.

'Let's go round the back,' he whispered to Jenna.

Still holding the spanner, Brook mounted the steps, conscious of the deep, oppressive silence in the house. She guessed she'd been down there a good ten minutes since that single shot, maybe even longer. During that time she'd heard absolutely nothing. But she also knew it could be a trap. Why else would someone have pulled the bolt across the door to give her an escape route?

She stopped when she got to the top of the steps and put her ear to the door. Finally, gripping the spanner tightly, she grabbed the handle and slowly pulled it open, half-expecting someone to be standing there with a gun. But as she slowly poked her head out, she saw that the hallway was empty, except for Chris Cervantes's body, which lay where it had fallen. Brook knew it was her actions that had killed him, just as they had Maria Reyes. It was a heavy burden to carry and, whatever happened after this, she'd be carrying it for the rest of her days.

She considered running out the back door and getting as far away as possible, but curiosity got the better of her and she crept along the hallway, unable to stop herself looking at Cervantes's corpse. His shirt was heavily stained, but there wasn't as much blood as she'd thought there would be. His eyes were closed, and in truth he looked like he was asleep. She thought about the fact that he'd gone out of his way to bring her pizza earlier. It had been a kind act. And one that had got him precisely nowhere.

It was when she reached the kitchen door that she saw Luis McPherson. He was lying on his back in the middle of the floor, one arm in his lap, the other splayed out over his shoulder as if he was doing backstroke. He wasn't moving.

Brook went over and looked down at him. The man who'd kidnapped Paige was dead. He'd been shot in the side of the head, close to his temple, leaving a large exit wound on the other side that had torn part of his skull away. He'd obviously been shot at point-blank range and there was a lot more blood, most of it in a pool around him. A gun – it looked like the one she'd seen on the kitchen table earlier – was lying a few feet away.

The first thing Brook thought was that McPherson had shot himself, but then she saw that the cellphone she'd given him was no longer sticking out of his front pocket. She leaned down to get a closer look, but the pockets were definitely empty. The tape-recorder wasn't there, either.

She looked round hurriedly. Neither item was on any of the worktops. McPherson's holdall was still on the table, so she pulled it open and looked inside, but there was nothing in there but some clothes and toiletries.

That was when she realized there was no way he'd killed himself, and that once again she was being set up, because the tape-recorder and the cell were the only items of evidence that proved her innocence.

'Shit,' she cursed aloud. 'Shit, shit, shit!'

She walked out into the hallway, her mind a maelstrom of confusion as she tried to work out what she was going to do now.

And then the decision was made for her, as she saw two figures taking aim and heard angry shouts of 'Police! Get on the floor now!' breaking the heavy silence in the house.

51

The police interview room

Now

Utterly exhausted, Brook finished her account and sat back in the hard seat. Her back ached and her mouth felt dry.

Detective Giant exhaled loudly. 'Well, that was some story, Brook. To be at three different crime scenes where, by my estimation, there were a total of five victims – and not to have participated in any of the killings – that's got to be a record.'

Detective Jenna King fixed Brook with a cold stare. 'Either you're the unluckiest person in the world or you're lying. And to think that your own lawyer's involved, too, seeing as she's the attorney of one of the victims and met up with Maria Reyes just before she was murdered.'

'She wasn't murdered,' said Brook.

Jenna shrugged. 'The fact remains that your attorney met her, and now she won't tell us what the meeting was about.'

'My client's already given you Maria Reyes's explanation for our meeting,' said Angie, 'and I don't want to add any more than that.'

'And I'm telling the truth about what happened,' said Brook, who knew how her story must sound to them. She looked at Angie, who gave her a nod to let her know that she had everything under control.

Angie turned back to the two detectives. 'My client is *not* lying to you and let's face it: what *is* her motive in all this? Yes, it's possible she may have had a motive for killing her husband. But let's assume for a moment she did kill him, then why start a fire to advertise her crime? Why not just dump the body somewhere?'

Detective King opened her mouth to say something, but Angie put up a hand to stop her. 'And if my client wanted to kill Maria Reyes, in revenge for the affair she was having with her husband,' she continued, 'why, having abducted her at gunpoint, would she drive to the family home to kill her in front of her husband and several other armed men? And what possible motive did she have for killing Mr Cervantes and his son? Or for dismembering her nanny, Miss Fernandez, a woman with whom she enjoyed an excellent relationship?'

'We don't know Ms Connor's exact motives yet,' said Giant, 'but you know as well as I do that spree killers are often illogical. The point is there's a stack of evidence against your client right now.'

'Really?' said Angie, raising her eyebrows. 'I don't think so. And let's talk about someone who's missing from this discussion so far. My client's daughter, Paige.'

'Stepdaughter,' said Detective King harshly. 'A stepdaughter she would have lost, if her husband had left her.'

'I'm assuming you've still found no trace of her,' said Angie.

'Not yet,' said King. 'But we have a major multi-agency search going on.'

'Look,' said Angie, as she consulted her notes, 'we know Paige was picked up from kindergarten at two p.m. on Wednesday afternoon by Rosa, and that was the last time she was seen by anyone. My client was at her office in Santa Cruz with her own clients at the time, and she didn't leave until seven p.m. Camera footage and witnesses will corroborate that. Are you suggesting that she'd cold-heartedly arranged the kidnapping of Paige, the murder of Rosa and that of Logan twenty-four hours later, and that Paige is now being held at an undisclosed location? If she wanted to get rid of her husband, why not just have him killed? Why go to all that trouble?'

'Some people like to show how clever they are,' said King. 'Maybe she thought it would work better like that.'

'By starting a fire in her own yard and then abducting her husband's lover? That doesn't sound remotely clever.'

Brook could see that Detectives Giant and King still looked completely unconvinced.

Angie hadn't finished. 'My client says Maria Reyes shot herself. Surely we can prove whether or not she did. Is the autopsy report available yet?'

Brook saw from their expressions that this had caught them out.

'Not yet,' said Giant.

'Okay. Please can you share its conclusion, when it's ready. And another thing: have you examined the gun used to kill Cervantes and his son – assuming it's the same weapon – for prints? My client claims she never touched that gun. And she was arrested at the scene without gloves on, so if she had shot them, her prints would be on it, wouldn't they?'

'We haven't had the results back yet,' said Giant. 'But we'll be sure to let you know them as soon as we do.'

'Please do,' said Angie, 'because they'll prove my client's innocence. You see, someone's set her up to take the blame for all of this. And it's the same person who killed Cervantes and his son, and who's almost certainly holding Paige against her will.'

'That's all well and good,' said Giant, 'but do you have any idea who this person might be?'

And this was their big problem of course, because in the end Brook knew that neither she nor Angie had a clue who lay behind this. And even as Brook was thinking this, she was wondering where Angie herself had been earlier that evening, and whether she knew more about Paige's abduction than she was letting on.

Angie looked at Brook, then at Detective King and finally at Giant. 'The person you should be looking for is someone calm, well versed in forensics and familiar with crime scenes. Someone well connected enough to cover their tracks as effectively as they have …' She raised her eyebrows at the two detectives in turn. 'Maybe a police officer.'

52

Giant gave Angie Southby a withering look. 'So now you're accusing us? You're getting pretty desperate here, aren't you?'

Southby shrugged. 'I'm just giving you some alternatives to your current theory. We still have the issue of the photo of you meeting up with my client's dead husband ten days ago.' She gave Giant the kind of probing look that he knew was meant to intimidate him. The fact was that he was worried. He hadn't expected Southby to bring this back up, and he knew that if there were any copies of the photo out there, he was going to have to destroy them, otherwise he was in serious trouble. In the meantime, though, he needed to head this off at the pass once again.

'I told you already,' he said, 'there must be some mistake. I've never met Logan Harris.'

'It was you,' said Connor with a certainty that unnerved him.

'Well, I'm telling you it wasn't. And be careful what accusations you make without evidence.'

'What are you going to do?' Connor answered petulantly. 'Lock me up?'

Angie Southby raised a hand to shut her up. 'Look, Detectives,' she said. 'My client's told you what happened. She's answered your questions. And she very strongly states her innocence. So if you're not going to charge her, then we'd like to go.'

'You know it doesn't work like that,' said Jenna.

Southby stared her down. 'Are you charging her?'

Jenna glanced across at Giant, who addressed Southby directly. 'Not yet, but she's not being released, either. I'm afraid you're going to be staying here tonight, Ms Connor.'

Angie Southby started to protest, but Giant terminated the interview and headed into the observation room, where the Chief and the lead marshal, Seamark Jeffs, had been watching proceedings through a one-way mirror.

The Chief looked as exhausted as Giant felt. It was now 2.30 a.m. and it had been a long day for all of them. Seamark Jeffs, however, was sitting ramrod-straight in his chair and looking totally alert. Giant knew that Jeffs was royally pissed off that it was he and Jenna who'd made the Brook Connor arrest, and not Jeffs's own team, and knew too that he wasn't going to get an apology. He'd expected to get a little bit of praise from the Chief, though, but that wasn't forthcoming, either.

'What the hell's all that about a photo of you with Logan Harris?' were the Chief's first words to Giant.

'It's just them pissing in the wind, sir,' answered Giant with a confidence he wasn't feeling. 'I don't know what the hell they're talking about. So what do you want to do, regarding charges?'

'Connor's story sounds like a crock of shit,' said Jeffs.

'I'd agree with that,' said Jenna.

The Chief looked at Giant. 'And you?'

The problem was that Giant still had plenty of doubts. 'According to the pathologist, Maria Reyes almost certainly shot herself, so that part of Connor's story sounds like it's true … And if Connor's prints aren't on the murder weapon from Luis McPherson's place, then I don't see how she could have killed them.'

Jenna shrugged. 'Connor could have used gloves when she shot Luis McPherson and Chris Cervantes and then hidden them.'

'My people are all over the house,' said Jeffs. 'If she hid plastic gloves anywhere, we'll find them. The tests show Connor's got gun residue on her hands.'

'The residue could have been from the gunfight the previous night at Reyes's place,' said Giant, who was almost surprised to find himself defending Brook Connor. 'She admitted she shot Reyes's security people.'

Jeffs shrugged dismissively. 'For my money, she's still the killer.'

'And mine, too,' said the Chief. 'At the very least we can charge her with the murder of her husband. I mean, he was found in the family car with a knife sticking out of him with her prints on it, and no amount of bullshit storytelling's going to get her out of that one.' He yawned and rubbed his eyes. 'Well, I don't know about you guys, but I'm pooped. I say we reconvene tomorrow, nine a.m.'

53

Brook sat in the cell on the single bunk facing Angie, who stood a few feet away, looking uncomfortable. The cell was bigger than she'd been expecting and was, thankfully, clean. She was also its only occupant.

She yawned. She was too exhausted to care about the fact that she was about to spend a night in jail for the first time in her life, but she still needed answers.

'How long did you know that Logan was seeing Maria Reyes?' she asked Angie. 'Because you must have known that him seeing a woman who was married to a Mexican drug lord was potentially putting Paige and me in grave danger.'

Angie's whole body stiffened. She looked more uncomfortable than Brook had ever seen her. She was silent for a few seconds before answering. 'I didn't know for very long at all,' she said eventually. 'Logan came to see me on Wednesday night. He told me about the affair then.'

'That was the night Paige was taken.'

'I know it was,' said Angie.

'And yet the following night you came round to our family home and I told you that Paige had been taken, Logan was dead in the car and that I was being set up. And yet still you didn't say anything about the Tony Reyes connection. Why not?'

'Because I wanted you to hand yourself in, and I knew that if I told you about Reyes, you might do something stupid. I also thought it was possible you might have killed Logan.'

'You let me down, Angie,' said Brook, her voice filled with disappointment. It felt as if she had enemies at every turn.

'I'm sorry,' Angie replied, but it was hard to tell whether or not she was.

'Logan was wearing Creed Aventus when he came back home on the night Paige went missing. He only ever wore that aftershave when he was trying to impress a woman. He used to wear it for me. Then he stopped. But he wore it for you.'

Angie didn't say anything. Brook could see that her jaw was set tight.

'You were seeing him, weren't you?'

Angie paced the cell, her heels clacking on the hard floor, trying not to meet Brook's accusatory gaze. 'It's not what you think, Brook. Wednesday night was the first time I'd seen Logan in a long time. He called me out of the blue and said he needed to see me urgently. When he turned up, he was terrified. He told me about the affair and said he was being blackmailed by the police about it.'

'So you knew about that, too?'

'I knew he'd been approached by someone, but I didn't know who it was until tonight. How sure are you that it's Detective Giant in the photo?'

With everything going on, it suddenly seemed hard to tell for certain. Brook rubbed her eyes, struggling to fight off sleep. 'Pretty sure,' she said.

'Where's Cervantes's file with the photo of Giant in it? Tell me you've got that.'

'In the glove compartment of the Rav4 I was driving.'

'Okay. I'll make sure no one touches it until I get there. This could be really helpful to us.'

Brook sighed. 'The most important thing is to find Paige. I know she's still alive.'

'And we will. But we need to get you out of here first. Look, I'll be straight with you, Brook. Logan wanted out of his relationship with Maria Reyes. He knew it was too dangerous. His plan was to take Paige and move to the other side of the country, well away from her. He didn't want anything to happen to Paige. Or to you, Brook.'

'Was he going to take me with him?'

Angie paused, giving Brook her answer. 'I don't know,' she said.

Brook shook her head wearily, feeling like the whole world had betrayed her.

'He was a weak man,' said Angie. 'I know that. But he had a good heart. He felt responsible for Maria, too, which was why he approached me to help her leave her husband, and which was why I went to see her last night at the restaurant. It was because Logan asked me to.'

Brook found it hard to keep control of her anger. 'Did you sleep with him on Wednesday night?' she demanded, her voice tight.

'No, of course I didn't,' Angie answered – too quickly.

'I thought you were my friend. What sort of fucking person are you?'

Angie's face darkened and she brought her face close to Brook's. 'I'm the sort of *fucking person* who's your last hope of of getting out of here, so treat me with some respect.'

Brook held her gaze. 'Do you believe my story?'

'Yes,' Angie said, standing back up. 'I do.'

'And will you get me out of here?'

There was a silence that lasted two heartbeats. Then Angie nodded. 'Yes, I will.'

But Brook wasn't at all sure she believed her.

54

Jenna had left her car at Luis McPherson's place when they'd brought Brook Connor in, so when she and Giant were finished for the night, he offered her a ride back to it.

As they got in Giant's car, Jenna turned to him. 'What Connor was saying in there, about seeing a photo of you with Logan Harris last week ... What was that all about?'

Giant wasn't sure if he could trust her or not, but he also knew he was going to need help if he was to destroy the evidence. He sighed. 'It *was* me in the photo. I wanted to get Logan Harris to persuade Maria Reyes to turn state's evidence against her husband. I followed them, in my own time, and took some photos of them together.'

She looked at him, and Giant couldn't tell whether she was angry or not. 'You were blackmailing him?'

'I don't know if I'd put it like that,' he said, even though that was exactly what it was. 'I thought it was the only way we were ever going to get Tony Reyes.'

Jenna actually laughed then. 'Shit! It seems the only person who didn't know what his wife was doing was Tony Reyes himself. I guess he must have trusted her. There's a real irony in that.'

'I'm worried the photo Cervantes took of me is going to show up at some point. If it does, I'm in a lot of shit.' Giant knew he wasn't being fair involving Jenna in what was a problem purely of his own making, but it was an undeniable relief to get it out there.

'Don't worry,' she said, putting a hand on his arm. 'If what Connor's saying is true, and Cervantes didn't want to be involved in the case, he probably destroyed the original photos. That means the only copy in existence is in the file he gave Connor. We just need to find it.'

Giant reversed his car out of the spot and drove onto the road. 'I figure it's only going to be in one of two places. The motel where Connor was staying or the car she was driving.'

'The place she said she'd left the car's only ten minutes away from here. Let's try there first. And we'd better hurry. The marshals will be impounding it for evidence soon.'

Giant felt a spasm of guilt, knowing he was breaking the law yet again by tampering with evidence. By destroying the photo, he was deliberately taking away another plank of Brook Connor's story. But as he drove, he justified his actions to himself, concluding that the existence of the photo didn't actually help her disprove her guilt, so it wouldn't actually do her any harm if it wasn't there. It would simply prove she was mistaken, that was all.

The Toyota Rav4 was parked exactly where Connor had said it was. There was no one around and Giant pulled up next to it.

'Shit!' he said, with a sigh. 'This is bad.'

'Come on. If we don't do this and it gets out, you'll be out of a job, and even more in Tony Reyes's bad books than you already are.'

Knowing she was right, he followed her over to the Rav4. He wanted to take charge of the situation, but found himself watching as Jenna slipped on a pair of plastic gloves and tried the driver's door. The car was unlocked and she switched on her flashlight and leaned inside, shining the light around before opening up the glove compartment.

'This looks promising,' she said, emerging with an A4-sized folder that she handed to him. 'There's a nine-mill pistol in there as well. That must be hers. We'll leave it for the marshals.'

Giant put on his own gloves and opened the folder up, looking through the typed reports and the photos, while Jenna shone the light down. The photos of Logan Harris and Maria Reyes together were exactly as Brook Connor had described. It was another part of her story that hung together perfectly, and it made Giant feel somehow unclean, standing here in the dark sifting through the evidence like a petty thief.

He stopped when he located the photo of himself at the tennis courts. It was a close-up shot of him walking in profile, and there was no doubt it was him, although on its own it wasn't incriminating as it could have been taken anywhere. The problem was that there was a second photo beneath it: the exact same shot, but taken from further away, in which it looked a lot like he'd just got out of Logan Harris's car, with the licence plate clearly visible. 'This is it,' he said.

Jenna took both photos from him while Giant skimmed through the rest of the file until he was satisfied there was nothing else that incriminated him. He closed the file and put it back in the Rav4's glove compartment underneath the gun.

Thirty seconds later they were back on the road, heading up towards Luis McPherson's place, and the guilt was hitting Giant hard again. Beside him, Jenna began ripping up the photos, her face expressionless. He wondered if she thought less of him for getting himself into a vulnerable position like this.

'Thanks for helping me out,' he said, as she finished ripping and scattered the little pieces out of her window, destroying the physical evidence of his wrongdoing for good.

She smiled. 'I hope you'd do the same for me.'

'I would.'

'And I know you were doing it for the right reasons.'

'I still feel bad about it. Connor was telling the truth about the existence of the file, and the photo. The location of her gun, as well. A lot of what she's told us is the truth.'

'Maybe so, but the best liars always mix their lies with the truth.'

Giant nodded, conceding the point, but the doubts he'd been having all evening persisted. 'You know, Jenna, I've got this theory about detective work, and it's served me well in the past.

A lot of criminals can act impulsively or irrationally, but overall there's a story surrounding the crime. And when you look deep enough, that story always makes sense. But my problem is that so far this one doesn't. I mean, what have we got? Brook Connor arranges either the kidnap or murder of her stepdaughter. She calls the kindergarten to report that Paige is sick, so we can assume that she's already dead or kidnapped. She then kills her husband that night, leaves him in the trunk of their car in the garage, calls her lawyer, tells her the same story she's told us about the kidnap and the set-up, then continues to leave him in the car for another twenty-four hours. Then she sets fire to her garage, flees, abducts Maria the next day, confronts Maria's husband, shoots two of his men, flees again and ends up killing the man she's hired to spy on her husband, as well as his son.' He exhaled and looked at Jenna. 'The point is, the story I've recounted just doesn't make sense. But the one Brook Connor herself told us: that *does* make sense. And right now I'm conflicted, because I believe it more than I do the alternative.'

Jenna gave Giant a sceptical look. 'If her story's true, then she's right and someone is setting her up. But who? Someone jealous of her success? Some cop who's got an obsession with her, like her lawyer suggested? Or this mysterious figure from thirty years ago who had something against her old man?' She shook her head. 'No way. It's a lot easier to imagine a vengeful woman finding out about her husband's infidelity, going completely crazy and killing the people involved – maybe even her own stepdaughter – and then going on the run. I don't know why she killed Lou McPherson and his father, Chris Cervantes, but there could be any number of reasons, and it still sounds a lot more likely to me than some kind of elaborate set-up. I'm a great believer in that old Sherlock Holmes quote: when you've eliminated everything else, whatever's left – however improbable – is the truth. Don't complicate it, Ty. Let justice run its course. We did well tonight. Even if the Chief didn't give us credit.'

But Giant remained unconvinced, and the more he thought about it, the more he saw the plausibility of Brook Connor's story. 'I don't like leaving loose ends, so I'm going to keep looking into it, even in my own time. It's a puzzle, and I'm good at puzzles.'

'I know you are,' Jenna said. 'But that's your problem, Ty. You're not a political enough animal. People need it simple. And look what happened the last time you did something off the books. We end up here, ripping up compromising photos of you.'

'I'll be a lot more careful this time. And if it looks like Brook Connor is actually guilty, then that's fine, I'll let things lie. But I'm not prepared to allow a miscarriage of justice to happen on my watch.' As he spoke the words he immediately felt better. If Brook Connor was innocent, helping her would erase his own guilt for destroying evidence. And if she was guilty, then what he'd done didn't matter.

'You're not going to let this go are you, Ty?' He looked at her and was surprised to see Jenna giving him a warm smile. 'You know, you're a good man.'

Giant felt a warm glow. Maybe things were going to work out for him after all. He felt even better when she leaned over and kissed him on the cheek, her breath warm on his face.

They were coming up to McPherson's place now. Yellow scene-of-crime tape blocked off the track leading down to the house, and two bored-looking marshals stood guard, while half a dozen police vehicles lined one side of the road, with Jenna's car at the end.

Giant waved at the marshals as he drove past and, recognizing him from the department, they waved back. He pulled up in front of Jenna's car, wondering whether he should try to kiss her now. They looked at each other for a couple of seconds. Giant told himself to go for it, but nerves held him back, and then the moment was lost and the atmosphere in the car was suddenly awkward, as if they both knew what ought to happen, but somehow couldn't manage it.

'Goodnight, Ty,' said Jenna, and Giant could have sworn she was blushing. But then she got out of the car and was gone.

He turned the car around and waited while she pulled in behind him, then began the drive back to Monterey, wondering whether he should just pull up at the side of the road, get her to stop, then go back and kiss her properly. She was definitely giving off signs of interest. He needed to take the lead for once. But Jesus, it was hard when you were as shy as he was. He hadn't been in a relationship for so long it was hard to remember what to do, and he was terrified of getting it wrong.

And then he saw in the rear-view mirror that Jenna was flashing her lights at him and he felt a burst of elation. It seemed she had the same idea as him. He pulled up at the side of the road, letting his window down as she drove in behind him and got out of her car, running towards him.

But elation gave way to disappointment as she reached the window and leaned down, her expression tense and businesslike. 'Jesus, Ty, I've just remembered something about Connor's story. Something we didn't think about.'

'What's that?' he asked, trying to keep the disappointment out of his voice.

And in that moment Giant saw the gun come up in Jenna's gloved hand and realized, with a sense of complete and utter shock, that Brook Connor had been innocent all along. A hundred different thoughts seemed to explode across his mind in that last second, but the one that stood out was that now Tony Reyes was never going to be brought to justice.

And then Jenna pulled the trigger and everything went black.

55

Jenna moved quickly.

After putting a second bullet in Giant's head, just to make sure he was gone, she threw the gun into the back of his car and shoved him across into the passenger seat, which was no easy task, given his bulk. She then reversed his car back up the road thirty yards, ignoring the fact that his legs were across her lap, until she came to the entrance to the corn field she'd spotted a few seconds earlier. She drove the car inside and parked it so that it was hidden from the road by a large hedge, before running back to her own car and driving off. The whole thing had taken about thirty seconds and, since it was gone three in the morning and this was an isolated stretch of road, there were no witnesses.

It was in many ways a perfect kill. The gun Jenna had used was an illegally owned pistol with the serial number shorn off, which she'd pocketed on a raid months earlier so there was no way of it being traced back to her. Also, after what had happened between Giant and Tony Reyes at the station the other night, there was a ready-made motive in place for Giant's murder. Even if Reyes's involvement couldn't be proved (which was unlikely, given that he'd nothing to do with it), the finger of suspicion was always going to be pointed at him.

Even so, Jenna wished she hadn't had to kill Giant. The fact was that she liked him. Not in a sexual way, of course. Physically he was the very opposite of the toned look she was attracted to, and he was also too soft, the kind of nice guy who always finishes last. But he'd been good to work for, and easy company. And he was a good detective, too, the type you want on your team, which of course was why he'd had to die. Driving back in the car earlier, Jenna could see that there was no way Giant would stop until he'd torn the case apart and put everything back together again, and that was when he'd have seen that the key to the case was Jenna herself. After all, as Mozzarella Man had proved in the past, he was nothing if not determined. And she couldn't have that.

The problem was, thanks to that bitch Brook Connor, Jenna's carefully laid plan (months – no, years – in the making) had come very close to falling apart. Jenna had expected Brook to give herself up as soon as she'd found Logan's body in the trunk of his car. At that point Brook's story really would have looked like bullshit, and it wouldn't have taken long for the affair between Logan and Maria Reyes to have got out. So she'd have had a gold-plated motive for his murder. The cameras that Jenna and

Lou had placed in her house had already been removed and there was no evidence they'd ever been there. It would have been a slam dunk.

Unfortunately Connor hadn't given in and, by trying to solve the case, she'd located Jenna's co-conspirator, the greedy and feckless Lou McPherson, and had got far too close to Jenna herself.

But as she drove back to her apartment now, still breathing heavily from the adrenalin-hit that always comes with killing, Jenna was confident that she'd overcome this latest obstacle. No one would think to connect her with Giant's killing because, as far as the world was concerned, she had no motive. And with Giant gone, the focus of the investigation would be back where it belonged: Brook Connor.

56

Sleeping on a cell bunk wasn't as bad as Brook had expected, and they even gave her coffee and a sandwich for breakfast. The coffee was bad and the sandwich worse, but she felt a palpable sense of relief that she was no longer on the run and had finally been able to tell her story. It was that, coupled with the remorseless stress of the previous few days, which made her sleep as well as she did.

Unfortunately, the fact she'd slept so well immediately made her feel guilty, because Paige was still out there, scared and confused and needing her mom. And as the morning passed and she was still stuck in her cell, without access to TV and the internet, Brook became more and more frustrated.

Finally, at 11 a.m. Angie arrived, looking pristine and ready for business in a conservative midnight-blue suit and matching heels. Brook was still wary of her, but even so, she was relieved to see someone who, at least on the surface, was on her side.

'They're ready for us in the interview room,' Angie told her. 'Now, don't say anything at all, okay? Let me do the talking.'

'I've got to get bail, Angie. At least then I can try to find Paige.'

Angie put a hand on her shoulder and gave it an affectionate squeeze. 'I know, babe. I've already got my best guy looking into the background of everyone connected to this case, to see if we can turn anything up. I'll do everything I can to get you out, but don't get your hopes up. There's still a lot of evidence against you.'

Brook nodded and followed Angie out of the cell, suddenly terrified of what might happen, because if she didn't get bail, she knew she'd get lost in the system and forgotten about for months on end, and all that time Paige would be out there somewhere, living a completely different life. She had a feeling that the next few hours would decide the rest of her life, and it wasn't a comforting thought.

They were led by two uniformed officers back to the interview room they'd been in the night before. Detective Jenna King was in there, looking as serious and austere as ever, but Brook didn't recognize the detective next to her, a younger Latino guy with a neatly trimmed beard.

'Detective Giant not here?' said Angie as she and Brook sat down opposite them.

'I'm afraid he's indisposed,' answered Detective King. 'This is Detective Padilla. We'll be running things today.' She made a play of consulting the handwritten notes laid out in front of her, before fixing Brook with a cold, officious look. 'So, Ms Connor. You've had some time to think. Are you going to persist with your story, or would you like to tell us what really happened?'

Angie let out a dramatic sigh. 'Please, Detective, let's not go through all this again. My client has already given you a full account of what happened. So if you're not going to charge her, then you're going to have to release her.'

'Is that your last word on the matter?' asked Detective King, turning from Brook to Angie.

Brook felt her stomach clench. She had an ominous feeling about this interview.

'No, it's not,' said Angie. 'I'd like to see the pathologist's report regarding the Maria Reyes shooting.'

It turned out that the pathologist's report wasn't available yet, but that in the pathologist's opinion, Maria Reyes's shooting had been suicide. Detective King gave this information reluctantly, and Brook felt her hopes rising as a part of her story was vindicated.

Angie then asked if the police had completed the fingerprint analysis of the gun used to kill Chris Cervantes and his son, and whether Brook's fingerprints were on it.

Brook knew the answer to that one but, given the thoroughness with which she'd been set up, it was still a relief when Detective King admitted that the analysis had been completed and that Brook's fingerprints weren't on the gun. 'However, that doesn't mean she didn't kill them,' she added.

'Well, you arrested her at the scene,' said Angie, 'and she wasn't wearing gloves. So how could she have shot them?'

'We're still searching the premises for evidence. It's an ongoing process.'

'In that case, I'd like you to release my client while that process goes on, since it's clear there's a lot of doubt surrounding her involvement.'

Brook felt her hopes rise still further, but Detective King's next words killed them stone dead. 'There's no doubt at all in our minds that your client killed her husband. The knife with her prints on it was sticking out of him in the back of his car, in their garage. So if you have nothing else to say, I'm charging you, Brook Connor, with the first-degree murder of Logan Harris on or about the third of May 2018.' Detective King looked at Brook as she spoke, and Brook thought she saw a malignant gleam in the other woman's eye.

'This is bullshit,' said Angie. 'We want a bail hearing as soon as possible.'

'Good,' Detective King told her. 'Because you've got one. Three p.m. this afternoon.' She got to her feet. 'Interview terminated.'

57

Jenna had enjoyed charging Brook Connor with the first-degree murder of her husband., the man she herself had actually killed. Logan Harris's instructions on the night he'd delivered the money at the nursery had been simple: he was to keep hold of the cellphone he'd been given and beat Connor up, until she was in a position where she couldn't fight back. Then, when Connor was questioned afterwards about her injuries, she'd have to admit that Logan had hit her, thus giving her a secondary motive for his killing.

Logan had managed to knock Connor out cold, but had somehow lost the cellphone in the process. As he'd walked back through the nursery, looking distraught and confused, Jenna had stepped out from behind a building, along with Lou McPherson, and had called him over. While McPherson had watched him with the gun, Jenna had told Harris to open up the bag and show her the money. As he'd gone to open it, Jenna had slipped the switchblade from the back pocket of her jeans and stabbed him between the ribs a number of times in rapid succession. It had all been surprisingly easy and Logan had fallen to the ground and died, almost without a sound.

Jenna didn't feel at all guilty about what she'd done. Logan Harris was a serial philanderer, and Connor deserved everything that was coming to her. It was just a pity they couldn't also charge her with the Maria Reyes murder, or the murders of Lou and his old man. But for the moment, at least, everyone in the department, from the Chief downwards, believed that Brook Connor was guilty of most, if not, all of the killings. Unlike Giant, they wanted the simple narrative – the one that Jenna had provided for them. In truth, she was proud of what she'd done. It was a pity about Giant. He was the kind of collateral damage she'd have preferred to avoid. But he, too, had played his part in Jenna's plan. For months she'd been plotting Connor's destruction as well as that of her nauseatingly happy family, but it had been Giant who'd provided her with the opportunity, when he'd told her about Logan Harris's affair with Maria Reyes. With that knowledge, she'd had a perfect motive for murder to pin on Connor. And it had worked, too. Maybe not smoothly, but they'd come to the right place in the end.

So far, Giant's body hadn't been discovered, which surprised Jenna, given that it wasn't exactly well hidden. Obviously Giant himself was missed at the station. In the nine months he'd been with the department he'd never missed a day of work and was considered highly reliable.

When he still hadn't turned up by mid-morning, the Chief had had little choice but to give her the job of charging Connor. It was even possible, she thought, that Giant's death would get her the promotion she'd always wanted. As they say, every cloud has a silver lining.

And for Jenna there were going to be several silver linings, starting with Brook Connor's bail hearing that afternoon, when she'd have the opportunity to watch as the woman she'd hated for so long was taken off to begin her new life in jail.

58

The bail hearing that afternoon was possibly the most nerve-racking hour of Brook's life, as she sat and listened while the state prosecutor and Angie argued in front of the judge about whether or not she should be given bail.

The argument against was strong. Brook was being charged with a capital offence and she was therefore deemed a flight risk, especially as she'd taken a quarter of a million dollars in cash out of her bank only four days earlier. However, Angie had a trump card. She'd found out from the police department that a hundred and twenty-five thousand dollars in cash had been recovered from Luis McPherson's house, and the serial numbers on the money matched that of the money Brook had been given. This made her look a lot less like a flight risk.

In the end, after a tense session, bail was granted at a cost of two million dollars. Brook had to sign over the money and the deeds to her house (which was still a crime scene) and surrender her passport. She also promised to stay at Angie's house until she found herself somewhere to live. Thankfully, she managed to avoid wearing a tag, even though the prosecution called for it.

Brook left the courthouse via the back entrance in Angie's Tesla, slumped down across the back seats. Even so, it didn't take long for half a dozen media vehicles to pick up their trail, as well as a helicopter. Angie seemed oblivious as she drove up Highway One, having a lengthy phone conversation about another case. When they finally arrived, an hour later, at her beautiful, architect-designed house on a hill looking down to the sea in Half Moon Bay, the half-dozen media vehicles had become a dozen, and Angie drove straight into the garage, letting the automatic door close behind them before getting out of the car.

'Don't worry about them,' said Angie, leading Brook into her house. 'I'll go and tell them that our hands are tied and we can't talk about the case. They'll disappear soon enough.'

They walked into the huge open-plan living area. A line of floor-to-ceiling windows looked out onto the Pacific Ocean, where a big orange sun was beginning its slow descent into the dark waters.

Brook felt the tension ease out of her as she took in the view. She couldn't relax. Not entirely. Not with Paige still out there and a murder charge hanging over her head, but the longer Paige was gone, the more Brook was growing used to the situation.

Angie fixed her a drink – a large gin and tonic, with ice and a slice of lime – and then excused herself to go down and address the camera crews. Brook sank into an armchair right next to the window and watched as a slew or reporters, backed up by camera crews, gathered around Angie at the bottom of the drive while she spoke.

It didn't take long. Angie finished and walked back up the drive to the house, while the reporters milled about, seemingly realizing they weren't going to get much of a story here. It felt strange for Brook, knowing she was the subject of so much interest, and she wondered for the first time what it had done for the sales of her new book.

When Angie came back into the room, she was on another phone call. She nodded at Brook, before going over to a desk in the corner and making some notes on a pad while Brook drained what was left of the gin and tonic, already thinking about the possibility of another one. She was tired of running; she was tired of worrying; she was even tired of thinking. She just wanted to drown her woes in drink for a few hours.

And then Angie walked back across the room as she ended the call and threw the cat right back among the pigeons.

'I think I know who set you up.'

59

For Jenna, the fact that Brook Connor got bail only showed how skewed the whole system was in favour of the wealthy. She'd been at the scene of a total of five murders, and yet still the judge had seen fit to release her while she awaited trial.

Back at the station there was disappointment that she'd been released, too, but no one felt it more than Jenna. Inside, she was seething, and for the first time it occurred to her that the bitch might actually get away with it. If she did get off, Jenna had no doubt she'd write a book about the whole thing and make millions once again. As it was, her latest book was selling so well it was predicted to make Number One on *The New York Times* Best Sellers chart that weekend. Even faced with all this shit, Connor had still come out in profit. It wasn't justice.

More than anything right now, Jenna wanted to kill her. To hold a gun to her head, make her beg for mercy and then blow her away. The thing about killing, as Jenna had discovered, was that it was very addictive and got easier every time. Killing Harris had taken willpower, because it had been up close and personal. Killing Lou McPherson, a man she'd been intimate with on numerous occasions, had been easy. Not only had he betrayed her by contacting Connor behind her back and trying to get the reward money, but he'd always been a liability and knew way too much for comfort. A quick shot to the side of the head and that had been that. Same with Giant.

But right now, killing Brook Connor was a needless risk, so Jenna knew she needed to bide her time. The right opportunity would present itself. In the meantime she decided to leave for the night, pleased that they still hadn't located Giant's body. Another murder on their patch would mean a lot more work for her, and she could do without another long shift.

Tonight, she was planning on enjoying herself.

60

'I'm pretty certain it was Detective Jenna King,' said Angie, sitting down on one of the comfortable chairs opposite Brook.

Startled, Brook frowned and put down her drink. 'The woman who's been questioning me, with Detective Giant? What on earth's she got against me? I've never even met her before.'

'I've had my best investigator on this all day. He tells me that Jenna King grew up in Massachusetts in a single-parent family. There's no father's name on her birth certificate. She was born in 1988, which is around the time that pregnant woman you told me about visited your dad. The mom had her young – twenty-two years old. At the time, she'd been working as an intern at Northeastern University. You said your father was a university lecturer and travelled, and that could be how he met her mother.

Jenna King was a police officer in Boston, but she transferred to California eight years ago.'

Brook swallowed. That had been just before her parents had died.

'We also know, from what Chris Cervantes told you, that the third suspect in the shooting incident that he and Jenna King were involved in was Luis McPherson,' continued Angie. 'What if she let him get away, or realized at the time that he was one of the shooters and blackmailed him later? It's conjecture, but the fact remains that Jenna King has a link with McPherson and, as a police officer, she had the means to plan this whole thing and frame you for it.'

Brook remembered the last photo she'd been sent of Paige, standing on a neatly kept lawn. 'Where would she be holding Paige? It looks like she's being held in a place where there's some private outside space.'

'King's address is an apartment in Monterey. I've got it written down.' Angie grabbed her notebook and laptop from the other side of the room and checked Google Maps. 'There's no obvious outside space at her apartment block. At least not somewhere Paige could play, without attracting attention.'

Brook thought about this. 'Do we know what happened to her mother?'

'I'll ask my guy if he can find out. It shouldn't take him long to get an address.'

Angie got up to make the call while Brook stared out of the window. Already the reporters were packing away. Her story would die down now until the trial. Unless, of course, Angie was onto something. It was a shock to think that the person trying to destroy her could be Jenna King, but Brook knew better than to get too optimistic about her involvement. At the moment they didn't have much.

Angie returned ten minutes later. 'The mother's name's Doris Barclay and she came to California at roughly the same time as Jenna. She's currently living in a place called Boulder Creek.'

'I know it,' said Brook. 'It's close to Big Basin Redwoods State Park, so only about forty-five minutes away.' She used Angie's laptop to bring up Boulder Creek on Google Maps, while Angie gave her Doris Barclay's address and zip code.

Brook zoomed in as far as she could go on the satellite map and saw a large, rambling wooden house with a big back yard put to grass, enclosed on three sides with pine forest. And now she did feel a rising excitement, because it looked very much like the place where Paige had been photographed two days previously. 'Paige is there, Angie,' she said, trying to keep the excitement out of her voice. 'We need to get her back now.'

Angie stood up and shook her head. 'No, no, no. It doesn't work like that, Brook. We've got no proof that Paige is there. What I need to do is get my investigator to arrange surveillance on the property. If that's where Paige is being held, he'll be able to get video evidence ...'

'That could take days, Angie. Maybe weeks. They could even move her in the meantime. We need to call the local police.'

'And say what, Brook? That we're convinced your stepdaughter's being held against her will by someone you've never met, and have no connection with? They don't believe your story, as it is. They definitely won't believe this. And it'll warn Detective King that we're onto her. Let's do it my way and be patient.'

'No. The past five days without Paige have been absolute hell. Every day she's gone will be damaging her mentally and helping to destroy the relationship we had. I need to know, Angie – don't you understand that? I need to see if Paige is there. If she is, I'm taking her back. If she isn't, then I'll accept the consequences.'

Brook stood, her mind made up.

Angie gave her an exasperated look. 'You could be putting yourself in serious danger. If we're right, Jenna King is a ruthless sociopath.'

Brook gave a hollow laugh. 'I've been in danger the whole of this past week. I'm getting used to it.'

They stared at each other in silence for a long moment. There was no way Brook was going to back down – not when she had a chance to be reunited with Paige – and she knew Angie could see that. 'Will you help me?' she asked.

Angie sighed and shook her head. 'Jesus, I've had some difficult clients in my time, but you're way ahead of them. What is it the Brits say? "In for a penny, in for a pound?" Okay then. Let's go.'

61

Boulder Creek was a pretty little town set in the midst of one of the last redwood forests in central California, and Jenna King's mother, Doris Barclay, lived about a mile outside, on the long, heavily wooded road out towards Big Basin Redwoods State Park.

Night had fallen and the traffic had long since faded away by the time Angie and Brook left the house in Angie's Tesla. According to Google Maps, the track to the house wound through trees for about a hundred yards, passing the driveway to another property that was set even further back in the forest.

When they were out of sight of the road, Brook told Angie to pull over.

Angie cut the engine and killed the lights. 'You know, you don't need to do this ...'

Brook smiled and put a hand on her shoulder, giving it an affectionate squeeze. 'Thanks for your concern, Angie. And thanks for all your help. But I do need to do this. Turn the car around and stay here. If I'm not back in fifteen minutes, dial nine-one-one and tell them what's happened.'

'You've got bigger balls than I ever gave you credit for, Brook Connor.'

'They've grown a lot in the last week,' said Brook and climbed out of the car, shutting the door quietly behind her. She no longer wondered if Angie had slept with Logan. She no longer cared. Angie had been there when she'd needed her, and right now that was enough.

As she walked quickly down the track, keeping close to the treeline, Brook felt a potent mixture of hope and trepidation, knowing that the line between success and failure can be paper-thin. If Paige was here, then they'd be reunited, Brook would be able to clear her name and the future would suddenly be bright. But if she wasn't – and they were making a mistake in blaming Detective King – then she'd be right back at square one and effectively without a future.

The house loomed up in front of her: an old timber-clad structure with a wraparound porch built on piles that looked in serious need of updating. There was an ancient car parked out front and the lights were on downstairs.

Brook walked around the side of the house and looked out across the back lawn. Even in darkness, it looked familiar and she felt certain now that she was in the right place. Taking a deep breath, she ascended the steps to the back door. There was a light on in the nearest room and, although the curtains were drawn and she couldn't see inside, the noise of a TV quiz show drifted out the open window.

She tried the door and it opened with a low squeak. Brook was unarmed, and she had no plan other than to simply creep inside and see if she could find Paige. If Doris Barclay had a dog, or good hearing, then Brook was in trouble, but as she'd kept telling herself on the way here, the time for caution had long since passed.

As soon as she was in the narrow hallway, she saw it. A bright pink child's soccer ball, like the one Paige had been playing with in the photo she'd been sent the previous day. She was here!

Forcing herself not to hurry, Brook crept past the half-open door to the TV room, feeling a powerful, illicit thrill at being in someone's house like this without them knowing. Then, as she reached the staircase, she saw that the door to the room next to it was open, and a whole host of kids' toys were strewn on the floor, including the Sylvanian house that had been in the first photo.

Taking a deep breath, she mounted the staircase, conscious of the creaking of the wooden steps underfoot. As she reached the top, she saw there was a door opposite and doors to either side of her, all bathed in the dim glow of a single lamp on a stand. All the doors were closed, but one of them had a big rainbow sign on it, with a smiling pink fairy at the end of it. Brook stopped outside, hardly daring to breathe. She put an ear against the wood, but could hear nothing from within. The only sound in the house was the faint, tinny blare of the TV from downstairs.

Confident that no one else was up there, Brook quietly opened the door and went in.

And there she was. Her darling Paige. Fast asleep in a tiny bed in the corner of the room, an unfamiliar teddy bear tucked up beside her.

Brook almost fell to the floor, such was the force of the emotion that hit her then. Relief; joy; hope; fear – they all seemed to strike her, one after another, like hammer blows. She steadied herself by concentrating on her breathing for a few seconds and then, as the reality of her current situation hit her, she hurried over, kissed Paige gently on the forehead and lifted her out of bed and into her arms. Paige stirred a little and then rested her head on Brook's shoulder, already asleep again, her breathing soft, yet audible, in her ear.

It took all of Brook's willpower to stop herself squeezing Paige too tightly against her and waking her up. Instead she crept out of the room and back down the stairs, teeth gritted at every little noise they made, knowing this was the most dangerous part of the whole venture because, with Paige in her arms, she was uniquely vulnerable.

But there was no movement downstairs and, when she tried the front door, it opened immediately, allowing in the cool, fresh air of freedom.

Closing the door behind her, Brook hurried back down the track, breaking into a run, not caring if she woke Paige up now, feeling an incredible elation as Angie's car came into view. Angie had turned the car around, as requested, so that it was facing the road, and Brook covered the last few yards at a sprint, climbing into the passenger seat, unwilling even to think about letting go of Paige as she strapped herself in. 'I've got her – let's get out of here,' she panted.

Angie didn't move.

Brook stopped what she was doing and looked at her.

Angie was staring straight ahead into the darkness, eyes wide open, unseeing. There was a deep gash across her throat that had leaked a thick curtain of blood all down her front and into her lap. More blood spattered the windscreen.

'Oh God!' whispered Brook. And then as she opened the passenger door and stepped out, still holding Paige to her chest, she heard movement behind her and a voice dripping with hatred hissed the words, 'Don't move or I'll slice you right open.'

62

Very slowly Brook turned around and saw Detective Jenna King holding a gun in one hand and a bloodied switchblade in the other. She was still dressed in the same jacket and white shirt she'd been wearing that morning, when she'd charged Brook with murder.

'The police know I'm here,' said Brook, unable to think of anything else to say, conscious now of the weight of Paige in her arms.

'No, they don't,' said Jenna with a wide, triumphant smile. 'If they did, I'd know about it. As far as the law enforcement of this state is concerned, you're a dangerous spree killer who should never have been bailed. Now let's go back to the house.'

'So you can kill me at your leisure? No, thank you.'

'I can do it here, if you prefer.'

Brook knew she was trapped, but the important thing was to protect her daughter. 'Paige is asleep. Let me put her in the back seat of the car. If you've got to kill me, kill me. But I don't want her to witness any of this. Or to know I was here.'

Jenna thought about this, then nodded.

Brook opened the door and laid Paige gently on the back seat, knowing that even though there was a body in the car, she'd be a lot safer here than back at the house.

'Okay, start walking back the way you've just come, and don't try anything,' said Jenna, following Brook as she started down the track.

Brook knew that she was almost certainly walking to her death. And yet she was more shocked than terrified, finding it hard to come to terms with the fact that someone could hate her this much. 'What have I ever done to hurt you?' she asked over her shoulder, needing to know.

'Your whole life hurts me,' answered Jenna, venom in her voice.

Brook had to try to create some kind of bond between them and personalize this, appealing to the detective's better nature. 'Did we have the same father? Is that what all this is about?'

'I have no father. But the man who impregnated my mother and left her as if she was nothing – who left *us* – is the same man who fathered you, yes. You had everything. I had nothing. It wasn't fair.' She spat out these last three words, and Brook could tell she was working herself into a fury, and that she'd probably rehearsed this conversation in her head a thousand times.

'You're a cop,' said Brook. 'You know that life isn't fair. And it's not my fault, either, that my dad left you and your mom like that. Did you kill him and my mother?' Jenna didn't answer, and Brook felt a flash of anger. 'Because if you did, you've ruined my life already.'

'But that's not what happened, is it?' said Jenna. 'You made money out of their deaths with your books, and your TV appearances, and all your New Age life-coaching bullshit. You didn't suffer. You've never suffered.'

Brook stopped and turned to face her. 'Of course I fucking suffered. I lost my parents. At least you have your mother. You murdered my parents. What sort of monster are you?'

'I'm not the monster here. You know who the monster really was. Your father. When I came here to California, I tried to connect with him. I turned up at his house one day when your mother was out. I told him I was prepared to forgive him, and do you know what he said?' She shook her head angrily. 'He said I must have made a mistake. That there was no way I was his daughter. Then he slammed the door in my face, just like he did with Mom. He slammed the door on his own fucking daughter.'

'And that was wrong of him, but please don't blame me for it. I'm nothing to do with any of that.'

Jenna King's expression turned cold. 'I don't want to hear it. Get moving or I'll do you here right now and leave you out for the animals to eat. No one will hear a thing.'

It was quiet out there. Brook couldn't hear anything except the crickets and the occasional cry of a bird. It felt utterly strange being threatened with death by her last blood relative left on earth. 'We could have been friends, you know,' she said, disbelief in her voice. 'It didn't have to be like this.'

Jenna's expression didn't change. 'Of course it had to be like this. You're the bitch who stole my life. And now I'm taking it back from you.'

'But you're not, are you? You're not taking back anything. By trying to destroy me, you're only destroying yourself. You can't get away with this. You can't simply bring Paige up as your own and hope for the best. She'll have to go to school. You'll be found out, and then the police will work out that you're the one behind all this.'

'No, they won't. They'll be looking for you and your lawyer friend and then, when they can't find you, the whole thing will just fade away. You'll be forgotten.' Her face twisted into an ugly sneer. 'One way or another, you die tonight. If you cooperate, it'll be quick. If you don't, I'll make it slow.'

Brook had a feeling Jenna wanted it to be slow, and that any appeal to her better nature wasn't going to work. She was too consumed by hatred for that.

They'd reached the house now, and Brook knew this was the end of the line. The whole gamut of emotions was running through her head again: fear, anger, relief that Paige was alive and unharmed, sadness because she'd never see her beautiful girl grow up.

King directed her to the edge of the treeline, off to the side of the house, and told her to stop.

Brook stopped. Waited. Wondering when the bullet would come.

And then she heard a voice call out, 'Jenna. What's going on? I can't find Little Boots.'

Brook turned around. Jenna was standing five yards behind her, too far away to charge, her gun raised. But now she could also see a woman in her fifties, wearing an old-fashioned dress, hurrying down the steps at the front of the house and coming over.

'Get back, Mom. I'm dealing with a complication. Little Boots is fine. She's sleeping in the car. I'll go get her in a minute.'

Her mother – Doris Barclay – was small and thin, with a long nose and birdlike features, and Brook realized there was something familiar about her.

Doris stopped next to Jenna, looking concerned. 'Oh, Jenna,' she said. 'This is going too far. We don't want anyone else hurt.'

'This is the only way, Mom. I'll bury her in the woods and, once she's gone, it'll all be over, and it'll just be me, you and Little Boots. You go back in the house and leave everything to me, okay?' Jenna gave her a mother a reassuring look.

Doris looked at Brook. There might have been sympathy in her eyes, it was hard to tell, but there was also a steely pragmatism there. She knew as well as her daughter that, now that Brook had found them, she had to die.

And that was when Brook realized that she bore striking similarities to the old woman in her dreams, with the hooked nose, beckoning from the forest. 'I know you,' she said, staring hard at Doris Barclay. 'We've met before. When I was a child.' Something lurched up from her subconscious, a memory suppressed since early childhood. 'You tried to kidnap me,' she said. 'When I was very, very young. It was *you*.'

Doris said nothing. She stared at Brook with her narrow, beady eyes, before turning back to her daughter. 'Make sure she's the last one, baby,' she said. 'I don't want you to become too hard.'

Brook almost laughed at that particular comment, but then, as Jenna turned to smile at her mom, she saw her chance and – knowing there wasn't going to be another one – rushed forward, keeping her body low.

She hit Jenna full-on, sending her crashing to the ground as the gun went off once, then twice, temporarily deafening her. Brook landed on top of the other woman, managing to grab her gun arm at the elbow, pushing it back as the gun went off a third time. Jenna screamed in anger and drove her body upwards, knocking Brook off. But as she scrambled to her feet, Brook lashed out with her foot, striking Jenna on the shin before she could get her balance.

She stumbled and went down on her ass. At the same time Brook rolled over, jumped up and sprinted for the trees, noticing as she did so that Doris Barclay was lying motionless. She'd been hit.

Two more shots rang out – both close to her – but Brook had already reached the shelter of the treeline. Keeping her head down, she tore her way through the thick undergrowth, ignoring the pain as the branches scratched her skin. Behind her, she heard a blood-curdling scream as Jenna realized that her mother had been shot.

Brook hit a branch at head height and stumbled, falling onto the soft forest floor, her head spinning. She could hear Jenna crashing through the trees only yards behind her, cursing and yelling. Ignoring the shock, Brook crawled on her hands and knees behind a tree.

'I will kill you, you bitch!' hissed Jenna, very close now. 'You can't get away. You're mine.'

Her footfalls became slower and quieter. She was only feet away. Any second now, she would see Brook and then it would all be over.

Next to Brook's feet was a dead branch about three feet long and perhaps a couple of inches thick. She leaned over and grabbed it, rising slowly to her feet, holding it two-handed and behind her head, like a baseball bat.

And then, as she heard Jenna's foot crunch on the dead leaves just on the other side of the tree, she swung the stick round with every bit of strength she possessed, striking the detective full in the face as she stepped into view. The stick broke in half, but Jenna fell backwards and the gun went spinning away, bouncing off a nearby tree and landing on the ground.

Brook still had hold of the bottom half of the stick and she hit Jenna again with it, three times in rapid succession, as she lay dazed on the ground. Then, throwing the stick away, she ran over, grabbed the gun and pointed it down at the woman who'd become her nemesis.

Jenna rolled onto her side, spat blood and glared defiantly up at Brook. Her nose was badly broken and she didn't look like she could fight any more. 'Go on, then,' she whispered. 'Do it. Kill me.'

Brook's finger tightened on the trigger. This was the woman who'd murdered her parents, her husband and her friend Angie, along with plenty of others, and had done everything she could to destroy her life. She didn't deserve to live. The world would be a far better place without her.

Anger seared through Brook. It was so damned tempting. Just pull the trigger... pull the trigger ...

And she did.

The bullet ricocheted off the ground beside her head, and Jenna screamed, throwing up her hands reflexively to protect her face.

'You're not worth it,' said Brook with a sigh and, still holding the gun, walked away from her.

Doris Barclay lay unmoving on the ground, bleeding from where she'd been shot in the head. Was she the woman from Brook's recurring nightmares? Had she really tried to abduct her all those years ago – something that might have prompted her parents to move to the UK? She didn't know. And she would probably never know now.

So she walked past Doris Barclay's body, putting her and Jenna King and all the other traumas of her life behind her, calling 911 and telling them to get there as fast as they could.

On the walk back down the track she kept turning to see if Jenna had come after her, but the forest was quiet, and there was no one there.

When she got to Angie's car, she stopped. Angie still sat motionless in the driver's seat, gone now for ever, and Brook felt the tears welling up at the sheer waste of it all. All those lives lost, and for what? A petty, teenager-like desire for revenge, born of a misguided jealousy. Jenna King was her half-sister. They could have been friends. It could all have been so, so different.

But out of all the negatives, there was still one huge positive. Brook opened the back door of the car as quietly as she could, relieved to see that Paige was still asleep. With tears running down her face, Brook lifted her up, held her tightly and together they waited for the police to come.

Epilogue
Four months later

It was the end of summer and a cool, bright evening as Brook stood on the beach, watching Paige run along it with their new German-shepherd puppy, Scout. The two of them were playing a game they both liked, whereby Paige held a stick just above her head, and Scout had to jump for it and somehow wrestle it from her grip. At the moment Paige was still very good at keeping hold of the stick, but that wasn't going to last much longer.

They'd got Scout just after it had all happened – partly for security, partly because they needed an addition to the family and something to take Paige's mind off everything that had happened. In truth, she'd got through the whole ordeal remarkably well. Thankfully, she hadn't really understood what was going on and had thought she was simply staying with distant family members she didn't know. It had been hard telling her that her daddy wasn't coming back, that in the time she'd been away he'd hurt himself and gone to heaven, and that Rosa had had to leave and go home, too; and for a while Paige had been terribly upset, but Brook had supported her by being there every day, never leaving her side. She'd put her whole life on hold, had refused all interviews and had set about the task of adopting Paige, a process that had finally been completed the previous week. They were now a proper family again.

Brook, too, had been scarred by everything that had happened. For weeks afterwards she'd been plagued by her recurring nightmare of the old lady at the edge of the forest, along with other, fresher nightmares, taken from those terrible days back in May. She'd considered moving house and starting somewhere afresh with Paige. Her house had felt tainted after what had happened, and it didn't help that it was only ten miles down the road from where Tony Reyes lived. But in the end she'd decided to stay put. Paige had always been happy there. She had her friends and her kindergarten, and her life had already been messed up enough. And Tony Reyes, from what Brook could gather by talking to the police, was keeping a very low profile after what had happened and wouldn't be doing anything that might draw the attention of law enforcement.

And so Brook had fought through the pain and now finally, months later, she felt she was coming out the other side. Her new book, not surprisingly, was selling incredibly well, which meant they didn't have to worry about money; and her agent, also not surprisingly, was pleading with her to consider writing an account of the events surrounding Paige's abduction. But Brook was holding off. It was far too early. She'd make the decision after Jenna's trial, which was set for November.

Jenna had been arrested at the scene that night, bent over the body of her mother. She'd tried to talk her way out of Angie's murder, as well as all the other crimes she was responsible for, but there was way too much evidence against her for that to wash, and she'd now been charged with a total of four counts of homicide, including that of her fellow detective, Tyrone Giant, who, it seemed, had got too close to her. Either way, it was unlikely she'd be walking free anytime soon. Incredibly, Brook still didn't feel any anger towards Jenna, even after all she'd done; just sadness that the whole thing had been so preventable, and regret that the woman who was her half-sister hadn't chosen a different path and tried to forge some sort of relationship between the two of them.

But that was life. You can only deal with your own issues. Other people have to sort their own stuff.

The sun was beginning to set over the Pacific and there was a chill in the air as Paige ran back towards her now, her feet splashing through the edges of the surf, Scout in hot pursuit.

Brook smiled at them, feeling a wave of pure happiness. It was time to go home.